KNEEL

THE RUIN OF SERPENTS

USA TODAY BESTSELLING AUTHOR
LILY WILDHART

To those of you, who like me, have started fresh a thousand times after what we thought were the worst things possible…

Light is at the end of the tunnel, you just have to believe you can get there. Strength is learned as you go, and it doesn't matter how many times you fall down.

Just so long as you get back up afterward.

To those of you, who like me, have started fresh a thousand times after what we thought were the worst things possible…

Light is at the end of the tunnel, you just have to believe you can get there. Strength is learned as you go, and it doesn't matter how many times you fall down.

Just so long as you get back up afterward.

Save youself before you fall

- Unknown

PROLOGUE

Talia

Blood trickles down my fingers as I pull against the rope that binds my wrists. Its pace mirrors the erratic beats of a heart trapped in a web of deceit. The welts on my skin tear open again as I struggle once more to free myself.

A bitter cocktail of anger and disbelief simmers beneath the surface, bubbling up as thoughts race through a mind that's been thrust into a nightmarish reality.

I trusted him.

I trusted all of them.

I should have known better.

The savage sting of betrayal gnaws like a relentless predator. Trust is a double-edged sword, capable of turning friends into foes and love into a weapon.

Amidst the darkness that threatens to swallow me whole, a flicker of determination sparks. Rising from the fires of anguish and humiliation.

The memories of this ordeal will serve as a haunting reminder of the price paid for my naïvety.

It's then I make a vow to myself, a promise whispered in the suffocating stillness of the room.

Never again will I be the helpless pawn in their sinister game.

They may have me captive now, but they underestimate the seed they have planted, blinded by their overconfidence.

And when the moment comes, when the stage is set and the pieces are in place, the world will witness the unraveling of their most guarded secret—one mired in blood, betrayal, and my bitter revenge that eclipses even the darkest of desires.

Weaving a map of my own version of justice in my mind, a dark smile hidden by the shadows, that seed takes root.

They'll underestimate me again. I'll make sure of it.

And it'll be the biggest mistake of their lives.

ONE

Talia

Staring out over the edge of the bluff, the wind whips around me as the waves crash below. Curling my toes into the long grass, I close my eyes and lift my arms, letting my mind drift away on the cutting breeze. *Dare You to Move* by Switchfoot blasts from the speakers of my car and I've never resonated with a song as much as I have right now.

It was his favorite.

He'd play it on guitar so much it would drive me nuts. Not anymore though. Now I listen to it on loop. Like my own personal torture.

That night plays out in my mind like a never-ending nightmare that's been on loop for the last year.

My stomach twists and I consider, just for a second, what it would be like to take another step. Right over the edge of the cliff. Would that fix everything?

Would it even make a difference?

The sound of the waves crashing on the jagged rocks below soothes me for a moment. The beach was Brody's favorite place and being here reminds me of him; the sounds, the smells, it's like he's here with me. In those seconds, I feel a little less... alone. Which is all I've felt for months, even if I've been trying to fill that hole with mindless distractions. But still... I'm alone, even when I'm surrounded by people.

And yet, it occurs to me that if I fell, no one would notice. Not for a while anyway.

I mean, Ruby might notice, since I've been staying with her since Dad abandoned me here with her to go off saving the world, but I'm supposed to be enrolling in my new boarding school, Arbour Academy, today, so more likely not.

My hair tickles my face as it gets caught up, dancing in the unseasonal storm's wind, and I open my eyes, staring out over the port on the murky, gray, cloudy day. The lighthouse in the distance attempting to light the safest route for the lost souls trying to find their way here is the only other real sign of life this far out.

Farther down the beach, I know the parties will be

starting. The flyers were all over campus when I went to look around first thing, but the place just felt wrong.

It wasn't home.

But then, I haven't known a real home in a long time.

Not since Mom left three years ago.

But at least then I still had Brody…

Everyone leaves eventually. That's what the last year has taught me.

Even my grandpa, before he died just before last Christmas, told me that no one my age should have to suffer so much loss, but then he left me too.

The chorus hits and tears well in my eyes.

I dare you to move, I dare you to move like today never happened.

I swipe away the errant tear that streaks down my face, the wetness stinging in the harsh wind, and take a step back from the edge.

This isn't what he would've wanted. He never would have wanted me to feel this empty. My sunshine was one of the things he loved the most about me…

Taking a deep breath, I steel myself once more, pushing down the darkness that I let free once I got out here, vowing again to not let it win. I've beaten it ever since it appeared. Since Brody died.

Don't let go of your sunshine, Tali. It's what makes us yin and yang.

His voice fills my head and I take another step away from the edge. Then another. And another. Until I reach the car, clinging to his voice, his favorite song playing on repeat still.

He was my constant in the whirlwind that was our lives. We might have bounced around the globe, but we always had each other.

I look down at the tattoo I got last week.

On the anniversary.

The first anniversary, and of course I spent it alone. I didn't even hear from my parents.

I'll always be with you. I'm the thunderstorm and you're the sunshine, Tali.

Yin and yang.

Balance.

My other half.

My twin.

Taken way too soon.

After I put my socks and boots back on, I climb back into the car that has become my personal fortress of solitude since I landed here in Spring Creek three months ago. The engine roars to life, the music as loud as it was when I got out, loud enough to block out the thoughts that chase me in the darkest of times—the one thing that saves me time and again—and I make the journey back to what is meant to be my new home for the next year.

For my senior year.

Maybe if summer hadn't been such an epic fucking shit show, I'd be looking forward to it more, but it was, and here we are.

Have a hot girl summer, they said. What's the worst that could happen, they said...

Fairly certain that when my dad dropped me off with his high school best friend, Ruby, for the few months before my new school would take me in, a summer of fuckery wasn't exactly what he had in mind, but well... he wasn't here to say a goddamn thing.

Except, my summer fling ended up being with the guy I wasn't supposed to fall for—fucked up there too— because it wasn't ever going to be anything serious. Well, he supposedly wanted to get over his ex, and me? I just wanted to forget... everything. The rest is history.

So here I am... my car packed full of all my stuff, my entire life boiled down to fit inside a metal box on wheels, heading to yet another boarding school.

Just under a week until the semester starts. Time that I'm sure will be full of parties that I won't attend, because instead I'll be building my schedule, meeting with my academic advisor and, of course, my in-house therapist to work out when to fit in my weekly breakdowns while still trying to graduate.

The drive doesn't take long and once I pull into an

empty spot in the somehow already jam-packed parking lot at the back of campus near the dorm buildings, I take a beat to soak it all in. Obviously, I saw it this morning, and I did a few drive-bys over the summer, but each time I've been here... well, the place kinda gives me the creeps.

It has that old, dark, gothic, haunted vibe. Which I could understand, what with all the crusty, dusty old white guys that fund this place—my dad included—but we're on the coast. There's more sunshine hours here than a lot of places in the country, yet we get the Addams Family mansion for a school.

Awesome.

I grab my bag off the back seat, along with my coffee from my little detour into town on the way here—I spent the summer working at Taylor's, Spring Creek's most popular bakery, and the coffee there is to die for. Of course, I armed myself with a cappuccino this morning—and take a deep breath.

Popping the trunk, I sling my bag across my body before grabbing my rucksack and suitcase out of the car, glancing at the boxes of stuff.

Definitely going to take more than one trip.

I grab the satchel, place it on my suitcase before locking up what would have been Brody's prized possession—our grandpa's Impala—and turning back to the dorm building that's at least a ten-minute walk from the main school, I pause.

Fuck. My. Actual. Life.

Somehow, because karma is killing me slowly, not only is my former summer fling, Dillon, walking across the parking lot—somehow him going here didn't come up in conversation, not that talking with him was exactly top of my list while trying to forget leaving my old life behind—but next to him is my ex, Evan, my very own not-so-Prince-Charming from my old city, who was supposed to be majorly in my rearview for, well, forever.

How the fuck do they know each other?

I mean, yes, they're both baseball players, but Evan is from clear across the country.

There really is no feeling quite like having your heart broken then having everyone forget you even existed... which is exactly what happened with him.

Grabbing my phone from my pocket, I snap a picture of them together, because there is no way Callie will believe me otherwise, then finish the last of my coffee before dumping the cup in a trash can.

Focus, Talia. New start, new you.

At least that's what I was telling myself the entire drive here while I listened to my sad girl summer playlist, trying to convince myself this year won't be that bad.

That was before this stellar update to my day, but still, it can't be that bad.

Can it?

Who am I kidding? This year is going to suck. Brody should be here with me. This is the first time I'm starting a new school without him. The pang in my chest is enough to almost take me to my knees as I white-knuckle grip my suitcase.

It's just one year, then I can escape to college and leave everything behind me. Fake it till I make it, I guess?

Come on, Talia. You got this.

Ha. My dad's voice in my head is about as useful as a chocolate coffee pot. He dropped me in this godforsaken place before running off to save the world and I don't even get to be mad at him because he's literally saving the world.

Stupid rule if you ask me, but then again, no one did. Ask me, that is.

No one ever has.

Not my mom before she took off.

Not my dad before he made all the decisions to go join Doctors Without Borders as part of his whole, mid-life crisis thing along with the divorce.

The only person who gave a fuck was Brody... and now he's gone.

Taking a deep breath, I shake off the woe-is-me shit, put on my practiced RBF, and head toward the building.

I guess it's time to face the music... and see if my roommate is as awesome as the start of my day has been.

Freaking yay.

The dorm is... not at all what I was expecting. After the whole goth vibe of the outside, the bright, open, and airy interior was a surprise.

Yin and Yang, Tali.

My room is on the top floor, which consists of three halls, each with twenty-four rooms, and most rooms hold two to three girls. Some have four, but they're not common. At least that's what the 'dorm sister', Nicolette, who welcomed me explained as she showed me to my room.

"Last room on the right, and you get a view overlooking the quad. So lucky." Her parting words as she opened the door, gave me my room key, then shot off back downstairs to welcome the next victim—I mean, student.

The room has two queen beds, separated by a giant window in the middle of the far wall. On the outer side of the beds, each side has a dresser, chair and mirror, a bedside table, with a desk on the wall opposite the bed that has a few shelves above it.

I take the bed on the left since my roommate is apparently not here yet, and well, ya snooze ya lose and all that.

After dropping my bags on the bed, I investigate the room, finding two separate closets, both on the right side of the room, but no bathroom.

Awesome, communal bathrooms for the win.

I make a mental note to thank Dad thoroughly for the stellar choice in dorm, because I guarantee some people have private bathrooms. This place reeks of money and there's no way some of the people here would share a bathroom.

Judgmental? Maybe. But also probably right.

I guess not being from old money and bleeding blue means that I get the communal bathroom despite Dad donating to the school and paying the, what I imagine to be eye-watering, tuition, but it could be worse.

At least, that's what I'm telling myself.

Upside, it should mean my roommate isn't a brat.

Please don't let her be a brat.

It doesn't take me long to make the few trips back and forth to my car to grab the rest of my stuff, unpack my suitcase into one of the closets, and start unpacking all of my stationary goodness onto my desk alongside my laptop. While I wait for it to start up, I put the picture of Brody and me from our last end-of-summer beach trip together on my bedside table, hiding my journal under my mattress, and pick up the welcome packet that was waiting for me on the desk.

A smaller white envelope falls to the floor, so I grab that before opening the welcome pack and pulling out the contents of it.

WELCOME TO ARBOUR! WHERE THE BRIGHTEST AND BEST EXCEL IN TAKING THE FIRST STEPS TOWARD THEIR EXCITING FUTURES.

Someone gag me.

I take in the map of campus, which is bigger than I thought it would be, the list of all the teams available to try out for, the classes available, including the selected senior-only elective classes to help with that last chance push for an Ivy.

Upside, they have a swim team.

Downside, no gymnastics, but they have cheer. Definitely not my go-to, but it's something close enough that I should be able to keep in shape. Double downside, it means being around the other sports teams, of which there are many.

I know this place is big, but holy crap, Batman.

Grabbing a notebook, I make notes of tryout times and potential classes I want to take, ones I really don't want to take, as well as ones I'll settle for.

Nothing quite like being organized.

Toying with the chain around my neck, I pause at the twang of sadness at the memory that hits, of Brody being the total opposite. So laid-back, never any plans, yet always succeeding.

I miss you, B.

My phone pings, drawing my attention, and I find three emails waiting for me.

ARBOUR: *Welcome to Arbour!*

N. Feldman: *Your appointment with your academic advisor.*

P. Bassett: *Talia! Let's schedule some time!*

I tap on the second one, adding my appointment to my calendar for tomorrow morning with Ms. Natalie Feldman, my academic advisor, and apparently head of year, along with a reminder that my uniform will be available to be collected at our appointment.

Different.

Then I open the one from Posey Bassett, the school's therapist. My new therapist. I drop her a message letting her know when I'm meeting with Ms. Feldman to see if she has time to meet after that appointment, then close down my email.

Day one at Arbour is almost uneventful so far. You know, if I ignore the whole Dillon and Evan thing. Which I entirely plan to.

I pack all of the info back into the welcome pack

envelope and remember the smaller white envelope.

My full name is written on the front in cursive, no post stamp, and when I flip it over, it's sealed with red wax, stamped with a symbol that looks almost like the school sigil thing.

Curiosity has always been one of my worst traits, but it wins out and I break the seal. Pulling out two handwritten pages, I skim over the first few lines.

Talia,

Welcome to Arbour. I do hope you'll enjoy your time here. When your father told me he'd taken my suggestion for your schooling, we were overjoyed. You'll be much closer to us here, so I hope we have a chance to visit.

What the hell?

I scan the rest of the drivel, then notice the sign off.

Theodore Gafferty.

My mom's dad. I would call him my grandfather, but I've met him all of twice. He wasn't a fan of dad's. I didn't realize he and my grandmother lived here, but it's nice to know who is responsible for me ending up here.

Thanks for that, Theodore.

I tuck the letter back into the envelope and stuff it in the drawer of my desk along with the welcome pack.

Debating between sitting and waiting on my roommate

or going out and exploring, I ask myself the same question I have all summer.

What would Brody do?

So, exploring it is.

Grabbing my keys and phone, I give myself a little pep talk while putting on my hoodie before braving the outside. When my phone pings, I smile when I see the name on my screen.

CALLIE

S'up bitchtits. This place sucks without you, no surprise there. Updates from the suckfest. Evan has moved away, his mom got a new job. Roan has officially taken his spot as pitcher already and the first day hasn't even started yet. Did I hook up with him at the back to school party on Saturday? You know I did. School might not start for another week but I'm making my mark LOL!

I'm still sad I missed your birthday over summer, but this obviously isn't news. Anyway, wreak havoc on that boarding school and make it your bitch. Tone down that sunshine and channel your inner me, you'll rule the school in no time.

Oh I spoke to my parents, and I'm totally heading your way for spring break. They wouldn't move on Thanksgiving or Christmas, but at least we have Spring to look forward to. Love your sunshiney face. Now, armor up, ice queen resting bitch face on, and strut into that place like you own it.

I cackle at her ferocity. Callie likes to pretend she's

an ice queen, but we both know she's a big softie. The way she took in the new girl last year when I landed in Summerville showed me that from the get-go. We've been friends ever since.

Not that she lets many people see her soft side. I was one of the very lucky few who she let see the real her and I'm going to miss her like crazy. Hell, she might've yelled at my dad louder than I did after the boarding school announcement.

If she was here, the fact that Evan and Dillon seem to be new besties wouldn't even matter. I could just borrow her confidence and bravado and it'd be easy.

Except she isn't here, they are, and I'm alone.

Again.

Leaving my dorm, I lock the door and head down to the giant green quad. Checking my map again, I figure this should be the quickest way to the cafeteria and I need more

ME

I know Evan left, he's here.

I send it to her along with the quick snap I took of him and Dillon earlier.

ME

This year is going to be so fun. *upside down smile emoji* I miss your face. Wish you were here.

CALLIE

Well holy forking karma. What did you do to piss off the universe? Is that him with NSDD?

I laugh again, this time loud enough that a few people walking past me turn to look at me like I'm crazy. Well, little do they know, I am. Not the psycho kind, at least I don't think so, but the fun kind. Still... crazy is crazy, right?

Shaking my head, I read her message again.

NSDD - Not so Demon Dick. Aka Dillon.

ME

Yes. Yes it is. The universe hates me. Obviously. Talk tonight?

CALLIE

You know it. I want all the tea.

ME

I'm hoping there's no tea. I just want a quiet day. A quiet life. No drama. God knows I've had enough drama to last a lifetime.

CALLIE

That you have. The whole Evan thing was bullshit. But that's in the past. You go seize the day and all that fuckery.

ME

Yes ma'am.

I slide my phone and keys into my pocket, glad for the hoodie since this weird-ass storm has dropped the temperature too far below what should be August weather, and stuff my hands in the front pouch.

I can totally walk and not trip. I'm a gymnast. I can walk.

Please, whatever god might be out there, do not let me trip.

After crossing the field outside, I duck inside the first door I come across on the main building and lean against a radiator to warm up a bit. Usually, I'm not averse to the cold, but yesterday was shorts weather, today I'm in jeans and a hoodie. Freshman year that we spent in England, I expected this mercurial weather. But here?

Absolutely not.

Grabbing my map, I try to work out exactly where I am.

The place is a huge maze.

Not exactly great for those of us who are directionally challenged, which, unfortunately, is definitely something I can be described as. My inner compass is officially broken. It took me all summer to come to grips with getting around Spring Creek, and now I have this place to work out.

Making sure my map is actually right side up, I head off in what I hope is the direction of the cafeteria, making note of where the pool is to head there next.

I've totally got this.

Won't get lost at all.

Coffee, then exploring. I mean, what's the worst that

could happen?

I shudder at the thought, because well, this is my life, and if the last eighteen months are anything to go by... the worst is a fucking hellscape.

TWO

Talia

Staring blurry eyed over the cafeteria, waiting for the coffee in my hand to reach my senses, I scroll aimlessly through yet another dopamine hit video on my socials, thankful for my AirPods so I can listen in peace. There's nothing quite like an early morning scroll to start your day after a night of almost zero sleep.

Apparently, my brain isn't used to the dorm situation again yet. Even playing my audiobook after triple checking the lock on my door didn't work. I swear I got about three hours sleep max. I feel about eighty and the bags under my eyes would require an extra charge if I was flying. Thank fuck no one is paying any attention to me.

Watching random people on the internet talk about

random shit gives me way more joy than it should, but it's a distraction, and since I can't go for an early morning swim yet—I discovered yesterday that the pool doesn't open to the bulk of the student body until Thursday. Makes no sense to me but go figure—this is my current routine.

Admittedly, for a Tuesday, there's been more people and way more drama than I would've expected, but I guess that's the joy of a new school, even one as supposedly prestigious as Arbour. Everyone has their shit, but rarely does it spill out quite so spectacularly as this. I've already seen two breakups and one very PDA make up.

So gross.

Pausing my scrolling, I look around as I sip on my vanilla latte, trying to observe these teens in their natural setting.

I choke back a laugh at the David Attenborough style voice in my head. Jeez, I'm a dork sometimes. Looking back up, thankfully no one is paying attention to me, but that doesn't mean I'm not paying attention to them.

It's the typical cliques from what I've seen so far. The nerd table, which is usually where I'd drift toward, but it's day two, so I'm still scoping the place out; the jock table, though mostly empty at the moment except for three guys who look like they've already been to the gym and are protein fueling now. At least, that's my assumption from the shakes and giant plates of eggs and sausage; there's the indie table; the alts; the musicians, all the usual players, and I'm sure when it's not ass o'clock in the morning there will be even more to fill the gaps.

The quiet argument I've been subtly watching play out for the last ten minutes between the dark-skinned jock-type guy and the tiny-yet-terrifying manic pixie girl who stormed in here before shaking her phone in his face is my current entertainment of choice. No idea who they are, but from what I can tell, he had a little fun over the summer and someone sent her a video.

Stupid decisions lead to stupid outcomes, Jock Type.

I am all for body positivity, but recording a girl going down on you, on her phone? Yeah, idiot move. Especially if you're the cheating kind.

"For fuck's sake, Trey," Pixie Chick screeches. "Keep your dick in your fucking pants. I never want to see it again. I swear, I am scarred for fucking life, you dumb asshole. You're just lucky I caught wind of it and shut shit down."

Okay, so not cheating? Color me intrigued.

"Come on, Allie. It's not that bad," he says, scratching the back of his neck. Oh, he's British. Sounds like an East London accent if I had to guess, and oof, do I love those. "But like, thanks I guess. I was wasted, letting loose, we'd just won the championship—"

"I swear if one more excuse falls out of your carpet muncher, Trey, I'll kick you in your oh-so-precious dick before sending this to Mom."

Ooh, siblings?

His eyes go wide and I press my lips together to stop from laughing. Never have I ever seen a giant jock type look so afraid of a tiny alt girl and seem genuinely afraid.

"Allie, you wouldn't. Don't be such a wanker."

She glares at him and a snort escapes me at the fear on his face caused by this tiny girl. They both glance over at me for a moment and I swear my heart pounds loud enough for them to hear it. After a second, they dismiss me and face each other again while I hide by continuing to scroll and keeping my head down... well, at least enough so they ignore me.

So I shouldn't be nosy, and curiosity killed the cat, but screw it. I am nosy.

Though I am intrigued. She definitely has an American accent... so maybe they're cousins, not siblings.

"Do not test me, Trey. We might be family, and family first and all that bullshit, but I did not work my ass off to get a side hustle here with the tech unit just to clean up your shit. Keep your dick in your pants, or at least off of the fucking internet. Fucking stupid penis-having asshat!" She storms from the room as fiercely as she entered.

A job here? She looks young enough to be a student, not staff.

Go figure.

I guess coming here instead of swimming might be a good idea. Maybe I'll figure out how this place works.

Upside to bouncing through schools, you know they tend to work the same, just with different players.

Downside, you never know where you're going to land with said players, and while the game is typically the same, the rules are always different. Learning can be the difference between surviving and thriving.

Last year, I thrived thanks to Callie.

Before that, I had Brody.

This year? Yeah, this year might just suck the worst, but I guess I'll just keep my head down as much as I can and try to sail through with no drama. I wince, thinking about how well that worked last year. And Evan is here.

Fuck my life.

I can so do this. I need to do this. One year, then I can go to college, one that I actually get to pick rather than having my life dictated to me.

Adulthood never sounded so good.

Looking around the room, I find Jock Type glaring over at me, so I decide to get out of here before he comes and says something. There's a rage simmering beneath the surface with him, I can see it in his eyes, and I *so* don't want to be the person that gets to experience it.

Closing the app on my phone and finishing the dregs of my coffee, I double check that I have my notebook and laptop in my bag before putting a different song on my playlist and checking that I have my AirPods case in my pocket before adding my phone along with it and head out of the cafeteria for my meeting with the academic advisor.

"Hey, Talia right?" I pause as the guy saying my name waves me down as I walk past him.

I pause, scrunching my brow as I run my gaze over him. I try not to panic that he seems to know me. "Do I know you?"

"Not yet," he says with a wink. "I'm Laurence. Welcome to the club."

"Club?" I ask, wide-eyed, wondering what's up with the cryptics and confused more than I was at him knowing my name.

"Oh, right," he says with a sly smile, tapping his nose. "You're right. See you around, Talia."

"Erm, bye?"

I'm thoroughly baffled, but I shove it to the back of my mind. Looking at my school map again, I search for the advisor's office and hope I'm not late as I haul ass to my meeting.

Thankfully, her office isn't far, so I make it with time to spare and take a seat on one of the chairs outside. I fiddle with the strings on my hoodie while I wait, trying not to feel scrutinized as people walk by, obviously staring at the new girl. I mean, I could totally be a freshman, except I definitely don't look like a freshman, and from what I've seen of Arbour so far, most people here know each other before they get here.

The joys of an elite boarding school, I guess.

"Talia Hayes?"

I look up, spotting who I'm assuming is Ms. Feldman. The jeans, t-shirt and cardigan combo makes her seem oddly... warm. Maybe it's the smile, or the kind eyes behind her black-rimmed glasses, or even how she clutches her cardigan around her, but she seems... nice.

"That's me." Standing, I grab my bag and walk past her when she pushes the door open and motions for me to enter. Her office is cozy. The desk in the middle, the plants dotted around the room, the art on the walls; it makes it look less sterile-school-office and more creative-at-home workspace.

"Please, take a seat." She smiles as she rounds her desk, sitting in the comfy-looking gray chair on the opposite side, and I drop down into one of the equally cozy chair-shaped beanbag things in front of me. "So, new to Arbour for senior year. I can imagine that's both exciting and tough, but have no fear. I wanted to make sure I saw you before anyone else so we could get you situated as well as possible. I've gone over your transcripts, looks like lots of schools from around the world."

"Yeah, my parents like to travel," I respond, trying

to seem upbeat and avoid the conversation of just how messed up my parental situation really is.

"Except for last year, you stayed in the States, and now you're here."

Her words are matter of fact as she glances over what I'm assuming are my records on her screen. I swallow past the lump in my throat, not wanting to explain why the sudden change, hoping it's all in there and she realizes that it isn't something I want to discuss today. Her smile falters and she looks at me, the pity in her brown eyes almost overwhelming.

Yep, it's in there.

Awesome.

"Okay, so great GPA to this point, a very varied study range. Have you thought about colleges already?"

Thankful for the change of subject, I dive into the conversation with as much enthusiasm as expected, letting her know that currently, I have absolutely no idea what I want to study at college, but that I absolutely want to go. We go through my past classes and extracurriculars and work out which of the classes I wanted as electives this year are still available.

She hands me the paper that comes out of her printer, my new schedule on it, and I let out a deep breath. "I think that just about covers it. I know you'll be disappointed we couldn't get you everything you wanted, but I think the alternatives will be just as useful, and maybe music and government can inspire you onto a career path. You'll get a copy by email too. You already have the time for tryouts this week?"

"I do," I reply with a nod, giving her a tight smile and tucking the new schedule into my bag.

"Oh, don't forget this," she says before standing, moving to the boxes that line one wall and handing me a garment bag. "Your uniform. You have blazers, blouses, skirts, and pants. If you need anything else, please just send me an email."

"Oh, right. Yeah. Thanks." I take the bag, folding it over my arm, and thank her for her time before hightailing it out of there.

Fucking music class with choir.

I can't sing to save my life. What a shit show. Definitely not the creative elective I was looking for, but at least it wasn't theater. A shudder runs down my spine at the thought. Absolutely not.

Checking my phone, I realize I only have twenty minutes until I need to meet with my therapist before this afternoon's swim team tryouts.

Let's hope this is one of those days that gets better as it goes on.

The worst I could do is drown, right?

The natatorium is... spectacular.

I mean, there's an Olympic-size pool at a fancy-ass boarding school, it was never going to be dingy, but it's like its own freaking area. The separate diving pool, the stands for meets, and a separate practice pool. It's kind of insane just how big this place is.

The echoes of shouts make me almost feel at home while I wait for practice to finish before trying to speak to Coach Summers.

She seems badass from what I've seen already. Supportive, competitive, pushy without being a total bitch.

It's just a first impression, but I've had enough swim coaches in my life to have seen a rainbow of types. My mom used to joke that I could swim before I could walk. There's something about being in the water that just feels like home.

Feels safe.

Brody had the beach, the ocean, I had the pool. Both water babies, but in very different ways. He couldn't stand the confines of a pool, the limitations of competing within the rules. He always wanted to be free, but me? Well, I thrive in structure.

Or I did.

Last year wasn't exactly a highlight of my life, but this year? This year I vowed to myself, and to Brody on the anniversary, that I'd get back on track. Reach for the life I always wanted. Regret the things I do in life, rather than the things I didn't do. I might only be seventeen, but there are plenty of things I've passed on because I was afraid.

Not anymore.

Life is too short.

It made me a little reckless last year. But this year, I can do that *and* not lose my head.

I hope.

Swim practice finishes and the team climbs out of the pool, heading for the locker rooms, so I rise from my seat in the stands and make my way over to the coach.

Seems I'm not the only one with the same thought, and I take in the squad of girls who will be my competition for joining the team. Usually, I wouldn't doubt my chances, but I just saw the team practice, and from that alone I can tell that they're the elite.

I'm getting the notion that that is Arbour's thing. Being elite.

I watch on from a short distance as the girls surround her ahead of me, all talking over each other. Coach's frustration builds each time she opens her mouth to speak and someone interrupts her. After about a minute, her patience expires and she blows her whistle loud enough that I wince.

Ouch.

"Ladies, sign-ups are going out via email later today. Tryout times will be emailed out in the newsletter next week. I appreciate you coming to try and argue your case, but kissing my ass isn't going to score you any points."

They all start speaking over each other again and I press my lips together to stop from laughing. Yeah, I am not one of those girls. I catch Coach's eye and nod before heading out of the building, hearing her blow her whistle again before telling everyone to leave.

This time I let myself smile before I leave. This day has definitely been interesting, even if I am just getting a small insight into the inner workings of Arbour.

I've been to plenty of schools—boarding and otherwise—and some things are always the same: the cliques, the politics. There are also some things about teenagers that just seem to never change, no matter where they are, and maintaining the status quo is one of them. The rules might be new, but the game is old. I've learned to use the first few weeks to keep my head down and try to figure shit out.

Brody's Lessons of a New School 101.

Learn the players. Learn the game.

I didn't follow his rules last year and it was a disaster.

This year... well, he's in my head and I refuse to drown.

This year is for him as much as it is for me.

Really, I need to figure out what comes *after* this year, so I can make the most of it, but for now, I'm just going to live. To thrive. And do it for the both of us.

Pulling my map from my bag, I decide to try and figure out this behemoth maze of a school and map out where my classes are. But first, I need more coffee. Heading back to the cafeteria, which is on the other side of this gigantor building, I grab another coffee and take the seat I vacated before, in the far back corner, a nice scoping point to watch the rest of the student body from.

There are more people here now, but my spot was still thankfully empty. Reject corner maybe, but I don't give a fuck if it means my peace continues for a little longer. Reject might be a happy banner I wear this year, especially if it comes with less drama than last year.

I pull my map out again, grab a pen and highlighters, and try to locate all my classes, marking them in different colors while I sip on my latte.

A wave of cheers go up on the other side of the room, and I watch on in horror as Dillon and Evan greet the jock from earlier. I duck down to make sure they don't see me before stashing my pens in my bag, grabbing my map and my coffee, and hightailing it out of the room.

I even almost make it, except just as I'm leaving I run into a wall.

A wall of human.

Fuck my life.

I manage to not spill my coffee, even if it feels like I've bruised my tailbone. Not that that has anything on the bruise to my ego from crashing and burning quite so publicly.

Looking up, I find three guys staring down at me. The one I ran into is so hot I forget how to speak, but he sneers at me, muttering "new girl" under his breath as he walks past me like I'm less than dirt on his shoe.

Why are the hottest ones always assholes?

The other two look at each other and the dark-haired one shrugs then follows asshole number one, while the blond rubs the back of his neck, staring after the other two. Letting out a huff, I move to stand as he offers me a hand. "Sorry about that, darlin'. He's had a bad morning."

I take his hand, because why not, and a shot of electricity seems to run up my arm when we touch. Like, damn he's pretty and I've heard of sparks, but shit. Pulling back my hand as quickly as I can, I try not to let it show. I already made an ass of myself once.

"It's fine," I respond, dusting myself off once I've stood, trying not to stare into those pretty blue eyes of his. "Thanks for the hand."

"Anytime, darlin'. See you around." He winks at me as he tips his head, his southern drawl making me think if he was wearing a hat, he'd be touching the brim of it, then strides across the room after his friends to where Dillon, Evan, and the jock I watched get cussed out earlier are.

Nope, not here to get involved in that, but I can't help glancing back as I leave, finding the guy who I ran into staring at me, and I can't tell if it's annoyance or curiosity on his face.

I don't know who he is, but I have a feeling I'm going to find out...

And I don't know if that's a good thing or not, but knowing my luck... yeah, it's going to be fucking awful.

THREE

Talia

I head toward my locker to drop off my books for today's classes. Whoever thought of starting the first school week on a Wednesday was either a genius or entirely crazy. I haven't decided which yet.

The first bell sounds before I get there, so I pick up my pace, knowing that my first class, English Lit with Mr. Hall is right next to my locker, so I should make it.

I glance back at my map, hoping I'm going in the right direction, when I walk into what feels like a wall before bouncing backward, dropping onto my ass with an *oof*, and let out a groan for my stupidity.

Looking up, I realize I didn't walk into a wall.

I walked into Evan, who is blinking down at me like

he's seen a ghost. "Talia?"

Freaking universe is killing me today. As if once wasn't enough. I really need to start paying attention to where I'm going.

"Hi, Evan." He offers a hand to help me up, which I take despite wanting to run the hell away, grabbing my bag once I'm back on my feet. Dusting myself off, I look anywhere but at him, wondering how I can make a quick getaway without this being any more awkward than it already feels.

"How are you here?" he asks, scratching the back of his neck, eyes not having left my face. I hate that he looks exactly like I remember, right down to the nervous bouncing from one foot to the other. After the way things ended with us, I half wished for Karma to hit him with the ugly stick or something. Turns out Karma was not listening.

I open my mouth to reply, realizing the silence is drawing out because I'm just staring, but thankfully the bell sounds again, saving me from this entire situation. "Got to go."

I see the number of my class on one of the signs ahead and grip my bag tighter, thankful that even though I didn't make it to my locker I was still at least going in the right direction.

Sliding into the room just before the bell finishes

ringing, I make my way to the first empty seat I spot toward the back of the room and plant my ass in it. Resting my forehead on my arms for a minute, I catch my breath, more from the awkward, panic inducing moment of running into Evan than from any sort of physical exertion.

The voices around me finally filter into my mind as the anxiety lessens and I lift my head to take note of the people around me. One upside of uniforms is that everyone's wearing the same thing, but it's still pretty easy to see who here is from money and who isn't from the way people have accessorized. Be it the Prada bags, or the Louboutin shoes paired with the black and blue uniforms, or just the air of *I own this place* that so many people here naturally have.

Most people in the room have that exact vibe, but they also all seem to be friends, or at the very least know each other.

The joys of joining a boarding school in senior year, I guess.

Keeping my head down, hoping for a less eventful rest of my day, I grab my laptop and my book from my bag before stashing it at my feet, prepping myself for starting my day with English Lit.

Seconds later, a polished young guy, who can't be much older than we are, in a black suit with his hair slicked back walks into the room and everyone goes silent. Without a word, he walks to the board at the front of the room and everyone moves to their seats as if on autopilot.

"Welcome to your senior year, most of you know me, but for those that don't, I'm Mr. Hall. Same rules as always: pay attention, do the work, and keep your phones put away. Follow them and we won't have problems. Break my rules, well, then we'll have problems, and I'd really rather not. I hope you all did the reading I set before summer, otherwise today's pop quiz is going to suck for you."

I look down at my hands in my lap, smiling. Teachers talking like they're teenagers is too funny, especially when he looks the way he does and somehow seems to have everyone's respect. I press my lips together and school my face before looking back up, glad I started the reading list already.

"Laptops and books away. We're doing this old school. Grab a pen, kids."

An errant groan from the next row draws my attention, and I see a younger version of the teacher sitting in a chair at the back of the room. His amber eyes glint in the sunlight, his square jaw set in defiance as he glares across the room. The only real difference between the two is the younger version's hair is a little longer and not slicked back. That and the ink I see poking up over the collar of his shirt.

Brothers, maybe?

I bite the inside of my cheek, curious as I watch the silent conversation that seems to take place in front of us.

"Really, Isaac?" the teacher asks, brow quirked as he stares at the guy behind me. I turn again, my focus bouncing between them, watching the interaction play out with intrigue. Isaac rolls his eyes and seemingly quits his part of the silent exchange and puts his laptop away. "Good. Let's get on with it, shall we?"

Class whirrs past without incident, which is nice considering it's my first of the year. What I've managed to determine so far is that Issac really is Mr. Hall's little brother, and most people here know him because he went to school here before college.

This place really does like the alumni thing.

I finish scrawling my answers on the paper Mr. Hall handed out, then make my way to the front to drop it on his desk as instructed.

"Thanks, Talia," Mr. Hall says with a smile as I drop the paper on his desk. His voice seems horribly loud in the otherwise silent room. I turn to go back to my desk, finding everyone looking up and staring at me. I want to shrivel up and pass away. Being the center of attention, at the front of class... absolute nightmare.

In fact, it's been the focus of many nightmares of mine.

I move as quickly as I can back to my seat without looking like I'm running, and as I slide into the seat, Isaac pipes up with, "New girl's a kiss ass."

My cheeks flame when the rest of the class starts to laugh and while he and Trey fist bump. Thankfully, the bell rings, taking the attention from me, but that doesn't stop the heat in my face.

"Try sucking up a different way, new girl. Teacher's pet isn't my brother's thing," Issac sneers as he stands.

"Better yet, be seen and not heard," Trey tags on. "Or not seen either. Both work for me."

I open my mouth to respond, but they walk away before I get the chance. Anger flares in my chest and I promise myself to not become a doormat to those assholes.

I've never been one before, I don't intend on starting now.

After a morning of dodging jocks as they bullied nerds and mean girls being bitchy to the outcasts, making the school hierarchy known afresh with the school year, I let out a sigh of relief as I take my seat back in the far corner of the cafeteria that I have claimed as my own. There's nothing like being the new kid to draw attention and become a target. I'm just thankful that I've somehow managed to fly *mostly* below the radar.

Long may it last.

Maybe if I can keep my head down, I can get through this year without any more scars and get off to college unscathed.

I'm not counting my literal run-in with Evan as conflict, mostly because I'm pretending it didn't happen and that he doesn't know I'm here.

Delulu is the solulu and all that other nonsense.

I take a bite of my chicken burrito and do a little happy food dance in my chair, then realize where I am and scan the room to make sure no one saw me.

Of course I'm not that lucky.

I smile at the girl who's sitting two seats down on the opposite side of my table. She's already smiling in that whole, trying not to laugh kinda way, so she totally saw. How the hell was I so in my head that I didn't see her sit down?

"Hi," I say with an awkward wave after taking out an ear bud. "I'm Talia."

"Tory," she responds, with a just as equally awkward nod. "You're new, right?"

Nodding, I try not to grimace. "It's that obvious?"

"Not really. Well, I mean, yes, but only because this place isn't that big and I've been here since freshman year. I'm a senior now, so I'd know your face at the very least. How are you finding the delight that is Arbour?" She tucks the loose strands of mousey blonde hair that have escaped from her ponytail behind her ear. I'm not sure why she's sitting all the way over here. She has that effortlessly pretty look, and she seems nice enough so far, which does make me wonder why she's sitting alone.

Maybe don't overthink every little thing on day one, Talia?

"It's okay so far, just getting the hang of navigating this maze of a building and the way my classes are structured. It's not like any boarding school I've been to before," I tell her honestly.

"You've been to others? Boarding schools, I mean," she asks politely before eating a few of her fries.

Pressing my lips together, I nod. "Yeah, I've bounced around the globe a bit, so I've been to a few. My parents like to travel, so I've been exposed to a lot of the world, even though I've been dumped at a different school every year. Guess I'm just lucky like that."

It's weird to say it's just me that's bounced, rather than me and Brody, but she doesn't need to know about him. Nobody here does. He's gone, so there's no point. I swallow down what feels like shards of glass in my throat at the thought and take a sip of my water to try and clear the feeling.

"Sounds fun," she responds with a shrug. "I've been stuck here forever. Same people, same drama, same bullshit."

"Is that why you're over here rather than with the masses?" I ask. It's nosy, but don't ask, don't get and all that.

"Something like that," she says with a shrug, that sunshiney exterior going ice cold. "People here are unforgiving, and they don't tend to forget either. Like I said, Arbour is a small place."

I glance across the room as Dillon and Evan enter with who I assume are other baseball players, considering the matching letterman jackets. "You're telling me," I mutter before taking another bite of my burrito.

She doesn't seem to want to talk anymore, so I put my earbud back in but leave my music off like before. How to avoid talking to people 101.

The rest of lunch is pretty uneventful; no one else joins the table, no fights break out in the cafeteria, it's just a normal, boring break in the day.

I'm not sure why I'm disappointed, yet, I am.

Scanning over my schedule for this afternoon again, I check my map to make sure I have some semblance of an idea as to where the hell it is I'm going, when shadows appear over the table. I look up and find a group of girls circling Tory, and they don't exactly seem like her friends.

"Made a new friend, Tory?" one of the girls snarls before sneering over at me. "Be careful, new girl. You better keep an eye on your shit if you're going to hang with this one. Nothing is off limits with her."

What is with the new girl thing? Here's hoping it doesn't become a thing.

"Fuck off, Lexi," Tory growls as she pushes her tray away from her. The other girls *ooh* and *ahh*, and I gulp.

So much for no drama.

My disappointment disappears quickly. While I might have enjoyed watching other people's drama, I like to enjoy it with popcorn from a distance, not get dragged into it.

"Oh, we're going, Tory. Don't know what we'll catch being here too long. Take our advice, new girl, stay far away from her. You don't want your tenure at Arbour to be over before it begins." Lexi smiles that ice queen smile at me and I just smile back, because what the fuck am I supposed to say or do here? Sure, I could tell her to go to Hell, but I just met this girl.

Dammit, I feel bad for not attempting to stand up for her or telling the ice queen to eat shit, but I don't know their business. I don't want drama.

Fuck, I hate high school.

"Go run back to Noah, Lexi," Tory says as she stands, pushing her chair back, causing one of the other girls to let out a screech as she collides with the chair. "Can't let your queen know that you're trying to steal her crown."

"She's not queen anymore," Lexi responds, a smug

smile on her face as the others all giggle like she just told the best joke ever.

Without saying a word, Tory grabs her bag and walks away.

It's only then I notice how quiet the entire room is, and how all of the attention is on this table. Glancing around the room, I spy Evan watching me, then I see Dillon, whose wide-eyed stare tells me that Evan didn't tell him I was here.

If they even know they both dated me. Well, kind of.

That'll be a fun conversation, I'm sure.

"Well, while this was just fascinating and informative, ladies, thank you for the warning, but I should get going too," I say, mourning the loss of the rest of my burrito as I wrap it up before putting the lid on my bottle and tucking it back in my bag. "See you around."

"We'll be seeing you, new girl," Lexi says with a saccharine smile. The threat in her voice isn't missed either.

Awesome. So much for flying under the radar.

Just another thing to look forward to this year.

Freaking yay.

FOUR

Talia

So I survived my first week at Arbour. It's finally Friday evening, and I let out a deep breath as I lie on my bed and stare at the ceiling. Still no roommate, but I'm beginning to think—and hope—that whoever it is, isn't coming.

It's been a week. Surely, no one's missing the first week of senior year. I suppose it's only three actual days of school, so that's not anything major I guess. But then, what do I know?

From what I've seen this week, the seniors seem to run the place. The jocks are almost top of the totem pole of hierarchy here. Topped only by the guys I bumped into in the cafeteria earlier in the week.

Nico, Dallas, and Trey, the jock type from day one that was arguing with manic pixie chick, along with Issac, the guy from my English Lit class.

Learning their names wasn't hard. Not when I've spent the week trying to listen to as many conversations as I can. Got to love my earbud tactic.

I haven't made friends, but I'm also not that worried about it. Friends were always Brody's main focus, but this year isn't about friends for me. It's about graduating with the best GPA I can, getting my extracurriculars in top form to keep my college applications padded while I decide what I actually want to do with my life, and somehow managing all of that with zero drama.

Shouldn't be too hard, right?

Which reminds me, I need to start making some decisions about where I'm applying and look over the requirements. Which also means I should probably start thinking about what the hell it is I want to major in.

Applications need to go in soon. I should've already started over the summer, but summer was kind of taken up getting lost in my grief and finding ways to distract myself from it.

Got to love a good wallow and pity party that lasts several months and has the potential to screw up my future.

Just the best.

Hell, I even ignored my birthday because celebrating it

without Brody just didn't feel right.

The door handle jiggles and I sit up straight, wondering who is trying to get in here. It's a Friday night, I figured most people would be off into town or something so I could get some quiet time.

The lock turns a moment before there is a human-sized wall of bags falling through the door.

"Shit!"

I try not to laugh at the cuss in a *very* English accent as I climb from the bed to the disaster at my door. "Hello?"

The tiny pale redhead in the doorway just blinks at me for a second before her cheeks turn a similar shade to her hair. "I am so sorry, I didn't know anyone was in here. What a mess. I'd love to say I'm not usually this messy, but I try not to lie. Sorry."

Apologizing twice in one sentence? Yep, she's definitely British.

Smiling and still trying not to laugh, I shake my head. "I'm a walking disaster sometimes too, don't worry about it. Are you lost?"

"No, just late." She lets out a deep sigh, blows her hair out of her face, and tries to step over the avalanche of bags between us before falling flat on her face. I dart forward in the hopes of catching her, but I am no Flash Gordon, so she slams into the floor with a squeal and I wince at the thud that comes with it.

I thought I had bad luck, but damn.

"Are you okay?" I ask quietly, realizing the door is still open. Thankfully, the hall is empty. No one needs an audience with this shit. She groans, lying face down, and gives me a thumbs up. "Do you want a hand up?"

Rolling over, she groans again, righting her black-rimmed glasses before covering her face with her hands. "No, I'm fine, just leave me to wallow in my humiliation. It's official, my parents should have just called me Klutz, not Kate. I mean, really? It's amazing I've even made it this far in life. I wish I could say this wasn't a perfect example of my entire life, but again, I try not to lie."

"Well, Kate, I'm Talia, known to my friends as a hot mess extraordinaire, so I wouldn't melt down too much. I'm assuming you're my missing roommate?" Part of me is disappointed that my solo room is no more, but it's quieted by the part of me that is thoroughly amused at her arrival.

She glances at me before covering her face again. "Probably should've covered that bit already." She sits up, turns to lean her back against the wall, and looks up at me. "Yes, sorry. I'm Kate Galloway, I've been at Arbour since freshman year, but I finally got to go home for the summer. Unfortunately, the last two weeks have been a typical nightmare and I ended up being entirely late to get back in time for the start of the year, then the airline thought they'd lost my luggage so I've spent the entire day frazzled, hoping to get my stuff, which, obviously, I did, but now, well, here I am." She lifts her arms in the air, in a sort of 'tada' motion and I finally give in to the urge to laugh.

"Well, Kate Galloway, I'm Talia, complete noob to Arbour, yet I've still managed to have a run in with my ex-boyfriend, Lexi and Tory, oh, and I literally ran into Nico in the cafeteria too. So I can't say that you've missed much."

Her eyes go wide and she just blinks at me again. "Oh, it sounds like I've missed plenty!" Scrambling from the floor to her feet, she starts dragging her bags in with my help. I'd be sad about losing the privacy of a room to myself, but so far, tonight has been entertaining. I'm just hoping she isn't a nightmare roommate.

Once her stuff is in and the door is closed, she seems a little less flustered.

"Do you want some help unpacking?" I ask, feeling a little awkward. Gone is my night of peace and pretending to myself that I'm going to get ahead with reading and caught up on homework from the first week.

At least now I don't have to feel guilty, I guess?

"No, no, it's fine. I'm sure you had better plans than that for your first weekend here. Are you going into town?"

I drop onto my bed and shake my head. "Nope, I've managed to avoid most people this week, despite the drama it sounds like. Just trying to get the lay of the land."

"Oh, well, if you want that then we absolutely have to go to town. Everyone will be at CoCo's, and I can fill you in on everything that is Arbour. Advantage to me being a long time wallflower here. I'm quiet and mostly ignored, so I find out everyone's business. It's amazing what people say when they think they're alone."

I laugh again as she wags her brows at me. "And here was me trying to stay under the radar, but who am I to say I know best? Plus, the burgers at CoCo's are to die for."

She jumps to her feet and claps her hands. "Yes, yes they are. Now, let's leave this disaster behind," she says waving to her mountain of luggage. "Let's go have some fun instead."

A trip to CoCo's appears to have been both a great and terrible idea. We ended up waiting for a table for an hour, so we stood around at the counter sipping on drinks with Kate filling me in on the who's who of Arbour that's here already.

"So, you met Lexi, her and her merry Barbie band are in a booth in the corner at the back. Have you met Noah yet?" she asks as I glance over the menu, already knowing what I'm going to order. I only came here twice over the summer, but twice was all I needed to cement my favorite item on the menu. I am not a boujee kind of girl and the chicken, bacon, and cheese CoCo masterpiece has my mouth watering just at the thought of it. That sandwich is incredible. The deluxe burger is a close second, real close, but the chicken is just... chef's kiss.

I look up and realize she's staring at me, waiting for my answer. "Oh, right. Erm, Noah. No, I don't think so."

"You'd know if you met Noah, trust me. Lexi is playing queen bee right now, but when Noah is around, she... well, you'll see, I'm sure. I wonder why she isn't here yet. Normally, wherever Nico, Trey, Dallas, and Issac are, she isn't far from." She pauses, taking a sip of her soda and glancing around the room. "You said you dated Dillon over the summer?"

"Dating is a bit of a stretch, but yeah," I say, trying not to roll my eyes. "And I dated his new bestie, Evan, last year at my old school. I had no idea either of them would be at Arbour this year."

"Yeah, Dillon lives around here, so I'm not sure why he actually boards, but I guess it's just part of the Arbour experience." She shrugs just as our server comes over and takes our order before disappearing. "If Nico and the other *Elites* weren't at Arbour, Dillon would be top dog—the baseball team here are kind of a big deal—so I'd usually say that would score you points, but he dated Lexi from freshman year up until school finished before summer, so if she discovers you and he were a thing, you'll likely find out just how much fun she is."

"Oh, fuck me sideways with a rusty spoon," I moan, cradling my chin in my hands. "Just awesome."

Kate laughs, snorting a little as she does. "I don't think I've ever heard anyone on this side of the pond say that before."

"I've spent some time in England," I tell her with a half-hearted shrug. "Picked up some of your random-ass phrases, I guess."

"You won't be alone. There aren't many international students here, but Trey, the tall, dark, beautifully terrifying god of football here at Arbour is also from back home. An East London boy. I don't know his entire story, but he moved to the States just before freshman year and has been at Arbour since. He's adopted, that much I know, though I don't quite understand the dynamics because he was adopted by an American family. Anyway, his sister Allie is all kinds of amazing, but that inner sanctum keeps their cards close to their chest. So while I can give you info on *the Elites*, I don't know *that* much."

"How mysterious," I tease, and she pokes her tongue out at me. Mental high five to me for guessing his accent right though.

"Hey, I know almost everyone's story here, but for such high profile people, they keep their shit locked down between them. The inner sanctum is no joke. They're friendly with other people, but the five of them... it's like an unbreakable circle. Which is why it's so weird that you've not seen Noah. I obviously royally messed up being late, turning up in more ways than one."

The door to CoCo's opens and, for a second, it's like the room is muted as the four guys she was just talking about enter the place... followed by a dainty, ballerina-type blonde, who I can only assume is Noah.

"The queen bee?" I ask Kate, who turns her head back around from gawking and nods.

"The one and only, Noah Carrington."

It's like they're royalty. The crowd literally parts for them and they head to the only open booth in the place, in the opposite corner to where Lexi and her friends are. The music and the sound of voices in the room seem quieter than before, but maybe that's just me being weird as I watch them take their seats, securing Noah in the back of the booth, surrounded by the rest of them, like her own personal bodyguards. "Are they always like that?"

"Not usually, they're protective of her, sure, but they're not her security team or anything," she replies, her gaze darting over to the group in question again. "From what I know, Dallas, Nico, and Isaac have been friends for like, forever. Noah and Nico come as a package deal since they're family, so she's always been with one of them, and Trey... well, he joined their group in freshman year. There were rumors of something with Dallas but like I say, they keep their stuff under wraps. But I wonder if this new level of protectiveness has something to do with why she's late to Arbour this year."

"Who knows?" I say with a shrug, dismissing it. "So, since you know the ins and outs, other than Lexi, who should I be avoiding at all costs, and just how hard is it going to be to get on the swim team?"

She chokes mid sip of her soda. It shoots out her nose and her cheeks turn plum as she darts for napkins. "Swim team?"

"Are you okay?" I ask, ignoring the question. This girl really is a bit of a walking disaster. I don't think I've ever come across someone who made my awkward ass look like an eloquent and graceful butterfly, and yet...

Brody would have had a field day here. He'd have fit right in, joined the football team, probably become captain or something insane and this poor girl would have been fodder for him.

The thought hits me out of nowhere and I try not to let the downturn in my mood show on my face. It's not that there's ever a day I don't think of him, but I've been getting so good at getting through the days and only thinking about him first or last thing.

"I'm fine," she says as she brushes the napkins over her face, then grabs some more to mop up the soda on the table. "You're trying out for the swim team?"

"Yeah," I tell her with a shrug. "Coach said tryout sign-ups come out this week. I've always been on my school swim team, and gymnastics. I don't intend on not competing just because I'm at another new school." Bit of a lie, I totally quit the teams halfway through junior year when my grief over Brody got the better of me, but otherwise, total truth.

"Lexi is the swim captain."

Well shit.

"Then let's hope she has no idea I was Dillon's fuck toy over summer, or if she does somehow find out, that she doesn't hold it against me." I shrug again, because there's fuck all I can do about it now.

"Good luck with that. Lexi is... well, she's honestly just awful. I've had my fair share of run-ins with her in the past. So have the few friends I have here at Arbour. I've managed to stay off her radar since sophomore year but it's like she communes with the devil, I swear."

"Surely she can't be that bad?" I ask, but continue before waiting for an answer. "Either way, I'm still trying out. It's not like she can keep me off the team."

"No, but she can make your life a living Hell. Just ask Tory."

I laugh softly and shake my head again. "Still so confusing. What's their issue?"

"Well, they used to be inseparable, best friends, joined at the hip as it were, but then, during one of their breaks, Dillon and Tory hooked up. This was like, the summer before sophomore year, and since... well, I mean, you told me you were front row to their ongoing spat."

"Awesome. Though, I mean, if they were besties, girl code states you don't get with your friend's ex."

Kate nods enthusiastically. "Exactly. Which is why Tory is pariah number one. I almost feel bad for her at this point though. She was young, it was one stupid make out session. But Arbour is small, as such, no one ever really forgets your highlight reel here."

"So keeping my head down was a good idea," I mumble and she nods again.

"Definitely."

Our server swings by with our food, refilling our sodas before disappearing back into the chaos of CoCo's, when shouts start up in the far corner.

I look over and see Evan squaring off with Trey. "Jeez, Evan is going to get destroyed."

Don't get me wrong, he's tall, but Trey is... well, he's huge. Taller and wider than Evan, and he looks pissed as hell.

"That's Evan?" Kate squeaks across from me, her eyes

darting from me to the commotion in the corner. "Well shit, Trey could eat him for breakfast. Not that Evan isn't like, the all-American type or whatever, but have you *seen* Trey? If he didn't terrify me, I'd crush all over him."

I laugh louder than I should, but she just grins at me. "Go you though, because Evan and Dillon? Yum in that jock type way. That's your type?"

"Not usually," I reply, shaking my head, trying to work out just what is going on in the corner, but we're too far away to hear much of anything.

She eyes me before a shout draws our attention back to the other side of the room, where Trey is taking a swing at Evan.

"Enough!" The bellow is so loud I swear my heart skips a beat. Nico is standing in front of Trey, a hand on his chest, and Evan is holding his jaw, Dillon and a few more people I don't know standing beside him.

"This tosser started—" Trey starts, but Nico cuts him off with a look before turning back to Evan.

"Leave."

Nico's declaration is low, but the entire place is silent enough to hear a pin drop. The menace in his tone is unmistakable. Evan opens his mouth to argue but Dillon claps a hand on his shoulder, shakes his head, and they all make their way out.

"Okay, so he really does have that sort of power," I say

to Kate when the silence dissipates as Trey and Nico take their seats again. *Color me interested.*

"So hot," Kate says, fanning her face, and I laugh until her smile drops and she lets out a sigh. "If only he wasn't a giant asshole."

FIVE

"After a somewhat disastrous start to the semester, I think I might just be okay."

"Disastrous start?" Josie asks and I nod, rebalancing my phone so she can see me on the call rather than my ceiling. "What happened now, Kate? You've only been back for two days."

I swear her British accent is thicker when she's shocked. Or maybe I just miss the sounds of home already. "Oh, sister of mine, don't you know I am a walking disaster with a smile on my face? Two days is more than enough to create chaos."

She cackles at me, shaking her head as she puts another pin in the deep-green material on the mannequin before her. My big sister, the designer. Not only is she beautiful and smart, she's creative and nice too. If I didn't love her so much, I might hate her. I mean, sure we look mostly alike; the red hair, the blue eyes. But she is tall, curvy, and typically pretty. I swear, she's all legs. I however... well, I'm short and curvy, which isn't really a great look in my oh-so-humble opinion of myself. Our brother, Charlie, the fierce lawyer who causes hell wherever he goes, well, he looks exactly like my dad, just with the red hair from Mum too. I am definitely the ugly duckling in this story. "Oh, I'm fully aware, but what happened?"

I tell her about the debacle of falling through the door when I arrived at my new dorm and met Talia, my run-in with the new editor for the school's newspaper this morning, and my soup exploding in the microwave just twenty minutes ago when I tried to fend for myself and get some lunch.

After laughing, she picks up her phone and looks at me with concern on her face. "Where is your new roomie? Are you getting on okay?"

"She's out, not sure where. She seems nice enough. We went to CoCo's last night and there was drama with the fabulous five—"

"When is there not with that lot?" She sighs, rolling her eyes.

"I know, right? But yeah, Talia seems nice. I have a

feeling we'll be good friends."

"I'm glad," she says, smiling. "Now, what is up with the new editor? She seriously thinks she can kick you from the paper because you arrive a week late? Have you spoken to Mr. Teller?"

"Not yet," I tell her, flopping back on my bed. "I don't know if it's worth it. Obviously, I want to be a journalist, and being on the paper is good for my college applications, but I could show initiative and start a blog, writing about stuff that actually matters rather than fluff for the school freaking pomp paper that rarely covers anything actually worthy of news." I'm almost panting at the end of my tirade, but I do feel a little better having got it off my chest.

"Well then, do that if that's what you'd rather do. No one ever said that path is the only one. Be bold. Stand out. That's what will get the attention of colleges with your application. Screw the new editor." Her indignation fills me with enthusiasm that maybe my idea isn't just a pile of rubbish.

"Thanks, Josie. I needed that."

"Anytime, little sis. That's kinda what I'm here for. Now then... are you going to tell Evander you have a crush on him this year? That is the big, glaring question that's been avoided." She wags her brows at me as she sits down on her sofa, grabbing her cup of tea as she gets comfy.

"Probably not," I tell her honestly, trying not to sigh. "I

saw him at CoCo's for a few minutes, but he and Callum were on their way out. Plus, Vann and I are friends. It works that way. He doesn't see me as anything more. Plus, high school crushes don't go anywhere. I'm better just stuffing down my crush and not getting boy crazy."

"Oh, Kate," she mutters, shaking her head after taking a sip of her tea. "You are so clueless when it comes to boys. I blame myself. I should've taught you better when I was there."

Rolling my eyes, I shake my head. "Hardly. Plus you were three years ahead of me. There wasn't much you could've said while we were here together that might have made me less awkward around the penis carrying species."

She giggles at me and I can't help but smile again. Nothing like my big sister to make me feel like being me is entirely okay. "Maybe, maybe not. But if you don't say something, you'll never know what could have happened. Better an oops than a what if, trust me. Regret the things you did, not the things you didn't. Just like Nana always said."

"Yeah, or not," I counter before I sit up. "As much as I love our chats, I should probably go. I need to catch up on the mountain of work I missed this week."

"Okay, buttercup. I'm here if you need me. Same time next week? I can fill you in on the gala that Mum is dragging me to. Not that I'm that mad, she'll be wearing one of my creations too, so hopefully I can drum up some business with the rich and fabulous for my designs."

I shouldn't be jealous of my sister and her success, but the fact that she's living back in London and jetting off to New York this week with my mum for some fundraiser definitely sounds more fun than high school. "Yes, send me all the pictures too! I hope you have an amazing time."

"Not long and you can come too! Well, unless you're off covering the news all over the world, of course." She winks at me before blowing a kiss at the screen. "Love you."

"Love you," I say back before we end the call.

How can I be homesick after just a few days? Especially when I'm at Arbour more than I'm home. This is my home away from home. My parents met here. Both Charlie and Josie came here because we Galloways are alumni and this is what we do. My dad just happened to be the American boy who fell in love with the English girl in his year and followed her back to London when he graduated because he couldn't stand the idea of being apart from her. They went to Oxford together, and well, the rest is history. You'd think with a story like that I'd be more of a romantic, willing to admit my three-year crush, but that's definitely not the case. It also doesn't mean I wish that I got to stay home for school like normal people.

But no, I'm here. Just one more year.

And I get my pick of college. That's the deal my parents made with my siblings and I. We go to Arbour, because we're alumni, and also, the opportunities from going here are unreal, but the rest is up to us.

Looking over at my desk, piled high with my books and the notes that Ms. Feldman gave to me when I arrived so I could catch up, my stomach twists. Catching up is going to suck, but it's just one week. I can worry about the paper or creating my own blog after.

My stomach rumbles, reminding me of my failed attempt at lunch before Josie called. As I ponder whether or not to make some ramen before working, the door to my room opens and Talia appears.

She spots me on my bed, hangs up her call, and grins at me. "Fun morning?"

"Just thrilling," I reply and her grin widens. I swear, she's peppier than I am sometimes and I didn't think that was possible. "Busy day?"

"Just scoping out the grounds some more. Wanted to grab my wallet before hunting down some food. Want to come into town?"

Thank you, Talia, for the perfect procrastination!

"Sounds great, let me get dressed. Have you been to Rico's?"

She shakes her head as she sits down. "Nope, haven't heard of it."

"It's just outside of town, but they make the best burrito of your life."

She barks out a laugh as I scurry into my closet to put on something that isn't my thick joggers and fluffy socks.

"I'll drive," she says once I'm dressed and pocketing my phone and wallet in my jeans.

"Oh, good." I grin. "Because I don't have a car here."

"No car?" she exclaims, her weirdly American-yet-not accent twanging in her shock, and I nod, laughing softly.

"My parents think it builds character."

"What, walking into town?" she asks as we head out of the dorms.

I nod, shrugging as I do. "That, and having to make friends so we can either walk together or they can drive. It's devious, really."

She shakes her head at me, bewilderment on her face. "It's definitely something. At least they care, I guess."

You'd think I'd be grateful for a free study period first thing on a Monday morning, but the get up and go kinda girl that I am hates that my week starts with a block of nothing. Yes, it means I can finish the reading I didn't get done yesterday, and yes, I can sit here in the library getting ahead on some of the other bits I know are coming, but still... not a fan.

The only upside is that this library is my happy place, my sanctuary of sorts, so starting my week in here isn't the worst thing in the world. It's quiet and comfortable, and Miss Perry, the librarian, mostly leaves me alone because she knows I'm trustworthy.

Kate Galloway would never step out of line or cause trouble.

I sigh at the thought. Sometimes I wonder if the troublemakers have more fun... but the thought of getting into trouble, I get anxious flushes even at the prospect of it. A rebel I am not. Never have been and likely never will be.

Even if that makes me a little boring. I guess I can live with that. Or I can reinvent myself at college. The problem with a place like Arbour is that reinventing myself, if I even wanted to, would be impossible. I've known these people too long to be someone new now.

Why are you thinking that you even want to change? You like your life.

And I do...

Honestly, I don't know why my brain is running down this rabbit hole today. I put it down to Monday morning emptiness. I have nothing to focus on and I'd really like to just jump in with both feet so I don't feel like I'm behind. Maybe it's Talia, the fact that she's new here, that she can be whoever she wants to be because no one really knows anything about her. Hell, I'm her roommate and I don't know much beyond the fact that she likes to eat, had a promiscuous summer, and has nightmares each night that she doesn't talk about—not my business, so I won't pry unless she says something.

That must be it. She's shiny and new and we haven't had someone new join our year since we started here as freshmen. Though Evan is new here this year too, and he happens to know Talia.

The journalist in me doesn't want to believe the coincidence, but really, what else could it be?

Leave it alone, Kate.

Letting out a sigh, I pack up my bag, waiting for the bell to sound. I flick through my junk email, considering shooting one off to Erica, the new editor on the paper, and my biggest competition on the paper since we both started. If I hadn't been late getting here, I'd be the freaking editor.

Thank you for that, Universe. Stellar planning there.

Maybe I should just accept my fate like I said to Josie; start my own blog, write what I want to. I was so full of indignation yesterday after Erica kicked me off the paper, but today? Today I want the security blanket of having the paper on my transcripts. I like finishing what I started.

Maybe I should speak to Ms. Feldman about it. Feels like snitching, but also, why would I care about that? This is Arbour, hardly a snitches-get-stitches kind of place. Plus, Erica is about as rebellious as I am, even if she is a power-hungry arse.

I type out an email to Ms. Feldman, hitting send just as the bell goes, feeling only a little gross about tattling to get my spot back.

What was it Josie said? Better an oops than a what if? Different circumstance, but it should still apply.

I gather my bag, slide my phone into the pocket of my blazer, and head out to the now-full halls of Arbour so I can make it to History. The grin on my face at the prospect of my second favorite class confirms just how much of a nerd I am, but I am self-appointed and proud. I like being a nerd. We read a lot, and plus, being a nerd means I get to know the gossip of Arbour without being a part of it.

Win, win if you ask me.

Not that anyone ever has.

Speaking of drama, the fabulous five that are Nico, Noah, Isaac, Trey, and Dallas strut toward me down the hall, wrapped up in their own conversation, and the sea of students part for them so they never have to even acknowledge that they're taking up basically all the space. I plaster myself to a wall as they pass, wondering why they all look so serious, and if it could be about what happened at CoCo's, just as the second bell rings.

Once they're gone, I pick up my pace and slide into

History moments before Mr. Torvito, parking myself in an empty seat in the third row.

Nothing like center of the room anonymity.

"Psst," sounds from my left and I look over to see Rosie, fellow nerd and library enthusiast. "Did you hear about the drama at CoCo's?"

My eyes widen and I shake my head. "Fill me in after class?"

She nods and I do an internal little jig.

See? Nerd network wins again. She's roomed with one of Lexi's friends, Bella, for years. Somehow, they've been dorm mates since sophomore year, so she hears all sorts of gossip. They ignore her and hardly even notice she's around. Sucks for her, but I've known her long enough to know she prefers it that way. They may ignore her, but it means they also don't pick on her.

Lord knows she suffered enough freshman year. We all did.

"Morning, you bright individuals. Who is ready for a start-of-the-year pop quiz?" Mr. Torvito interrupts my inner monologue with his announcement, causing a groan in the room, but not from me. I love a pop quiz.

"I hope you all did your reading and thought to read ahead, because you're going to need it for this!" he declares with a grin before handing out the quizzes he has in his hand. I do a mental fist pump at my thoughts to read ahead this morning. A rebel I might not be, but once again, team nerd wins.

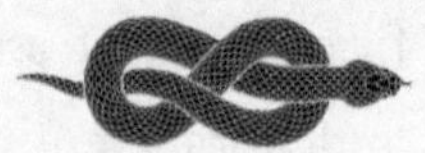

A knock on my bedroom door pulls me from my reading. AP English Lit is no joke, and I'm already behind. I expect to find Talia minus her keys, but am shocked to find Vann standing at my door. "Oh, erm, hi."

Could I be any more awkward right now? Game face, Kate!

"Hey, Kate," he says, smiling while tugging down the sleeves of his jumper. "We didn't get a chance to catch up yet since you were late to school, so I thought I'd swing by, but I probably should've called or texted first."

"No, you're fine." I try to smile, like it's casual and oh so normal that he's here. This is Josie's fault. I can hear her in my head going on about being oblivious when it comes to boys, but Vann is my friend. He's seen me ugly snot cry, for goodness' sake. I have nothing to feel weird or awkward about.

Yet I do.

He stares at me and I realize I stopped speaking but am still standing in the doorway. "Right, yeah, come in!"

I take a step back, letting him enter the room and

pushing the door closed, leaving it unlocked because Nicolette is a stickler for those pesky rules when it comes to having the other sex in your room.

"So, your new roommate seems nice," he says before taking a seat at my desk.

I move toward my bed to sit, then pause, my mum's voice in my head about being a good host. "She is. Do you want a drink?"

"No, I'm good." He smiles at me, his hair falling in his eyes, and for a minute, I'm stunned stupid. Obviously, I haven't seen him since the end of last year, and summer was *good* to him. "You have a good break?"

"Yeah, it was great," I say as I finally drop onto my bed, tucking my legs beneath me as I get comfy. "Josie moved closer to London, so we spent a lot of time together. Charlie even managed to make it home for Mum and Dad's anniversary. It was good. Did you?"

"It was okay." He shrugs. "I spent a lot of it with Callum. He basically forced me into the gym with him everyday, but we mostly just chilled at the beach. Mom and Dad spent the summer hopping around Europe, so it was mostly quiet. Especially with Sam doing the whole charity thing over in Africa."

"Oh right, I forgot she was doing that!" His older sister is a little out there, but she's spent the last three years bouncing around the globe working for different charities, either building houses, teaching, or helping with rescue relief. Her life sounds a little crazy, but super fulfilling.

He picks up the remote to the TV Mum had shipped here earlier today–which I excitedly unboxed and set up on my desk straight after class–and starts flicking through the channels. "Scoot over," he says as he moves over to the bed. "Have you seen the latest season of *Invincible* yet?"

"I didn't know it was out!" I shimmy over to the left side of the bed, making space for him beside me, while trying not to overthink what is a perfectly normal thing for us.

He grins as he drops onto the bed beside me, dropping an arm over my shoulder as he flicks the show on. "Well it is, and we have limited time to catch up!"

I get comfortable leaning against him and we lose a few hours watching the first two episodes of the show. At one point, I laughed so hard I snorted, which just made him laugh harder. After that I relaxed into our usual groove and managed to actually enjoy myself. I missed just hanging out with him. He gets me and my nerdy ways, and he never makes me feel lesser or judged... even with the snot crying and snort laughing.

I've found that it's rare to find a person you can truly be yourself with. Which is exactly why I'm good with us being just friends.

Anything more than that would make it complicated

and I don't want to lose this.

His phone vibrates in his pocket, and he frowns when he looks at it. "I should probably get going."

"Oh, okay," I murmur as he pulls his arm from around my shoulders before climbing from the bed. "Everything okay?"

"Yeah, I just forgot I told Callum I'd go to the gym with him tonight. Apparently he needs a spotter, so he can't go alone."

"Okay, I should probably get back to studying anyway," I reply with a smile. "I'll see you soon?"

"You will," he says, leaning down to hug me and kissing my cheek. "Be good."

"I always am."

He winks at me and heads for the door. Do I discreetly check out his ass? Of course I do, I'm only human.

Just. Friends.

I shake my head, hoping my thoughts aren't written all over my face as he moves to leave. The door opens as he reaches it, the swing of it only just missing him as he comes face to face with Talia. Stepping to one side, he lets her in before turning back to me. "Later, Kate."

"Bye," I call out as he closes the door behind him.

Talia drops her stuff on her bed then looks over to me, a smile toying on her lips. She lets out a wolf whistle and I duck my head into my chest. Apparently, she can see what

I thought was very inconspicuous written all over my face. "And who, little Kate, was that?"

SIX

Talia

Staring out the window while I'm supposed to be focusing on what it is Mr. Lancaster is talking about in my history class probably isn't the best use of my time, but my nightmares kept me up most of last night, so now I am flagging.

I'm grateful I didn't seem to wake Kate up, but I really wish I'd have gotten more sleep. We spent most of the weekend unpacking her stuff, and her showing me parts of Spring Creek that only someone who's lived here would know. Like the cute little vintage clothing boutique, BoHo's, down a tiny little offshoot alley that I had no idea existed but managed to spend way too much money at on Saturday afternoon. It was nice hanging out with her and having a friend, even if it is mostly because she's my roommate. I know friends weren't exactly on my agenda, but I also hadn't realized just how much I've isolated myself since I moved here.

Sure, I was friendly with people, and there was the whole Dillon thing, but really, he didn't know me. Not properly. None of his friends are my friends, they're just people I spoke to occasionally if I was out with him. Which wasn't often.

But what really has my attention is the football team. They're practicing on the field just outside the window I'm gazing out of.

"Miss Hayes?" I jolt hearing my name and blink as I face Mr. Lancaster.

My cheeks heat as I realize everyone is looking at me and I want the ground beneath me to open up and swallow me whole. Center of attention is so not my thing. "Sorry, what was that?"

"Maybe if you were listening to me, you'd already know." He scowls at me and I feel the red on my cheeks deepen as I curl in on myself.

"Maybe she's just a bit slow, sir," Lexi calls out from across the room, laughter sounding at her words, and I roll my eyes. "I have the answer though."

Of course she does.

"Go on then." The teacher encourages her to speak

up and I start actually focusing on the lesson, scowling when I realize I did know the answer, just not the goddamn question. For the next thirty minutes, I try to focus and take notes on the Gold Rush, despite the fact that I've already covered it and think it's an entire snooze fest. One thing I've learned about bouncing around schools is, same subject just with different details required on tests.

When the bell rings, I let out a sigh of relief. It's lunch and I finally have time to caffeinate and prepare for an afternoon of U.S. Government. So freaking thrilling. What I am looking forward to is swim team tryouts. They're tonight at seven and I am *so* ready to get back in the water. Technically, the pool was open this morning for general use, but I was rotting in bed, so there was no pool time for me.

Just another thing I need to get better at.

By the time I pack up my things, most of the class is empty and I find Kate in the hall waiting for me. She takes one look at me and winces. "Ouch, bad morning?"

"Do I really look that bad?" I ask with a sigh.

She shrugs and tries for a smile that absolutely looks like a grimace. "I mean, I've seen worse?"

"Upside, I guess." I try to straighten out my uniform, realize my shirt buttons aren't aligned, and drag Kate into the bathroom.

"Not like I haven't looked like this all morning.

Seriously, how does no one point this shit out?" My grumble is more at myself as I undo and redo my buttons, straighten out my pants, and redo my ponytail. My messy bun was about the only messy thing on me that was meant to be askew.

"Forget about it. Who cares, really?" Kate says as she leans against the wall. "I have gossip that might make you feel better?"

"Caffeine will make me feel better," I tell her as I pick my bag back up and sling it over my shoulder. "Gossip is a good second though."

We head toward the cafeteria and Kate fills me in on her morning, sans gossip, because apparently hall gossip is beneath us.

Once I have a burger, fries, chips, Coke, and chocolate, I feel a little better. Kate finishes paying for her stuff and rallies beside me. "Let's go."

"I usually sit—"

"Oh, I know, you told me," she says, rolling her eyes. "But we're avoiding Lexi drama, remember? So you're not sitting there. We can sit where I've always sat."

She drags me over to a semi-full table and says hi to the people sitting there, introducing me to them as I sit, but not one name registers. Probably good to stay off Lexi's radar, considering Dillon and her jab this morning in History. Though, the jab earlier could have been because she knows about Dillon, but I have no idea. I ask Kate and she grimaces at me. "Yeah, maybe. But it could also just be because you're new and she's seeing if she can. Got to love the mean girl mentality."

"On Wednesdays, we wear pink," I snark, and she giggles at me.

"Exactly that. My big sister loves the original *Mean Girls*. I swear I heard, 'You go Glen Coco' more than anyone ever should when I was younger. But as for Lexi, just try to stay under the radar, unless you have grandeur ideas about knocking her off her princess throne and being Noah's new underling, of course."

The soda I just took a sip of catches in my throat as I laugh at her and end up coughing. Thankfully, the rest of the table are in some heated debate about their new D&D campaign that is meant to be starting this week.

"Yeah, not on my agenda. Though, I can't avoid Lexi entirely if she's captain of the swim team. Tryouts are tonight and I'm determined to get a place."

"And I will be there in full cheerleader mode, obviously." She grins at me before taking a bite of her sandwich and stealing a few of my fries.

"Obviously," I reply after taking a bite of my gooey cheesy goodness burger. "Anyway, you said you had gossip."

Her grin grows wider and she nods while finishing her

food. "Yes, yes I did. It's not like, *major*, but I found out what the Evan and Trey thing was about. Apparently, your ex knows Noah."

My brows shoot up and I blink at her for a second before remembering how to speak. "He does?"

"Apparently so, and he made a comment Friday night, hence the throwdown that followed."

My curiosity piques, so I steal a glance over to the table where Noah is sitting with her four bodyguards. Then I notice the table next to them, with Lexi and Co., along with Dillon, Evan, and their group of friends. Evan has a black eye and one of Lexi's friends is sitting in his lap, fawning over him, but he keeps looking over at Noah.

"Small world," I murmur. "What did Evan say to her?"

"That much I don't know," she responds. "But whatever it was, it made the five of them lock down tight. The fact that Lexi isn't attached to Noah's ass, and the fact that the football team isn't sitting with Trey is telling too. Something has happened, but everyone is keeping tight-lipped about it."

"I could ask Evan," I suggest, and her eyes light up.

"You totally could," she responds, nodding. "And then we can try to piece the puzzle together. Just try not to end up on Noah's radar. I know you already had a run-in with the guys, but that was nothing. If they're really at odds with Lexi and the baseball team, being associated with them could end up badly for you. Got to love high school politics."

I chew on my bottom lip, wondering if working out the gossip is worth interacting with Evan. "I might just steer clear. Evan and I... well, that's not the best history either."

Kate nods, her eyes softening. "Totally get that. Who needs gossip? We just need to graduate with no drama, that's your mantra, right?"

"Absolutely," I tell her with a nod before shoving a few fries in my mouth. "Zero drama."

"Then we stay right here, at the nerd table, and you can join my covert wallflower club. Simple."

I glance over at Noah's table again and find Nico staring over at me intensely. I hold his gaze until it's uncomfortable and glance down at my plate of food.

"Well," Kate says quietly. "Maybe not so simple."

I spend the afternoon trying not to decipher why Nico was glaring at me at lunch, and attempting to focus on class and the fact that tryouts should be where my brain is at. Obviously, I mostly failed at that, but I'm now in the changing room for the pool along with a dozen other girls who are also trying out for the team.

Unsurprisingly, I recognize almost no one. One of Lexi's friends, Bella I think her name is, is in here, but most of the other girls are from the years below me, I think, and I can't say I've spent much time paying attention to people outside of those I might come into contact with normally.

Redoing my ponytail, I make sure it's slicked back then fiddle with the zipper on my jacket. My swimsuit is beneath my loungewear, but it's absolutely freezing in here, so nobody is in just their suits. I swirl my goggles on my finger, recheck that my locker is padlocked tight, then bounce on the spot, trying to shake off my nervous energy.

"Ladies!" Coach's voice sounds throughout the room moments before she appears in the doorway. "I hope you're ready. I'm going to split you into teams of two, you'll do four laps of each stroke, then out of the pool for the other team before doing the next stroke. Your times will be taken and I'll let you know by email this week who made the team. I hope you're prepared, competition is hot this year and there are only two spots open. Good luck!" She blows her whistle and leaves the room. People start stripping down to their suits and grabbing their towels, so I follow suit then walk out to the pool with everyone.

I blink when the voices register, then look over to the bleachers and realize they're not exactly full, but that is a lot of freaking people.

Since when are tryouts a spectator event?

Just another thing about Arbour to get used to, I guess. Coach points at me and calls out, "two." So I move to the side where the other twos are waiting and try not to fidget too much.

The two girls next to me are whispering between themselves, but not so quiet that I miss their conversation. "Have you seen Jenny in the pool this year? I swear it's like she's on something. She's going to make the team for sure."

"I don't know, Lexi has never liked her. You know Coach listens to her opinion on most stuff. Plus, if she is on something, she'll be dropped anyway. Drug testing is mandatory for all sports teams."

"Oh, I know, but still. She had a major glow up over the summer. Someone said she went to a swim camp with the Olympic coaches. She's chasing a scholarship or the Olympic track, supposedly."

I have no idea who the hell Jenny is, so I tune out their conversation, but bear in mind that if Jenny is that good, there's one spot left, and it has to be mine.

That thought is the one I cling to and take a deep breath as I try to focus. Brody used to be at my tryouts, or at least with me beforehand. He was my biggest supporter in everything. I haven't been in a pool for a while, so hoping that I'm going to beat out everyone here is probably foolish, wishful thinking, but then, I've never doubted my ability in the water.

You've never taken this long off either.

I shut down that new voice and pay attention as the first group lines up at the edge of the pool. The whistle blows and they're in the water. I focus on the timer on the wall, knowing what my best times were before, hoping like hell they're going to be enough.

One girl pulls ahead dramatically and nerves shake me. I guess that's Jenny.

Shit, she's fast.

The first group finishes and my heart sinks a little. The times are close as hell, and tight to my old times. I probably should've tried swimming over the summer. But there's no time for those regrets or thoughts now as Coach calls us to the edge of the pool for freestyle.

I pull on my swim cap and goggles and get zen as I step on the platform. The whistle sounds and I dive, shutting out every thought but my breaths and moving as fast as I can through the water.

A peace I'd almost forgotten about slides through me as I cut through the water. There is no sound, no pain, no sadness, just the here and now. I reach the far side, twist, and push off for the second lap.

Breath in. Breath out.

My arms ache in a beautiful way, right along with my lungs, and a pinch of joy joins the peace.

I can do this.

I push myself as hard as I can, not paying attention to the others in the water, just reaching the end of the pool as quickly as possible.

Pushing off for the final time, I dig down as deep as I can, pulling on parts of me I haven't engaged in a while, and try to push even harder.

When I reach the end, I grin as I pull myself from the water and glance at the timer.

"Go Talia!" Looking up at the bleachers, I spot Kate and her fiery hair bouncing around as she calls out my name. I wave before grabbing my towel and heading back to where the others are standing.

I was first out of the water. Not by much, but by enough. Close with the first team though, and there are still more strokes to go, but I feel more confident than I did a few minutes ago. This does confirm I need to get back to the gym though.

"Good time." I glance in the direction of the voice and see the girl who was fastest in group one.

"Thanks," I reply with a small smile. "You too."

She nods as Coach calls her group back to the pool. I look back over to Kate, who is waving at me, so I wave over to her again, then turn my focus back to the water.

An hour later, I'm exhausted, cold, and my hair is wet, but I'm dressed again, hoping I did enough to make the team, even if I did totally choke doing the butterfly. Cramp struck on the last lap and I ended up being sixth out of the water.

I head out of the pool after Coach tells us about the practice schedule if we make the team; daily gym sessions except for Thursday where we'll have evening swim practice, along with early morning practice on Tuesdays and Saturdays. I'm still chastising myself over my performance when I stumble into Kate. "You did so good!" she exclaims before hugging me tightly. "Swimming superstar!"

I hug her back, thankful for her cheerful exuberance. "Thanks, I did okay. Just got to wait now."

"You did better than okay. Or at least, it looked like it. The closest I get to water is when I go out on my dad's boat, but that's it. Sports and I aren't exactly friends, and I hate the water. I can't swim."

I snort a laugh. "Of course your dad has a boat."

She blushes, but I nudge her with my shoulder, smiling so she knows I'm only teasing.

"At Arbour, everyone that isn't on scholarship has a boat, or a jet, or something insane. It's ostentatious, but that's just this place."

"I do not have a boat or a jet and I'm not on scholarship either," I point out.

"I guess not, so you can be the exception to the rule,"

she teases before looping her arm with mine. "Now, let's go get cake and/or ice cream, because I'm starving just from watching you work that hard."

My stomach grumbles in response to her suggestion and we both giggle. "Maybe we should get some real food too," I suggest, and she nods.

"Nuggets and ice cream. The meal of queens. Let's do this! To the cafeteria!"

I can't help but laugh at her silliness. She's like this whether there are people around or not and it's refreshing. Everyone else, myself included, seems to dampen their personality here at Arbour. Well, excluding certain cliques anyway, but who knows what they're really like behind closed doors?

Making a vow to myself to stop toning myself down, I join her exuberance as we almost skip down the hall toward the cafeteria, a smile on my face wider than I've had since before Brody, feeling for a moment that maybe this year can be more than just graduation.

Maybe I'll find myself again.

Maybe I'll discover who I was meant to be, and actually find happiness again, too.

Groaning as I roll over in bed, frustrated that I once again cannot sleep, I tap on my phone and huff when I see it's two in the morning.

This is bullshit.

I kick off my blankets and slip my feet into my slippers before grabbing my robe from the end of my bed. Maybe a hot chocolate will help me sleep. I grab my keys and phone as quietly as I can before creeping from the room, trying not to wake Kate. That girl could probably sleep through a hurricane, but still, if I did wake her, I'd feel awful.

It's only Monday—technically Tuesday, but I haven't slept yet, so I refuse to acknowledge that out loud—but this can't set the tone for my week. Week three of the year can't be where I start messing up. Especially with music, chemistry, and math on my schedule tomorrow. They are not even remotely my strongest subjects. Decent sleep is necessary for a day like that.

Making my way down to the ground floor where Kate pointed out a small kitchenette area that I hadn't seen before she turned up, the place is eerily quiet. Could be the dark only lit up by the flashlight on my phone, could be the lack of sleep and my wild imagination being a terrible combination, but I feel so on edge.

Once I reach the bottom of the staircase, I push open the door toward the hall where the dorms link up and the kitchenette is tucked away and pause, hearing a voice.

"We made a start. One meeting was complete and no, it wasn't okay. Not even remotely." The voice pauses and footsteps fill the silence. "What is it that you expect me to do here? I can't just get rid of them, there are laws about that, apparently. Plus, you told me to keep it low key. Students disappearing isn't low key."

What the hell?

"I'll think of something," the voice says, and I consider turning around and going back to bed, but it's like I'm frozen in place. "Yeah, fine. I'll update you when I have news. Bye."

I'm still frozen in the doorway when Nico appears before me. My mouth opens then closes while I try to think of something to say. He stands before me, arms crossed, glaring at me like I'm his worst enemy.

"How long have you been there?"

His question jolts me from my stupor and I take a step forward out of the doorway, then stumble as my foot twists in my slipper and fall right into him. He catches me, keeping me upright, and I swear I want the ground to open up and swallow me whole for the second time today.

"Sorry," I mumble as I step out of his hold, looking at his feet, since apparently looking at his face makes my feet stop working, because that's twice now.

So awesome.

"How long have you been there?" he repeats and I shrug.

"Just a second, I pushed open the door and then I saw you." The lie rolls off my tongue and he raises a brow.

"You shouldn't lie to me, Talia. I'll always know."

I blink at him, wondering how the hell he knows my name before I start to stutter. My cheeks heat at my inability to make words, so instead, I clamp my jaw shut and nod because apparently I am too sleep deprived for whatever this is. "Just stick to that. You didn't see me and you didn't hear anything. Understand?"

I nod again, deciding being mute is the only thing that's going to work for me now. He steps into my space, grabs my chin, and pulls up, looking into my eyes. "Make sure you do."

His grip is tight enough that it hurts and he holds me there for a few extra seconds before releasing me and walking away in the direction of the adjoining dorm.

"That was unfortunate." I jump at the voice and find Noah standing behind me. This day is just full of surprises. "Try not to get on his bad side."

"I wasn't..." I trail off as she watches me before she shakes her head.

"Of course not, why else would you be down here like that at this time of night?" Her icy gaze rakes over me and I grip my robe tighter. I hadn't considered what I was wearing to be an issue, but suddenly I feel self-conscious about my robe hitting me mid thigh and my bare legs being out, despite being entirely covered elsewhere. "You're not his type, new girl. Try someone more in your league."

Without another word, she walks around me into the kitchenette. Letting out a sigh, I decide that hot chocolate just isn't worth this kind of hassle, but if I disappear now, she's going to think I was down here looking for Nico. How or why I'd think about finding him here at this time of night is beyond me.

Clenching my jaw, I follow her into the small space, grab a mug from where Kate showed me her stash, and tip in a pouch of hot chocolate before grabbing some milk from the fridge. I stir it together and put it in the microwave, trying not to look over at Noah, who I can feel watching me.

The microwave beeps and I grab the too-hot mug, cursing myself out for not thinking to grab some paper towels to handle the mug.

"Oh, yeah. You're so out of your depth," Noah says with a cold laugh. "Stay in your lane, new girl," she says before leaving the room with a bottle of something in her hand.

Not my circus, not my monkeys.

I grab a few napkins, cover my mug with them, and

head back upstairs. Turns out middle-of-the-night hot chocolate isn't worth the sleep. Because even with it, I have a feeling that sleep is going to evade me after that.

Because what the hell was Nico talking about, and why would Noah think I'd be down there looking for him?

Questions for Kate, maybe?

But again, not my circus, not my monkeys.

I repeat the mantra until I'm tucked back in bed, earbuds in, hot chocolate in hand, and fall down a social media rabbit hole. Maybe something online can tell me more about the people at my school.

Who needs sleep anyway?

SEVEN

Noah

I can feel the new girl's stare of rage on my back as I leave, flicking my blonde hair over my shoulder before I find Nico waiting for me in the doorway back to my dorm. Pausing, I quirk a brow at his knowing gaze and that smile toying on his lips. Freaking boys. "What?"

"Nothing, Ice Queen. Good to see your claws are still sharp and your crown is still atop your head."

Rolling my eyes, I flip him the bird. He laughs and tucks me under his arm before silently walking me up to my room. Once we're inside, he lets out a low whistle. "Good to see you still have your throne room."

"Will you stop with the queen stuff?" I ask with a sigh before dropping down onto my bed. So what if my room is twice the size of most, with a king bed and every luxury a girl could ask for? Being a Harrington has to come with *some* benefits, fuck knows it comes with enough downsides. "What was with you and the new girl?"

"Nothing," he replies just a little too quickly, then shrugs. "There's something about her. I feel like we know her, but obviously we don't. It's nothing major. I'm sure I'll figure it out."

I press my lips together, watching him closely, trying to work out if he's lying to me or to us both, but I let it go for now. I think I'll keep an eye on them though. Because if he's lying to himself too... well, that's not going to end well for anyone.

Unfortunately for us both, our futures are already laid out before us, whether we like it or not.

"You doing okay? For real?" he asks, sitting on the sofa opposite the end of my bed. "Being back here, seeing Lexi after everything that happened..." He trails off, like he knows that he doesn't need to remind me of what happened over the summer.

I relive that nightmare every day, awake or asleep. It's why they're being so extra this year. They're normally protective of me, but after what happened with Scottie... well, I know Nico has blamed himself for not "saving" me since it happened.

"Noah." I shake my head, pulling myself from the

memory and back to my dorm room. Where I'm safe. Nico watches me and I shrug. "I'm here, I'm carrying on. That's what's important. I'm just trying to forget about it and get on with my life."

"Noah—"

"Stop it, Nico. I went to therapy, did the stuff Dad wanted me to, I was even late to school because of it. I just want to get on with my life. What happened was bad enough. I was violated... whatever, can we just move past it? I don't need to be reminded of it."

"You were raped—sorry, assaulted—Noah." He rolls his eyes and I know it's at the new phrasing because I refuse to use the word rape. "By Lexi's brother, and he isn't in jail, or even facing charges. You wouldn't report it, and he could do it again. You see Lexi every day, you're going to be reminded, and I'm worried about you."

Pinching the bridge of my nose, I let out a sigh. Usually, I adore how protective he is of me, how protective they all are. We've been thick as thieves our entire lives. One of the many benefits of our parents running in the same circles was us being thrown together since birth. Trey slid right in as our fifth musketeer when he came to Arbour freshman year after he stepped in and helped Dallas before he got in some serious trouble... but right now? Right now I wish they'd stop hovering. I swear, outside of being asleep, I haven't had a moment to myself and they're driving me insane. "I get it, I do, but I really just want to move on from it rather than let it rule my entire life."

He watches me closely, like he's waiting to see if I'll break. Yes, what happened over summer was fucking horrendous, maybe even the worst thing I've ever experienced, but it's far from the only terrible thing I've lived through. Definitely far from the worst thing Nico has ever lived through. If he can survive what he has without being coddled, then so can I.

When I say as much, his jaw clenches along with his fists and he starts to pace. "This is bullshit."

"I know, but this is our entire lives. It's worse for you than it is for me. I'm not even supposed to know about your boys' club, what with me not having a dick and all."

He laughs and scrubs a hand down his face, and I relax a little because he seems to have given up on his original tirade. "Let's not talk about your lack of dick, or my having one. You talking about my dick is—"

"It's fucking gross, I know," I tease, relaxing a little more. "Now, can I please go back to sleep? Lexi and her clones will love using me looking like shit against me."

"Do you need me to step in?" he asks, concern marring his face again.

"You mean like you did at CoCo's? Yeah, let's not." Standing, I move to the door, unlocking it again. "Now let me sleep, please."

"Fine, I'll go, and I'll keep my mouth shut, but that doesn't mean I won't worry about you."

I hug him tightly and he stiffens for a moment before relaxing. Touch isn't exactly his favorite thing, but he's usually fine with me. A moment after he softens, he hugs me back before kissing the top of my head. "Lock the door after I leave."

"Yes, sir," I mock, curtseying, and he barks out a laugh. "You're a dick."

"I am, but you love me anyway," I tease as he leaves. I do as he asked and lock my door once he leaves, then throw myself back on my bed, putting my music on softly. Opening the drawer in my nightstand, I take two of the sleeping pills from the bottle my therapist gave me, then lie back and close my eyes, trying not to relive that night before the drugs pull me under.

"You have got to be kidding me," I murmur as I hand over the cash for my vanilla latte. Lexi, Emma, and Vanessa are less than three feet from me, watching me, giggling and whispering. Oh, how quickly things can change here. Less than eight weeks ago, those vapid bitches followed me around like their lips were surgically attached to my ass.

Now, instead of believing me about what happened with Scott, they're closing ranks with Lexi. Nothing quite like blaming the victim. Straightening my shoulders, I take a sip of my coffee, hold my head high, and shoot off a text to the group chat with Nico and the guys.

ME

Told you I'd be fine, so here I am, being fine.

My phone buzzes almost instantly.

TREY

Chin up, Your Highness.

ISSAC

Failing that, stab those bitches with those claws of yours

DALLAS

Of course you go straight to bloodshed.

ISSAC

It's the best way to handle two-faced, betraying assholes.

ME

Truth.

NICO

Let's try to get through just one day with no bloodshed?

I laugh at their messages, take another sip of my coffee,

and slide my ice queen mask into place, the one I wear every day in this hellhole, the one that so few people see past. The one that keeps me safe here…

Well, safe-ish.

Phone in one hand, coffee in the other, and purse balanced on my forearm, I head toward my locker, which just happens to be behind where Lexi and Co. are converging.

Taking another sip of my coffee, I weave around them before opening my locker and grabbing my chemistry textbook. I balance my coffee on top of it, using my elbow to shut my locker as someone knocks into me from behind.

My coffee spills down my blouse and all over my textbook. I lift the cup, shaking off my book as I turn around.

"Oops, sorry. Didn't see you," Emma says with a giggle, the other two laughing along with her. "You seem to have something…" She trails off, waving at my chest, where my now-wet blouse is showing my red lace bra.

Fuck this.

I hold her gaze and smile that venomous smile I perfected long ago. Her eyes widen, a flash of panic in them as she gulps. I shouldn't enjoy her reaction, but I do. "Thanks, you finished off the look I was going for today. I couldn't quite place what was wrong."

"I mean, it was…" She falls over her words, so I quirk

a brow, not taking my eyes from her until I let out a sigh and look down at my freshly done manicure.

"Cat got your tongue, Emma?"

My words are as icy as my stare, and she shakes her head quickly.

"Either of you got anything to say?" I ask, looking to Lexi and Vanessa, who are noticeably quiet. As is the crowd that has congregated around this failed little power play. "That's what I thought. Now get out of my way. I have somewhere to be."

I hold my ground until they separate, then walk between them, the click of my heels the only sound as I pass by. The crowd parts for me as I reach them, and I make sure to keep a sway in my hips as I sashay away from them.

Dropping my half-empty cup into a trash can, I divert back to my room, change again, and groan at my ruined textbook.

Fucking bitchy mean girls.

Yes, I might be the top bitch here, but that doesn't mean I'm an asshole. I might not have stopped their antics in the past, but I never took part, either. Don't get me wrong, I'll tell people what I think, and it might be blunt as hell, and *they* might think I'm being a bitch, but I'd rather be honest and hurt someone's feelings for a minute than lie and let them get hurt worse later somehow.

Some of us don't need to belittle others to feel good

about ourselves.

I've always thought that was for the weak minded, those unable to truly believe in themselves. And one thing I've never had a shortage of is faith in myself. Not to say I'm exactly nice, but I also learned a long time ago that being nice in this world is often viewed the same as being weak.

Weakness is something I'll never show.

Once I'm clean and fresh, I dart back to the halls, groaning as the second bell sounds.

Awesome, I'm going to be late. Letting out a sigh and accepting my fate, I make my way to chemistry with Mrs. Potter. The halls are empty and it's almost peaceful. Part of me wishes I could stay here in this quiet, but I shut that part of me down. I don't need to hide, not here, not anywhere.

Walking into class, I glance around the room and groan inside my mind. Of course the only free seat is with the new girl.

Being late back to school is having more consequences than I intended.

"Mrs. Potter," I say quietly as I step toward the teacher.

She presses her lips into a straight line as she looks down at me. "Yes, Miss Harrington?"

"I had an unfortunate accident this morning, do you have a spare textbook?"

Tutting, she glances over at the new girl then smiles.

"Looks like your desk mate has a book. I'm sure you can share until yours is replaced."

"About that—" I start, but she cuts me off.

"Seating is final, Miss Harrington. Maybe if you made it to school on time, you'd have had your choice of partners. Now, if you're done wasting my time, I have a lesson to teach."

"Of course." The words are tart, but arguing with a teacher isn't going to improve my day. Instead, I straighten my shoulders and head over to the table where the new girl is practically gaping at me.

"I guess we're partners," I mutter as I drop my bag onto the table before sitting in the empty spot beside her. I feel her watching me, so I turn to face her, evaluating her as much as possible in the brief moment of silence.

It takes less than a second to realize she's not a threat, but that doesn't mean I'm in the mood to play nice. Last night, I found her panting after Nico, and today, I'm paired with her. If I was more naïve, I'd consider it a coincidence, but my daddy taught me that coincidences don't exist. She opens her mouth to speak, but I shake my head to cut her off. I don't care to hear whatever it is she has to say right now. Instead, I interrupt her, hoping to scathe enough that she learns her place. That, or she slips up and shows me what her game is here. "You better not suck at this class. I will not carry you, and I do not tolerate idiots."

EIGHT

Talia

Coffee cup in hand, I walk into chemistry first thing on this gray Tuesday morning, head down, bleary eyed, and head over to my table. I got about ninety minutes of sleep after my adventures last night, and there isn't enough caffeine in the world to wake me up for this class.

Unpacking my bag, glad I was the only person not paired up last week—thank you odd numbers—so I don't have to be Little Miss Sunshine and speak to anyone for whatever today's lesson of delight holds for us.

Other students filter in, but I keep my eyes on my textbook, trying to remember what Mrs. Potter talked about last week and coming up blank. Instead, I sip at my coffee and pray to whichever god might be listening for a miracle.

Sick teacher? Fire drill? Anything like that would just be stellar.

Unfortunately, Mrs. Potter enters the room, followed by the last few students. I pinch the bridge of my nose, hoping like hell the tired headache eases and my aspirin kicks in soon, and when I open my eyes again, I see Noah talking to the teacher, who shakes her head firmly. Noah rolls her eyes before walking over to my table.

Oh, goodie.

"I guess we're partners," she mutters before dropping her bag onto the table with a thud that makes my brain shake as she sits on the empty chair. "You better not suck at this class. I will not carry you, and I do not tolerate idiots."

I give her a one finger salute with a tight smile, wondering exactly what I did wrong to end up with this karmic delight today.

She pulls out her laptop along with a notebook and pen, all of which look like they cost more than my car. Not that that would be surprising from what Kate said about boats and jets, but still.

Don't be so judgmental, Talia. You don't know anything about her.

Brody's voice in my head sobers me and I finish my coffee, chugging down a nice helping of guilt with it for being so judgy, then turn my attention to Mrs. Potter.

The class is a blur of sharp comments from Noah. Thankfully, it was a sit and listen while taking notes kind of class rather than a practical one, because while Noah might not "deal with idiots", she seems like a bit of a princess and I don't want to deal with a meltdown if something spills on her. She might be wearing the same uniform as me, but her shoes and bag... yeah, they're not Walmart specials. I don't even want to think about the fact that I could probably put a deposit on a house with the cost of them.

I make it halfway through the class without issue, but I pick up my water bottle to try and stay focused on the dull-ass lesson and the lid comes off. My bottle drops.

Then spills.

All over Noah's laptop.

"Fuck!" she hisses, jumping to her feet, lifting her laptop from the desk as the waterfall from my bottle streams across the table.

"I am so sorry! I didn't mean—"

"Girls!" Mrs. Potter shouts. It takes a second, but then she's at our table with a giant roll of paper towels, helping to mop up the river that has Noah glaring at me.

Once it's dealt with, the lesson continues, but Noah almost vibrates with rage beside me. I get that I spilled the water, but it was an accident and this seems like a gross overreaction.

It's just some water, and her laptop seems fine.

I think.

The rest of the lesson passes with tension between us thick enough to cut with a knife and I barely manage to focus on anything but the storm cloud beside me.

Once the bell finally rings, she hightails it from the room faster than I thought she'd be able to move in those heels, but when I look up, Trey is waiting for her in the doorway. He glares over at me before dropping an arm over her shoulder and escorting her away.

I wonder if they're dating...

Shaking off the errant thought, I pack my things away before heading to my locker to swap my chemistry book for my math one.

Taking the same seat as before, I get my stuff together, trying to scan through my notes from last week. I try not to pay attention as Nico and Dallas enter the room but I swear it's like my eyes are drawn to them, no matter how much I don't want to look.

Noah's words from last night filter into my brain and my lips twist.

'You're not his type, new girl. Try someone more in your league.'

She doesn't even know me. Though maybe that's her point. Her family and his obviously have money. The fact that the football field is named after her and the main auditorium has his surname on it tells me enough to know their families have deep pockets. Not that mine doesn't, but I don't come from their levels of money and I sure as hell am not known in these circles.

Despite not wanting either of them, despite my distaste for their friend, hell, my abhorrence of Nico after last night, I still find myself watching them as they cross the room and take their seats to my left in the row in front of mine.

Perfect stalking position if that's what I wanted.

But I don't.

Thankfully, Mr. Miller walks in and interrupts my thoughts. "It's a new day, ladies and gents, let's make some magic with numbers, shall we?"

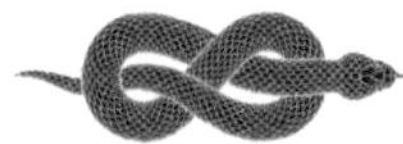

I walk into the cafeteria, flustered from a morning of barely managing to focus. After the disaster in chemistry with Noah, I've been trying to keep my head down. I still haven't worked out how Nico knew my name last night, or how Noah knew who I was, and to say it's bugging me is an understatement of epic proportions.

God, I miss Brody. He might have been a storm cloud, but he was *my* storm cloud, and I'd never have to navigate shit like this with him around. His personality was the type where he'd be king of the castle within a month, which made me bulletproof by association. It always made me laugh that he was so popular when he was such a grump, but I swear, his confidence mixed with his grump were like kryptonite to everyone he met. Is it selfish to miss that? Maybe, but I feel like I'm losing who I was without him. My sunshine is stuck behind gray clouds and I'm suffocating in them.

The smell of food perks me up a little as I trudge toward the line.

Grabbing my phone and earbuds, I stick one in my ear and put my playlist on repeat. Once *downfall* by Mvssie is blaring in one ear, I pull up my text thread with Kate.

ME

> Hey, are you coming to the cafeteria today or are you back in the library?

The three dots show on my screen almost immediately.

KATE

> Heading your way. Bad morning. There had better be chocolate pudding today. THIS FREAKING SCHOOL!

ME

> If I see some, I'll grab extra, just in case.

Well shit. I wonder what could have Kate upset enough for all caps.

I work my way through the line, grabbing myself some cheesy, veggie pasta thing that makes my mouth water, as well as some garlic bread and as many pudding cups as I can fit on my tray in preparation for Kate's upcoming meltdown.

Once I've got everything, I mindlessly walk through the masses and head to the counter to pay.

"Pay attention!" I snap to focus and find Trey glaring at me.

"I, er, what?" Feeling a little frazzled as I try to work out why he's barking orders at me.

"Fucking exactly," he growls. "Stay the hell away from me, new girl."

The sneer he throws in my direction sends an icy shiver down my spine before he storms out to the seating area.

Shaking my head, I turn to the woman at the counter who smiles sadly at me. "Be careful with that one, he has a temper. You nearly tripped him up when you stepped into line. I guess the skills that keep him on the football field are why you're not wearing his lunch right now."

Oh.

Yeah, I guess that'll explain it.

"Thanks," I murmur to her quietly as I pay for the food and head out to find a seat.

Kate appears beside me, cheeks red, hair looking like she's run her hands through it all morning, with nothing on her tray but pizza and pudding cups. "Should I ask you what has you so flustered, or should I wait until you've had cheese and chocolate?"

"Cheese and chocolate first." Even her voice is higher pitched than normal. Whatever happened this morning has her wound tighter than an eight-day clock. I nod in response then wait until she's done the same and follow her to the table where her friends are already sitting.

I say *her* friends because they only really acknowledge me when I'm with her, which is fine, they don't know me, but it's hard not to feel a little like a tag-along. I might have been that with Brody, but he never made me feel like it.

A pang hits my heart. I miss Callie. Last year might have been a disaster of epic proportions, but she always had my back.

Once I'm sitting, I pull out my phone again and send her a text.

ME

I miss your face. Catch up later?

Tucking my phone into my pocket, I take a bite of my garlic bread after dipping it in the creamy pasta concoction and try to decide if talking to Kate is a good idea yet. She's still silently simmering beside me, eating her pizza like it personally offended her.

"Oh, I forgot, this came to the room after you left for

swim practice this morning." She reaches into her pocket and hands me a folded over white envelope. I flatten it out and notice my name scrawled on the front in cursive. Flipping it over, I see the red seal again, then tuck it into my bag without opening it. Kate eyes me, the silent questions swimming in her eyes barely contained by the twitch of her lips.

"It's from Theodore," I tell her, drawing out his name in the snooty ass way he did the last time I heard from him. "My mom's dad. I've barely had any contact with him my entire life, but this is the second envelope I've received with that seal, and the last was from him. Same handwriting. I am so not inclined to read his drivel."

"Fair enough," she says with a shrug before turning back to her pizza.

"Ready to talk yet?"

"Nope."

I nod in understanding and tune into the conversation at the other end of the table. They're talking about their weekly D&D game again, something about a paladin and a master, but it's enough to make me tune back out. I have no freaking idea what they're talking about, and I don't know that I want to.

My phone buzzes and I smile when I pull it out and see Callie's name on the screen.

CALLIE

It's a fucking riot here this week. New girl turned up with her Chanel shoes and tried to make the cheer team. Two days in and she already had paint tipped on her head. I miss you, we could sit on the bleachers and laugh if you were here.

I blink down at the phone. Holy shit, I almost forgot how ruthless some of the people were at my old school. That is straight up *cold*.

ME

Paint? What did she do to deserve that?

CALLIE

She tried to take Lizzie's spot on the squad.

ME

Wait, Lizzie isn't on the team?

CALLIE

Broke her ankle at a party over the weekend, no team for her for at least this semester.

ME

So the new girl was just trying out?

CALLIE

Yeah, but she was good. Better than Lizzie. I think she was worried her spot wouldn't be waiting for her.

ME

Holy shit. I can't say I miss that shit, but this place isn't any different.

CALLIE

What's wrong? Do I need to rock up with a bat and smash some shit up?

ME

Calm down, Harley Quinn. I'm fine, just new girl politics. Typical shit, but nothing like having paint poured on me. Just the Queen Bee here hating me instantly, plus typical shit.

CALLIE

You might be a plane ride away, but if you need me, just call. I'll be there in the however long it takes to fly to you.

ME

I love you. But stand down for now.

CALLIE

Love you too. We both know you won't call if you need me, such a pacifist, but I'll stay on standby. Gotta run, it's meatball sub day.

I cackle at her last message and tuck my phone away. Callie and her love for that sub is... well, it's a little nuts. Somehow, I think if Noah didn't hate me so much, she'd remind me of Callie. They both seem utterly ruthless when it comes to protecting the people they care about. Thankfully, Callie is my friend. Noah? Yeah, not so much.

Tuning back into the conversations around me, I spot Kate hanging up her phone, tears running down her face. She stands up in a rush, grabs her bag, and runs from the room.

"What did I just miss?" I ask the girl opposite me, whose name I think is Rosie.

The girl rolls her eyes and me and turns to the girl beside her, completely ignoring me. *Fucking bitchy-ass girls everywhere.*

Swiping the pudding cups that haven't been touched into my bag, I take off after Kate. Thankfully, her bright red hair isn't hard to spot and I try to move through the crowd in the halls without hitting anyone in my haste to reach my friend.

I end up chasing her across the quad and over to our dorm.

"Kate!" I shout out, but she either can't hear me or ignores me as she rushes up the stairs.

My lungs burn as I rush up after her. Apparently, swimming and running are not equal, or I just haven't worked out enough lately.

The slam of our door rattles down the hall as I reach the top of the stairs and I hesitate before turning the knob and pushing our door open. I find Kate face down on her bed, sobbing.

I close the door softly, put my bag down on my desk,

and move toward her. "Kate, are you okay?"

Sitting beside her on the bed, I feel awkward as hell because I don't know how to comfort crying people. Add to that the fact that I don't know her that well yet, and I quickly come to the conclusion that I have no idea what she needs. Obviously, she's not okay, but what am I supposed to say?

She cries through the bell signaling the start of afternoon classes, and while I feel torn about missing class, being here seems more important. I grab my phone and shoot off an email to Ms. Feldman letting her know that something has come up and that Kate and I will be missing this afternoon, could she please mark it down and we'll check in with teachers tomorrow.

My phone pings with her acknowledgement and I tuck it back away, turning my focus to Kate. Her sobbing has turned to quiet tears as she pulls her face from her pillow and turns to look at me.

"What happened?" I ask as she tries to catch her breath, which is shaky at best.

She closes her eyes, pressing her lips together as more tears stream down her face.

"Is there anything I can do?"

She shakes her head before turning over and sitting up, grabbing her pillow and hugging it to her chest. "There's nothing... oh, Talia... I don't... There was an accident."

NINE

"An accident?"

Talia stares at me, waiting for me to elaborate, but saying the words... it's like I've lost the ability to speak. Instead, I nod, taking another deep breath as I swipe the tears from my puffy cheeks.

"My brother, Charlie. He was in a car accident. Mum called just then, and this day was already awful, but... he's in surgery, my dad is flying over now, but they don't know if he's going to make it."

Her pain at my plight is almost palpable, and for a second a flicker of a thought pops into my head, wondering who she's lost, but her words interrupt the trace of a question. "I'm so sorry, Kate. Do you need to go too? Do you need me to cover for you?"

"No," I tell her, shaking my head, wiping at my cheeks again. "I just need a distraction for now. Going there isn't going to help anything. Mum and Dad told me to stay put, so I just need to hope he's okay."

"Are you guys close?"

Taking a deep breath, I climb from the bed. My uniform feels like it's suffocating me, so I grab a pair of sweats and a jumper from my drawers and change while I answer her question. "Not really, I'm closer to my sister, but Charlie is... well, a typical big brother. He's eight years older than me, so I was just his annoying baby sister, but he's also the guy who will look out for me if I need it. He'd be here in a heartbeat if I called. He's a hot-shot lawyer in New York, but he'd drop and run for family."

I sit back down on the bed, pulling my sleeves down over my hands and bunching them in my fists. "He's a great brother. I really hope he's okay."

"I hope he is too," she tells me, her voice croaking like she's feeling my pain as viscerally as I am. "What sort of distraction is going to help?"

Shrugging, I wipe at my face again, the tears still wet on my cheeks. "Usually I'd work on an article for the paper, but thanks to Erica, the she-witch, that's a no go."

Her eyes spark for a second and she chews on her lip.

"So, something like a missing student would be a thing for you?"

"A missing student?" I ask, my curiosity piqued. How have I not heard about that?

She shrugs before moving to her closet and changing into jeans and a hoodie. "I overheard Nico on a call talking about a student being missing. I didn't think much of it because I haven't heard anything, but then, I only really talk to you here."

"He said something about a missing student? From here? Did you get a name or when?" The journalistic inquisitor in me shows itself and I grab a pen and notebook.

"No, sorry," she says, grimacing. "Worst lead and source ever."

I laugh at her, but it's empty. "Maybe we can still look into it. I've never heard anything, but it's weird that Nico would be talking about it. Where did you hear him?"

She squirms awkwardly as she sits cross-legged on her bed, facing me. "Erm, yeah, about that."

Quirking a brow at her, I can't help but be intrigued. "You holding out on me, roomie?"

Laughing, she tucks some of her insanely long dark hair behind her ear before looking down at her lap as she toys with her thumb. The worry for Charlie is still there, front and center, but the distraction helps. Even if it is a weak one.

"So, erm, about two o'clock this morning in the kitchenette."

I close my eyes and shake my head as my face scrunches. "I'm sorry, what?"

Shrugging her shoulders until they practically touch her ears, she presses her lips together. "Yeah, last night was a joy of Nico and Noah in the kitchenette. Let me tell you, hot chocolate when I can't sleep... sooo not worth it."

"Care to elaborate?"

She huffs and pulls her hood over her face before tugging on the strings and hiding her face. "Not much to say, Nico being a lofty jackass, Noah accusing me of stalking him and telling me I'm punching out of my weight class with him. Was a great little thing to mull over as I tried to sleep."

Not much...

"Holy shit, and you didn't say something this morning at breakfast? And here was me thinking you loved me."

She barks out a laugh, then rolls her eyes at me. "Call it intuition, I didn't tell you then, because you needed to know it now."

"And I thought I was the one of us with a love for woo woo. Next, you'll tell me you're fully an Aries. You scream Aries energy."

Her smile is wide and mine grows to match it. I needed this. A real friend. Someone who chases me when I'm crying rather than ignoring the fact that I was sad because it might inconvenience them.

"I'm a Leo," she replies, and I let out a cackle.

"Yeah that makes sense," I say with a wink. "Now, I'll do your birth chart and cards later, but for now, back to the missing student. You didn't get anything else from Nico?"

"Not a thing," she responds, shaking her head. "Sorry. It sounded important, but surely if no one is saying anything... maybe I misheard."

"Maybe you did," I tell her. "But I'm intrigued enough to look into it anyway. I need a distraction, and really... what's the harm in looking? Actually, we should head to the library. Probably better not to research this on your personal laptop."

"Good thinking, Batgirl."

"With this hair, I should totally be Poison Ivy."

She laughs at my grumble. "Yeah, maybe, but it doesn't roll off the tongue quite as well."

We get ready to go to the library, which doesn't take too long, but I nearly run into Talia's back as we're leaving. "Everything okay?"

She leans down before turning around holding a vase with a bouquet of what looks like purple anemone with baby's breath. "These were at the door."

I take them from her and put them on my desk. "There's no note."

"They could be from the staff if they heard about your brother?"

Smiling sadly, I shrug. "Yeah, maybe. Come on, let's go. We can worry about who they're from later."

After two hours in the library with Talia, researching people missing in Spring Creek as well as anyone who has ever gone missing from Arbour, we've come up mostly empty. With the exception of a story that's like, thirty years old about a student who went missing after a supposed hazing gone wrong. He was found washed up on the beach a few weeks later and his death was ruled accidental because of his blood alcohol level.

Part of me wants to call my dad, ask if he knows or remembers anything, but I know he's in the air, on his way to Charlie.

Tapping the screen of my phone again, I let out a sigh. Still no updates from Mum. She said she'd text when she heard anything, but I guess Charlie is still in surgery.

That can't be good. Or is no news good news?

Taking another sip of my caffeinated, bubbly goodness, I turn back to the old newspaper article and rub at my tired eyes. Bone tired doesn't quite cover just how exhausted

I feel, but it's barely dinner time, going to bed isn't an option. Sleep also won't be my friend until I know more about Charlie.

"I brought supplies," Talia whisper shouts at me, opening her backpack to show off the contraband hidden inside.

"So many snacks!" I hiss happily. "Did you get cheese puffs?"

I cross my fingers and wave them in her face as she laughs at me. "Of course I did, I'm no amateur."

"Yes!" She passes me the puffs before pulling up a chair beside me. I got lucky that they had started posting newspaper articles on the internet around the time of this kid's disappearance, but I didn't want to use my own laptop just in case. Missing students, especially students nobody knows about, is weird as hell. People at Arbour have money, the type of money that makes problems go away, so I didn't want to leave a trace of my searching for it.

Which I'm glad for now that I've seen the story about the supposedly accidental death. I mean, it totally could be, but my journalist nose and general cynicism are screaming cover up, but I have no proof. No witnesses. Nothing.

I tell Talia as much and she sighs, a little like I did when I discovered there was nothing else.

"Maybe I just misheard?"

"Maybe," I agree, though something doesn't sit quite right about it. "I can always see if I can find something out from the staff. Upside of being me, I'm enough of a nerd to have 'friends' in the faculty."

"You're an awesome nerd. Nothing wrong with that," she replies with a smile. "But if you think you can find something out about a missing person that doesn't seem to exist anywhere else, then sure, go for it. I'm starting to think it was a fever dream illusion or something."

"What was a fever dream?" I startle as Isaac Hall appears behind us, a hand on the back of each of our chairs as he studies the screen in front of us. "Research?"

"Something like that," I say, trying to keep my voice steady as I close down the screen. Something about him always makes me feel off kilter. He's never done anything to me, but he's like a predator who wholly makes me feel like prey. He watches me closely and I squirm beneath his gaze, my flight or fight instinct screaming at me to run the hell away from him.

"And you are?" Talia asks curtly, pulling his attention from me. Part of me is relieved, but the other part is terrified.

For her.

He turns that predatory stare to her and smiles, but it's the kind of smile that sends an icy shudder down your spine.

"Oh, new girl, let's not pretend like you don't know exactly who I am. Who my friends are. Or maybe you like games." He pauses, licking his lips before tracing a finger down her face to the nape of her neck, toying with her hair. "I can think of a very fun game we could play."

She rolls her eyes at him and I swear I stop breathing.

It's like she's a gazelle facing a lion, but with zero fucks.

Me, I'm a bunny rabbit—I hide from all the lions and they tend to ignore me. But she draws their attention. So taunting the lion? Such a bad idea.

My phone pings and I've never been more thankful to have my phone actually make noise. Relief floods through me, but then I realize it's not my mum and my heart sinks again.

"No games wanted here, whoever you are," Talia says, dismissing him and pushing her chair back, forcing him to step aside. "Now if you'll excuse us, we have places to be."

She stands, and he moves in front of her, toe to toe, but he stands at least a clear foot taller than her. Folding her arms across her chest, she looks up at him, jutting her chin, and I think I'm going to vomit. I feel like I'm going to have a freaking panic attack right here in the library watching them. Talia is definitely a distraction, I'll give her that, but facing off with one of the Elites of Arbour is not how we go about fitting in.

Remind self: talk to roomie about who NOT *to piss off.*

"I'll be seeing you, new girl," Isaac says after what feels like an eternity of watching them stare each other down.

"Not if I see you first," she retorts and I swear my heart stops in the seconds between her words and him barking out a laugh.

"Oh, I do love a good challenge. Laters, Kate. Maybe I'll see you around too."

A squeak falls from my lips as he turns and leaves, threat fully registered, and my cheeks heat, turning a shade of red that I'm sure matches the hair on my head as he leaves the library.

"What an asshole," Talia huffs, grabbing her bag. "You okay?"

"Erm, I'll let you know when my heart stops thinking it's a hummingbird."

Her laugh in response is light. "Oh, come on, he's just a boy."

"Isaac Hall is not *just* anything. Nico and his little band of buddies? They are the Elite. I know I told you about them some, but I guess the warning of *do not fuck with the Elites* didn't quite hit. Jeez. I thought I was going to vomit all over your shoes."

"Please do not vomit on me," she says, wincing a little.

"Me and vomit? Not friends. I'd love to be the friend that holds back your hair in those situations, but I'll gag, then I'll vomit too, and it's a bad time for everyone."

Her smile is wide, even though I can tell she's telling the truth.

"So, now that we have no leads, and douchebag number four, aka Isaac, has disappeared, does this mean we save the snacks for later and we go for dinner? Watch a movie? Grab ice cream? I am a pro at procrastination and distraction, ya know."

"That sounds incredible," I tell her, looking back down at my phone. A message from Vann, the one that pinged a few moments ago, stares back at me. "Two minutes."

VANN

You okay? You disappeared. Need to talk?

ME

Charlie was in an accident, no news yet. Just going to head into town with Talia. You want to come?

The three dots bounce on my screen and my stomach twists, but this time in that girl-has-a-crush anxiety kind of way, rather than the whole I-might-die kind of way from when Isaac was here.

He's just my friend. We are just friends.

Maybe if I tell myself and everyone else that enough, it'll be true.

VANN

Sure, I'll get changed and meet you guys out front.

ME

Great! See you soon!

"So, are you good if Vann comes too?" I ask Talia, who is already looking at me with a knowing smile.

"Oh, you mean the floppy haired, nerd-type dreamboat of a friend you definitely weren't drooling over before? That Vann?"

My cheeks heat again, but it spreads to my chest too. "Yes him, and stop it. He is just my friend. We are friends."

"Uh-huh, you keep telling yourself that. Me, I'll draw my own conclusions," she teases. "But yeah, it's fine. If you're just friends, I'm not third wheeling, not that that would stop me anyway."

I giggle at her. "You're a little weird, you know that? And coming from me... well, that probably means you're a lot weird."

"Eh," she sounds with a shrug. "I happen to like being kinda weird. Now let's go, my fire-haired friend who isn't totally crushing on the nerd-boy. We have places to go and things to eat!"

I laugh again as she loops her arm through mine, grateful that Talia is my roommate this year. She's exactly the kind of friend I've always needed, and I get the feeling that this year... well, it's amazing what can happen in a year.

Especially at Arbour.

TEN

I deadpan at Kate as I close the door to our room with my foot. "You are just what a girl needs after a harrowing day."

She grins at me from where she's sitting on her bed in her pj's, cross-legged, her wild red hair in a messy bun atop her head, laptop cast to one side, and a sleeve of cookies on the other. "I am an unwavering beacon of truth along with being the best kind of cheerleader. I never promised you'd love everything that comes with that." Her grin widens as she winks at me.

Rolling my eyes, I drop my bag on the floor beside my bed and drop down face first. Hell might be an understatement for the day I've had. Maybe the week. I swear, ever since my run-in with Nico, it's like I became public enemy number one with each and every person at Arbour and I have no idea if I'm being paranoid and delusional, or if today's events were something entirely unrelated.

"Bad day, cupcake?"

"Ughhhh," I groan into my pillow, wanting to scream, but two terrible days aren't enough to beat me. If I've survived all of my worst days to this point, I'm sure as hell not going to let demonic trolls in boarding school skins beat me. "Can it be summer yet?"

"It's not even Halloween yet, sunshine. Wanna talk about it?"

I flop over onto my side, mock glaring at her. "Trying to tell me that your little network of gossip didn't already tell you?"

"I would never discredit my sources that way." Her eyes brighten as she tries not to laugh and I roll my eyes at her again.

I swear I used to be sunshine, but Kate makes me look like an overcast day. I just can't tell if it's this place tearing down my usually sunny disposition, or if it's the lack of Brody and his storm cloud ways in my life now creating some weird imbalance in the universe.

"Any news on Charlie?" I ask, trying to distract us both

from my hellish day. It's been three days since his accident, but when I left this morning, he still hadn't woken up from his surgery. She didn't say it, but I could tell how worried she was.

"He's awake," she says, beaming. That explains the super star shine brightness when I walked through the door. "He's awake and he's talking. It's great news. The doctors said it's a miracle, he's on his way to being good as new."

"That's amazing," I tell her, genuinely relieved. I know the pain of losing a sibling all too well, and as much as I've tried to be there for her, be a bright light and give her some of my old style sunshine, it's been selfishly hard. She doesn't know about Brody. No one does. He's like my own personal dirty little secret, my personal guilt, my own little shame-filled secret to live with. "I'm so happy for you. For all of you."

"Thanks," she says, smiling wide. "Dad said he'd video call me tonight with Charlie so I can say hi. I'll introduce you. Mum and Josie fly in tomorrow for a gala, but they'll be staying with Charlie until he's out of the hospital, cause Dad's got something to sort back home for work."

"You'd think they'd give him a break," I utter, trying not to be as cynical as I feel. My parents used work as a shield, a place for them to hide from their problems rather than seeing or caring how it affected me and Brody, so her dad running back to work so quickly just... touches a nerve.

"Charlie is practically climbing the walls to get out of the hospital, swearing he's fine. He's basically shoving Dad back home." She says it with a laugh, like this is par for the course for them. I don't know her family, hell, I only really just know her, so who am I to judge?

"So are you going to the gala this weekend too?"

She shakes her head and shrugs. "No, I don't have an invite. That's a Mum and Josie thing. *So* not my scene. I'm more likely to trip over my own feet and make a spectacle of myself than help with whatever charity they're fundraising for. If Charlie wasn't recovering so well, I might've gone to visit him, but he is, so I'll be staying here."

"Well then, we should do something." I prompt. "Distraction extraordinaire, remember?"

"How could I forget?" She giggle snorts then covers her face with her hands. "Let's pretend that didn't happen, just like we'll pretend you didn't fall asleep with a tub of ice cream and wake up in a puddle of it."

I roll my eyes again, then get up and grab my shower bag. "Yeah, let's pretend that didn't happen either. I'm going to shower, then we can plan. Get your thinking cap on, Batgirl."

"My nerd is rubbing off on you," she teases.

"I was always a nerd."

"But also, tomorrow is the first football game of the season. Here, against our biggest rivals. We have to go. School spirit and all."

I blink at her. I'm pretty sure I'd be less shocked if she told me she'd committed murder. "You want to go to a high school football game?"

"I mean, yeah. I usually go to all of them. It's just a thing to fill the time. Plus, the atmosphere is fun. I go to hockey, baseball, and basketball games too. Plus, if you make the swim team, I'll be adding that to my roster."

"Kate Galloway, I did not know you were a sports girlie."

She shrugs again but blushes softly. "I'm a complex nerd girl journalist with a wide range of interests." She pushes her glasses up her nose, almost as if for effect.

"Well, can't say I saw it coming, but sure, we can do football. That just leaves the rest of the weekend to fill in this tiny nowhere town. I'm sure we'll think of something."

"Uh-huh," she says, rolling her eyes. "Go shower before the bathrooms get overrun, then we'll grab food and talk."

"Sounds great." Pulling a pair of sweats, a hoodie, and two towels out of my closet, I double-check my wash bag before heading down to the communal bathroom. Usually, I wait until the dead of night to shower because the bathrooms creep me out, but the last few nights the water has been icy cold and I really need to wash my hair.

Three of the five stalls are already in use, so I slink into the one at the end and lock the door behind me. Sure, there are lockers to put my clothes and stuff in, but the thought of leaving my stuff out there... yeah, no thanks. Walking naked through the halls doesn't sound like a fun time to me. I don't hate my body, but I don't exactly love it enough to flaunt it like that. Being in front of people in a swimsuit is bad enough, thank you very much.

Turning the knobs to full, I sigh happily as the water starts to steam. Undressing quickly, I fold everything up onto the shelf farthest from the water, slide into my flip flops, and slip beneath the blissfully hot stream of water. The joy is enough to block out the gossip in the other stalls and for me not to care when even more voices join.

I don't rush through my shower, but I don't laze in here either, as much as I want to. Icy showers aren't fun for anyone and with as loud as it is in here now, I don't want to be singled out any more than I already have been.

A shudder runs down my spine when I think about how many times I've caught Isaac watching me since our little run in in the library. He both creeps me out and fascinates me.

Though, I guess that's true of a lot of people here.

Of the entire school even, maybe.

Shutting off the water, I wring out my hair before

wrapping it in a towel, then pull my other towel around me and make sure it's secured tightly. I grab my stuff and head out of the stall.

The voices grow quieter, as if they had forgotten an outsider like me existed. Though I think I'm more shocked to find some of the cheer team in here. I'd have thought they'd have the cushy rooms with private bathrooms.

Guess I was wrong.

I hear a click and see someone with their phone pointed at me, but I know I'm covered. So what if they have a picture of me in my towel?

Go them, I guess.

I quirk a brow at the girl in question, one I don't recognize—though that's not all that shocking—then roll my eyes at her before leaving the bathroom, head held high.

Maybe a hot shower isn't worth dealing with the heinous masses of Arbour.

But then I think back to how good the shower felt and take it back.

Here's hoping I make the swim team because then those showers are open to me for the entire year. Which reminds me, I should hear tonight.

Deciding that sticking around in here to get dressed isn't a great idea, I pick up my pace back to my room where I left my phone and pray to the gods I don't believe in that, for more than one reason, I make the team.

"—catch you later, Kate." I turn into the hall and spot Vann leaving our room. Smirking, I catch his eye as he turns this way to leave after closing the door. "Oh, hey, Talia."

"Hey, Vann, fancy seeing you here." His cheeks heat when I pause in front of him, like he just realized I'm in a towel. Bless his heart.

"Just checking in on Kate."

"Oh, I bet you were. That was some serious tension with you guys the other night." I tease, playfully.

"I, er, we're just friends."

"Yeah I know, but you like her, right?"

His cheeks turn a darker shade of red and I take pity on him, though I'm happy to confirm what I'd already worked out. "Don't worry, I won't tell her. But you should."

"I, erm, maybe…" His words sound more like a question than a statement, but I let him off the hook, very aware that I am standing here in a towel.

"Don't stress, Vann. Secret's safe with me, I'm a vault." With a wink, I slink around him and into my room, kicking the door closed and trying to ignore how cold it is in here when I'm basically naked, then scramble to my phone where it's charging by my bed.

"Where's the fire?" Kate jokes as I dive across the room. "Everything okay?"

Dropping my clothes and shower bag, I dive onto the bed. "Yes, just forgot that today is swim team day."

"Oh, shit!" she exclaims, sitting up straight, eyes wide behind her glasses.

"Oh yeah," I mumble as I open my email app, refreshing it while cursing the slow-as-hell connection. You'd think with all the money in this place, we'd be able to get a more stable signal. Glancing over at her, I smile as I take the wrapped towel off my hair, trying to refresh my email again. "Once I check this, we can talk about Vann stopping by."

My phone finally pings as my email updates, and when I see one from Coach, all of a sudden I'm nervous. Like I don't want to open it.

"Well?" Kate asks, scooting to the end of her bed. "Do you have it?"

"Yup," I answer as butterflies take flight in my stomach.

"So, what does it say?" she asks as I drop my phone back down. "Talia?"

Jumping to my feet, I slide on my underwear before pulling on my hoodie and jeans. "Can't open it. Why am I this nervous? It's just swim team."

"Because it's obviously important to you, even if you're downplaying it. Which, by the way, makes entirely no sense to me. Especially since it's just us here, and even if it wasn't, you don't seem like you care much about what people think about you." She bounces over to my bed and picks up my phone. "Passcode?"

"My birthday," I reply, not expecting her to know it, but she taps away on my screen with a wide smile, tucking some of the hair that's escaped her messy bun behind her ear. I chew my bottom lip, way more nervous than I should be.

"You're in," she says loudly, but it still takes a second to register.

"What?" I ask, blinking at her before crossing the room and taking my phone from her outstretched hand. "I got on the team?"

"You got on the team!" she exclaims excitedly. "We're on the swim team, Talia."

"Holy shit," I almost whisper. I'd hoped but hadn't dared to actually get excited, not when so much has gone wrong the last year and a half.

Of course you did it.

Brody's voice in my head is like a blessing and a curse, but I smile softly anyway before looking back up at my new friend, who apparently knows me better than I'd realized. "I got in."

"I cannot believe we're at a football game," I mumble as I climb the concrete steps of the outdoor bleachers. The sheer number of people here is nuts. Admittedly, it's not just our esteemed students—wow, my internal sarcasm is on point today—the opposing school seems to have brought their entire student body too. And I think there are actually parents here.

Real ones.

Visiting their kids as they play.

That might be more shocking than me being here.

Maybe.

"Cheer up, Star Bright. It's going to be a wonderful evening, you'll see. Look at you with your hot dog and soda. If we got you a jersey, you'd be one of us. One of us. One of us." She chants with a wicked smile before heading down a row where Vann and the rest of her friends are already sitting. He waves at her when he sees us, hugs her when we get there, and I give him a knowing look as he does. He blushes at me and I swear, it's adorable.

Matchmaker has never been on my bingo card, but maybe, just maybe, here it will be.

Stranger things have happened.

Once I take my seat, my entire body aching from today's first gym session with the swim team, I try to take it all in: the masses, the teams warming up out on the field, the cheer squads. I spot Trey out on the field in his gear, except it looks like he's being shouted at by the tiny manic pixie chick I saw yelling at him on my first day here.

"Who is that?" I ask Kate, motioning to the field.

"Erm, that's Trey?" she responds, sounding confused.

"I know that," I sigh. "I meant the girl with him."

"That's Allie, his sister. Adopted sister. She's the year below us and part of the tech team at Arbour. A literal genius. Not sure why it is exactly she's here instead of somewhere that would nurture that genius, but she's kinda awesome. Why?"

I shrug, still watching the exchange between the two of them on the field. "Call it curiosity. I saw them together, arguing, before you got here. I don't remember all of it, but he looks... well, kinda terrified of her. He's a six foot, lean, mean muscle machine from what I can tell. Mildly terrifying if he tried I'm sure, and yet, that abjectly beautiful dickhead—from what I've seen of him—looks like he's going to pee his pants."

Kate and Vann burst out laughing when I finish my little tirade and I turn my focus to them instead of the field. "Abjectly beautiful dickhead, someone put it on a bumper sticker."

I stick my tongue out at Vann, glad to see his playful ways back after our conversation in the hall yesterday. "I mean, I'm not wrong."

"I don't see it," Kate says with a shrug. "Also, he's like

six foot six. Absolute giant, especially compared to me, and to Allie, but she is kinda terrifying. Especially with her tech wizard ways. Some of the rumors... yeah, like I said, she's awesome."

"Good to know," I respond with a nod just as music starts blaring around us and everyone is suddenly on their feet, cheering as the teams face off with each other on the field.

"You realize I have no idea what's going on right?" I shout at Kate, who grins and nods.

"I'll elbow you when you need to cheer. Just follow my lead."

She's practically glowing in her leggings, jersey, and braids. It could be the game, it could be how close Vann is standing to her, despite her arguments that they're just friends.

Yep, I think I might just add matchmaker to my bingo card for the year.

After the game, I make my excuse of trying to find a bathroom to give Kate and Vann some time alone after the rest of her friends disappeared. Except, in my moment of genius, I forgot that I have no idea where anything is on this side of the campus yet.

Rather than interrupting what I'm hoping is some good old fashioned one-on-one time for Kate, I meander through the concrete building that sits below the bleachers, hoping to stumble across a bathroom.

It's a school, there has to be a bathroom, right?

After wandering for about five minutes, I find one and distract myself for an extra ten minutes before my phone buzzes.

KATE

You're not that slick ya know. I see you and your tricks. We're heading to get food, you coming?

ME

Me, tricks? I know not what you mean :p who is we?

KATE

Me and Vann.

ME

Nope, you guys have fun, I think I'm going to grab some pizza and watch a film. I've had enough outside peopling for the night.

KATE

You sure?

ME

Positive. Have fun. Don't do anything I wouldn't do ;)

KATE

Sure thing, mum.

ME

I won't wait up!

Grinning, I pocket my phone again and head out of the empty bathroom, hoping to find my way back to the dorm building alone without getting lost especially since it's dark out.

Next time, bring a map, matchmaker genius.

I follow the sound of voices, wishing my internal compass was better calibrated, hoping I'm going in the right direction, when I stumble across Trey, Allie walking away from him in the direction I'm heading.

"Why are you here?" he barks, that accent of his making him sound so much harsher than it should, and I start. Looking up at him, I wish he was shorter because holy shit he makes me feel too freaking small and breakable when he shouts like that.

Shaking it off, I meet his gaze and fold my arms over my chest. "I'm trying to get back to my dorm. You might've missed it, but I'm new here."

My sass seems to piss him off more, if that's even possible. We won, he ran that ball to the end zone like a pro baller according to Kate.

"Stay away from me and my friends. Your type isn't

welcome with us." He moves toward me, backing me against the wall, using his size to herd me into a corner where the wall meets an arch, and I'm essentially trapped.

Trying not to let that intimidate me, despite my lack of escape, I latch on to my inner Callie, my inner Brody, and pull on the sass that landed me in this situation. "Maybe *you* should stay away from *me*. I was just walking. You're the one who started talking to me. Moved me here. Do you want to be close to me, Trey? Is this just some pent up frustration?"

I lift a hand to place on his chest, to add to my mockery, but he moves wicked fast, like a coiled snake, and grabs my wrist, squeezing hard enough that it feels like my wrist might snap. "Do. Not. Touch. Me."

His words are low, little more than a murmur, but the veil of his threat is as clear as the pain in my wrist.

"Hey! Dude, let her go!"

Relief floods me and Trey drops my wrist like I burned him. Cradling my wrist, I sidestep, pushing past his brutish size, finding Evan watching me, his brow scrunched in concern.

Did not expect him to be my knight in not-so-shining armor.

"You okay?" he asks me, holding out an arm toward me.

I nod as I move next to him and he steps forward, as if

protecting me from the big bad Trey.

"Everything okay here?"

Oh, great. The rest of the goon squad.

Nico, Dallas, and Isaac join our fun little face off, standing next to their friend when Nico speaks again. "Well?"

"Fine," I tell him, still holding my wrist. He frowns momentarily when he notices before turning his attention back to Evan.

"Cunningham, anything to add?"

Nico using Evan's surname throws me for a second, but Evan speaks before I have a chance to process that they know each other well enough for that.

"Maybe you should ask your friend," Evan retorts, his bravado obviously shocking Nico.

I shudder as Isaac eyes me up and down, but he stays quiet, and Dallas doesn't even bother to look at me. Nico turns to Trey, who just says, "We're fine."

"Well then, I guess this little meeting doesn't need to be dragged out any longer then, does it." Nico's dismissal riles me, but my wrist aches enough that I keep my mouth shut, whirl on my heel, and head off in the direction I was originally going as quickly as my feet will move.

"Talia, wait," Evan calls out, and I pause, turning as he jogs to catch up with me. "Are you okay?"

"I'm fine, Evan." I sigh and continue walking. He falls

into step beside me in silence. "Thank you."

"You don't have to thank me," he replies quietly. "I didn't know you'd be here. At Arbour I mean."

I let out a sharp laugh, relief filling me as he leads me across the green and I see the dorm building on the other side of it. "Yeah, me either. You or me."

"Are you really okay?" he asks, pausing a step ahead of me, forcing me to stop as he turns to face me.

"I'll be fine," I tell him, leaving out that I really need ice. My wrist being out of commission when I need to be in the pool tomorrow doesn't work for me at all.

"I'm sorry, ya know," he starts, and my stomach twists. I *so* don't want to talk about this.

"Don't," I say, before he continues. "Not here. I don't want to talk about it. Ever."

"Okay," he says, a sad smile pinching his face. "I won't talk about what happened. Or about what I know. We all deserve a fresh start."

"Thank you."

He reaches up, touching my cheek, and I freeze when he strokes a thumb across it before tucking my hair behind my ear. "But I really am sorry. I miss you."

"Evan, I—" He steps closer and cuts off my words, pressing his lips against mine. I push him back, taking a step away from him. "Evan, no."

"I'm sorry," he says, pushing a hand through his golden

locks. "I didn't mean—"

"I should go," I tell him and turn away from him before he gets a chance to speak again.

When I reach the dorm building, I startle when Noah appears in front of me. "Looks like you're getting around, new girl."

Gritting my teeth together, I push out a breath. "That is not my name, and you have no idea what you're talking about."

"How is your wrist?" she asks, and I shake my head, trying to figure out how she knows. She must see my confusion because she speaks again. "Nico."

"Of course."

"So, how is it?" she asks again, like I'm wasting her time.

I am running out of patience with this night. I should've gone to dinner after all.

"Your friend is safe, I'm not about to broadcast his brutish, manhandling ways. I'm going to go grab some ice and head to my room. I'm fine."

"Back corner of the first cupboard in the kitchenette."

"I'm sorry?" I ask, wondering if I hit my head at some point, or if this evening is just turning my brain to cheese.

"Instant ice packs, new girl. Keep up." She eyes me up and down as if assessing me.

I am so over this.

"Right," I retort. I've only taken a few steps when I hear her voice again.

"Be careful, new girl. But well done. Keep going like this and hell, you might even survive Arbour."

ELEVEN

Noah

"**B**e careful, new girl. But well done. Keep going like this and hell, you might even survive Arbour."

I can practically *feel* her rolling her eyes as she walks away from me despite the compliment, and once she's out of sight, I drop Nico a message to let him know the coast is clear. I'm not sure exactly what the new girl has done to rile Trey up so much, but I'm about to find out.

I laugh at my obviously genius wit as I slide my phone into my pocket and wait until I see the four of them waltzing toward me through the quad. One day, they'll fully let me in on their secret boys' club and mysterious rendezvous. Control is kind of my thing, especially since I lack it in *so many* areas of my life, but with this? I half like not knowing.

Not that I'll ever admit that to them.

I think they secretly enjoy my little tantrums about it.

Just like they are loving their extra-protective crap this year. I swear I can practically see their inner cavemen beating their chests like, we men, we protect.

So stupid.

"Ready for your little boys' club secret meeting?" I tease when they reach me.

"Oh yeah, you're missing out on so much fun, little queen bee," Isaac teases right back. "You know you're really dying to come with us."

"Even if I was, I'm not allowed." I pout at him before sticking my tongue out.

"No, you're not," Nico adds, exasperated. "For your own good."

Rolling my eyes at him, I fold my arms over my chest. "Yeah, yeah. Whatever. You ready to be my bodyguard for the evening?" I ask as I turn to Trey. Because that's how Nico explained it to me, as Trey watching over me, not me defusing the bomb that's a small vibration away from going off.

"Yeah."

The one word is barely more than a grunt, but I ignore the obvious rage simmering beneath the surface and loop my arm through his. "Be gone, the rest of you, with your secrets. Trey has to deal with me moaning about my waistline while we eat pizza and I paint my nails."

"Good luck with that," Dallas says, clapping a hand on Trey's other shoulder before the three of them head to the parking lot.

"What's got your panties in a wad?" I ask as I half drag him toward the dorms. "You won the game, I thought you'd be riding high and let me paint *your* nails tonight."

I mean, I'll do it anyway, I rope all of them into it when I'm trying to decide which color I want to go with, and because they adore me—as they should—they put up with it.

"Nothing," he grunts again as we head inside. He leads me up to my room, checking it once I've unlocked it, like some big bad monster is hiding under my bed, then locks my door again once I'm inside.

Nicolette will have an aneurysm if she finds out, but I don't care enough about that to leave it unlocked. If it makes him feel better, then that's more important to me.

"What kind of pizza do you want?" he asks as he drops

onto my sofa and pulls out his phone.

"Cheese. Lots of cheese."

He rolls his eyes as a smile tugs at the corner of his mouth. "What is with chicks and their addiction to cheese? Is it a hormone thing? Cause you guys are insane for the stuff. Allie and my mum are the same. Marnie too."

"You know you love us, really. But honestly, it's just the best ever."

He laughs as he places the order for us on his app while I grab us a can of soda each from my mini fridge. "So, ready to tell me about your run in with new girl yet?"

The joy drops from his face, and usually I'd feel bad, but I want to know what it is about this girl that has the four of them so off kilter. Isaac and Dallas haven't said anything, but I've seen them when she's around.

It's fucking obscure.

The four of them don't tend to go for the same kind of girls. Never have. And if more than one of them has been into the same girl by some miracle, they've always agreed to leave it alone because their friendship is worth more than some strange????.

"There is just something about her that gets my back up. She reminds me of the girls back home. Like, there's the girl you see, and then the real monster beneath. She was eavesdropping on me and Allie the first week of school, and since then, she just seems to always be there.

Watching us."

"You think she's actually up to something?"

He shrugs as he runs a hand over his super short hair, then lets out a deep breath. "I honestly don't know, but there's something about her that feels off. And I know you haven't missed the way the others are just drawn to her. She's trouble."

"She's just a girl," I say, trying to dismiss it. "Not some evil mastermind."

Though, even as I say it, a flutter in my stomach tells me I could be wrong.

"Maybe," he agrees, nodding. "But we both know that nobody is what they seem. Especially at Arbour. And her dropping in out of nowhere this year, with everything else…"

He trails off, so I wait for him to continue.

"Everything else?

"Nothing. I just mean it's suspicious." His phone pings and he looks relieved, like he's saved by the goddamn bell. "Pizza is here, I'll be back in two minutes."

He practically runs for the door, and I stay seated, watching him closely as he goes.

There's definitely something they're not telling me about because Nico said something similar the other day. If she's wrapped up in it, well, then maybe I was wrong before.

Trey is right about one thing: no one at Arbour is what they seem, so I think I'm going to be keeping an eye on new girl.

If she's up to something, I'll find out, and if she tries to mess with my guys…

Well, she'll live to regret it.

TWELVE

Talia

"**S**hit."

I glance over at Kate, bleary-eyed and still half asleep. I didn't even hear her come in last night. Once I got back from the game, picked up the new noteless bouquet of purple anemone with baby's breath that was waiting outside our door and placed them on Kate's desk next to the last one, I face planted on my bed and actually slept for a change.

Picking up my phone, I notice that it's only five in the morning. On a Saturday.

"Is the world ending?" I croak as she continues to curse under her breath. It sure as shit better be if she's waking me up this early.

"Sorry," she sighs, scrolling her phone. "But yeah, kinda."

"What?" I ask, sitting up, hoping my brain fog clears.

She climbs from her bed and drops onto mine. "Lexi knows."

"Want to elaborate?"

Lord, I need caffeine.

"About Dillon. You and Dillon."

Yeah, that'll bypass the caffeine requirement. "I'm sorry, what? How do you know?"

She flips her phone so I can see the screen and part of me wants to shrivel up and die. "That's your feed?"

Nodding, she gives me a sad smile. "I've been trying to report every post I see, but I'm one person and this is the Internet."

"That's not me," I groan, staring at the supposed naked pictures of me. They're pixelated in the right places but obviously photoshopped. Well, as far as I can tell anyway. I take her phone and scroll through, wanting to disappear. There are so many with different tags, different descriptions, but the comments, from what I've seen, are vile. I spot a few that are of me from the beach, where I'm in a bikini, but they've also been edited to look like I'm naked in someone's bedroom. What the actual hell? "Okay, some of them are me, but they've also been messed with. How do you know this was Lexi?"

Kate grimaces as I hand her phone back. "You'll never be able to prove it, but let's just say I've seen some of her work before."

"All this because I screwed some guy who she wasn't even dating? Is she certifiable?" Picking up my phone, I head to my social feed, only to find it looks similar to Kate's. The fact that I've been tagged in what feels like every post is just... thrilling. "How do I fix this?"

"You go to swim practice like nothing happened and I... I'm going to call in a favor."

Looking at her wide-eyed, bewilderment hits me. "You have a favor that can fix this?"

Kate shrugs, looking almost sheepish. "Remember I told you about Allie being a tech genius? Trey's little sister? Yeah, she owes me one."

"Are you sure she can fix this? That you'd call in your favor for me?"

"That's what besties are for," she says nonchalantly. "Now get up and get your shit together. Practice starts at six right?"

"Yes," I groan. Coach is apparently a sadist. Practice at six on a Saturday. So awesome. "Hopefully my wrist doesn't crap out on my first practice. Lexi is going to be there too. Double fun."

"She won't do anything with Coach around," Kate

replies confidently. "Go and act like nothing happened. Though, I daresay the staff will already be notified about it. Indecent pictures of a student being posted online, especially since you're not technically an adult, are going to be looked at."

My phone starts to ring almost like the universe heard her words and wanted to torture me some more. I flip my phone to show her the screen and she winces. "Have fun with that, I've gotta go wake up a genius."

"Thank you!" I tell her before answering my phone. "Hi, Dad! Everything okay? This is early, though, is it for you? Time differences and all that."

Kate waves as she quietly slinks out of the room, closing the door behind her.

"Talia Hayes! Why am I getting calls about naked pictures of you being posted online? I didn't send you to Arbour so you could become some party girl—"

"No, Dad. You abandoned me here so you could run off and pretend that life didn't happen to us."

"You listen here, young lady!" He starts his tirade, so I put my phone on my pillow and lie back, not listening to his bullshit, chiming in with an 'uh-huh' when he pauses. "Talia! Are you even listening to me?"

"Would it really matter?" I ask, trying to stuff down the urge to cry. I've lived through worse than an online troll campaign. I refuse to shed tears over this. "Do you even care that it's not me? Or do you just think that's who I am? The girl that takes nudes and lets them be leaked. Awesome parenting there, Dad. You haven't even asked if I'm okay, if they're me, what's going on that could lead to this? No, you just jumped in on your holier-than-thou crusade where I'm in the wrong. So ya know what, Dad? Go back to saving the rest of the world and leave me to the pit you dropped me in and ran from. I'll save myself."

I hang up before he has a chance to respond, then put my phone on do not disturb so it stops all notifications except for Kate, who I put on emergency bypass.

I haven't even been here for a month and I've already made enemies. I don't know that I'd consider Noah an enemy, but she doesn't like me—not that I know why—add that to her Fantastic Four followers who might as well be her guard dogs. Dallas might not be an asshole, but the other three... yeah, let's not go there.

Now I have Lexi to deal with, all because I banged a guy a few times over the summer who failed to mention her even once.

Just awesome.

Trying to push it from my mind, I grab my swimsuit and a bag for practice, stuffing my clothes and shower things in it before changing into my suit, adding sweats, a tank, and my hoodie over the top. Checking the time, I realize I have ten minutes to haul ass down to practice before I'm late, so I slip on my Converse and grab my phone and keys. After locking the door to our room, and checking it twice, I practically run down to the pool locker room, gliding in with two minutes to spare.

"Let's go, ladies!" Coach shouts through the locker room as I jam my things into an open locker and undress. "Sixty seconds!"

With no time to spare, I rush out to the pool, finding Lexi glaring at me from the edge of the water.

Oh yeah, this is going to be so much fun. Not.

After a practice from Hell, followed by a two hour nap, I'm finally awake, dressed, and hunting down Kate. Eventually, I find her in the cafeteria with Vann and Allie, tucked away in a different corner than normal.

Rather than grabbing food, despite my gurgling stomach, I beeline for them, hoping that there are some updates. Sliding into the seat next to Kate, I glance over at Allie, who is tapping away on her laptop.

"Hi," I say, trying not to be rude. Allie doesn't even look up at me, so I keep talking. "Any luck?"

"We're getting there," Kate says with a sad smile. "But removing all traces will be hard. People will have saved them and stuff. But Allie is doing what she can to scrub the internet of them. But it's the internet, once it's out there, it's out there."

I groan and drop my head onto my forearms on the table. "Just awesome."

"I'm really sorry this is happening to you," Vann says quietly. Turning my head, I glance over at him and smile softly.

"Thanks, Vann. Me too."

"Have you eaten?" Kate asks, and I shake my head. "Didn't think so. I came back to the room and you were asleep. Didn't want to wake you up, so I left pretty quickly. You should eat though."

"Probably," I mumble, my stomach gurgling again. Kate gives me what I'm forever now going to call 'the mom look'. Holding my hands up in mock surrender, I push my chair back and stand. "I'm going, I'm going. You guys want anything?"

"Fries, please." Allie's words are short and clipped, but considering what she's doing for me, I'd get her a lifetime worth of fries.

"Done," I reply, then turn to the others. "You two?"

"Cheese puffs and a Coke?" Kate asks with a smile and I nod.

"I'll come with you, help you carry it all." Vann stands before I have a chance to object, but the way Kate smiles up at him like he hangs the moon would keep my mouth shut anyway. Am I going to take the chance to ask him what his plan is? Absolutely I am. Distraction from my personal shit show? Yes, please!

"Sure," is what I say instead and he matches pace at my side as we walk across the room. Glancing over at him, it occurs to me that he's almost walking like he's trying to protect me from the room. "Wait, did Kate ask you to watch out for me or something?"

"No, I just figured getting food for four was a lot to carry."

"Uh-huh," I say, side-eyeing him. "If you say so. How is that 'just friends' thing going for you?"

He laughs softly, shaking his head. "Just as well as it has the entire time I've known Kate."

"Uh-huh," I parrot again, and this time he laughs.

We join the line for food, which, thankfully, isn't too long. I grab two portions of fries while he grabs cheese puffs and Coke for Kate and a slice of pizza for himself. Once we've paid, we head back out into the hall and I groan when I see Lexi across the room. She beelines toward us and I groan again.

"Oh, look, it's little miss drop her panties for anyone who asks," she announces loud enough for the entire room to hear.

I lock my face into what I hope is a mask of indifference

and try to channel my inner Callie. *God, I wish she was here right now.*

"Slut shaming. Great way to start your day, Lexi. Anything more original or controversial than me having a sex life?" I retort, trying to seem unbothered, hoping to God it comes across better on the outside than it does internally. Because inside, I want the ground to open up and swallow me whole.

"I don't need to be original when I have the truth on my side. You've fucked half the sports teams from what I've been told, and there are pictures... then panting after Trey and Nico. Desperate for some outside validation are we, Talia? You should probably see a therapist about that."

"*I'm* desperate? You're the one here supposedly blasting my business across the school like someone dying for attention. Does it make you feel on top to put others down, Lexi? Maybe I'm not the only one who should be seeing a therapist. I can recommend you mine, she's great."

Lexi's mouth opens, then closes, and I smile. "That's what I thought. Better luck next time, wannabe queen." Without giving her the chance to speak again, I flick my hair over my shoulder and strut away from her, glad I'm holding the tray of fries so no one can see how badly my hands are shaking. Vann scrambles to stay by my side as I hustle back over to where Kate and Allie are watching. Kate's mouth is open in shock, but Allie's grin is wide.

Might've made a new friend. Upside.

Glancing around the room, I notice Nico and Noah watching me. I can't read them at all, but they obviously saw everything. Then I notice both Dillon and Evan sitting with the baseball team.

Nice of either of them to stand up for me. Douchebags.

Vann and I take our seats as voices start up around us again, and Allie winks at me as she grabs a plate of fries from my tray. "Now *that* was freaking epic. I am so team Talia."

"Well thanks," I reply, dipping a fry in the ketchup bowl on my tray and taking a bite. "Hopefully nobody could tell I was shitting my pants the entire time."

"Not at all," Kate replies, sounding slightly stunned. "That was kinda incredible, not going to lie. Balls of freaking steel, my friend. Of *steel!*"

I laugh, trying to eat another fry despite the churning in my stomach.

"And I think I've cleared the pictures too," Allie chimes in. "Two points for team Talia."

I let out a deep sigh, relief mixing with my jumbled insides. "Thank you, Allie. Saving my life today."

"Eh, it was no biggie," she replies with a smile before looking at Kate. "I'll still owe you one, today's entertainment was worth it all on its own. I freaking loathe Lexi. After what happened over the summer, which no, I will not give details on, but let's just say her entire family is toxic and anything I can do to go against her, I will."

"Thanks, Allie," Kate says with a grin. "Team Talia for the win."

I laugh again, shaking my head. "Let's just hope there's no more need for teams."

Allie laughs in response and my stomach twists. "Yeah, I doubt you'll be so lucky. I have a feeling the games are only just beginning."

THIRTEEN

Noah

Well, that was some interesting entertainment for a Saturday lunchtime. Who knew the new girl had some fire? Especially after Lexi's pathetic attempt to humiliate her online. Anyone who saw those pictures would know they're photoshopped. It was a pitiful attempt at bullying, but after today, seeing the anger on Lexi's face at her failed humiliation, I have a feeling her war with the new girl is only just beginning.

May the best woman win.

By that, I mean the new girl, because Lexi and her entire family are scum.

"Where'd you go?" Nico asks, pulling me from my

thoughts.

"Huh?" I ask when he motions to my hands.

Shit.

I hadn't even felt it. I unclench my hands, my nails leaving divots in my palm and just a hint of blood where I broke the top layer of skin. "Just thinking about the fireworks at lunch."

"Fireworks?" Isaac asks as he sits on the sofa opposite me in the boys' room. "What did we miss?"

Nico fills the three of them in while I scroll through my phone, smiling when I see that Allie was obviously with the new girl, helping her at lunch, because all the pictures of her have disappeared.

"Looks like Allie helped the new girl with her picture problem too."

Trey frowns, shaking his head. "How has this chick managed to infiltrate so much of our lives already? The semester has barely begun."

I shrug, more curious about the new girl than anything. "You're the one manhandling her."

"I didn't mean to hurt her," he mumbles, running a hand over his buzzed black hair. "I was pissed at Allie, hyped from the game, and honestly, it's all a bit of a blur."

"The joy of adrenaline," Isaac purrs. "But there's something about her that is... intriguing."

"We should leave her alone," Nico adds. "We have

enough to deal with this year."

The four of them glance at each other, Dallas the only one remaining quiet in this conversation, which in itself is telling enough.

"Enough to deal with?" I question, wondering what mess they're in already.

"Nothing for you to worry about," Nico responds before anyone else can. His "I rule the world, my word is law" thing is getting really tiring. "You just worry about you."

"I'm trying to forget about my bullshit," I object. "Yours will be a fun diversion."

"We don't have anything we need your skills for," Isaac says with a wink, and I roll my eyes.

"If you say so," I say with a sigh before standing. "I'm going to go, let you boys have your secrets for now. We all know I'll find out eventually. I always do."

"You don't have to go," Nico starts, but I shake my head.

"It's good, I've got studying to do. I'll catch you guys later. Are we still grabbing dinner before the open mic?"

"I've got a meeting," Isaac adds. "So does Trey."

"We'll be there," Nico replies as I pick up my bag and pull the strap over my shoulder.

"Great, see you later." I head out of their dorm, not sure why they chose to room together when they could have a suite each if they wanted, but they've always had a weird co-dependency between them.

Everyone thinks we're all thick as thieves, and while that's mostly true, I'm definitely on the outside of their little boys' club.

I head down the stairs of their dorm and out to the quad. I really do need to study, but first I need to clear my head, and fresh air helps.

At least it always used to.

"Oh look, it's the girl who cried wolf."

Steeling myself with a deep breath, I pull on that ice queen mask of mine and turn to find Lexi and Co. a few feet behind me. "I called rape, not wolf, asshole."

She steps forward but I refuse to take a step back and let her gain ground on me. "It's not rape when you're a whore. Runs in the family, I guess."

I clench my fists and my jaw tics as I take another breath, loosening it before responding. "I'm a whore. Talia is a slut. You sound like you're stuck in a loop, Lexi. I thought you'd have more ammunition than this. I guess you didn't learn as much from me in the last few years as I thought. It's almost disappointing, this failed attempt at belittling. Better luck next time."

"Scottie said you were a lousy lay," she snarks. "I guess you're losing your touch, Noah. Better run to Mommy and ask for some tips."

Quick as a whip, I strike out, slapping her face, my palm stinging as she lets out a squeal. "I'd only be a lousy lay if it was rape, you two-bit, brain-dead bitch. And maybe you should ask your dad about my mom. I've heard him beg her plenty just to be sent away. I guess being trash runs in the family too. Every single one of you."

Turning, I sashay away, as if unaffected despite my insides quivering. Being called a liar infuriates me. A liar is one thing I am not, nor will I ever be. And who doesn't believe a rape victim? I know it's her brother, but dammit, she knows what a piece of shit he is.

So much for clearing my head, a walk isn't going to cut it.

I need to hit something. Hard.

You'd think with the money I have, and with my mother being who she is, that getting ready for a night at a cafe/ restaurant thing for an open mic night would be easy. I must have all the clothes in the world for something so simple.

And yet... my bed currently holds a mountain of discarded clothing where I've changed outfits a dozen times and now I'm starting to sweat from the workout of it all.

Ladies don't sweat, they sheen.

Rolling my eyes at my mother's voice echoing in my head, I drop into the lounge chair in my underwear and groan.

Getting dressed shouldn't be this hard.

But doing anything in this town, while at Arbour—hell, during my entire life—is like living in a fishbowl. I'm watched with such scrutiny, and honestly, I'm sick of it.

Sometimes I'm envious of people like the new girl, of the people who are mostly unknown, can go places without someone taking their picture and putting it online, forever criticized for what they're wearing, how they look, or God forbid, their hair not being done.

All because of who my parents are.

Really, my dad is a nobody. He just happens to have a lot of money. But my mother, well, she's a model turned TV reality star turned household name. Being her daughter comes with expectations that I really want nothing to do with.

Being a model or a TV star is not what I want for my life.

Not that I'm sure what it is I want. I've never really been given the chance to think about it or figure it out. I'm sure that's partially a blessing, so I'm not pining after something I can't have, but a bigger part of me resents my mother.

Sure, my parents being who they are has given me a somewhat easier life, but anyone who thinks growing up with money means that life is inherently easy... well, let's just say everyone has their own battles. Mine might not be worrying about if I'm going to be able to eat, or where I'm going to be sleeping, but more it's about what I'm allowed to eat, if anything at all, the societal hoops, along with the pressures that any woman lives with about how they look, that we should be seen and not heard, that we should look after everyone else while also looking after ourselves but allowing men to provide for us while not being a brattish princess type but not being too masculine either.

It's exhausting.

If my mother could see me now, the rolls of my stomach on display rather than hidden beneath a corset or tight shapewear, well, she'd likely have an aneurism.

Sighing, I pull myself from my pity party. I grab a pair of black wide-leg jeans, a black corset-style tank, a red leather jacket, and black knee-high boots with a red sole. Casual, but stylish enough that if I'm seen, I won't be crucified or wake up to a torrent of messages from Mother belittling my choices and how it makes her look.

I throw the ensemble together along with a dozen

rings, necklaces, and bracelets, finish my makeup, and put my hair up in a messy style ponytail, letting my butterfly bangs hang down and surround my face.

Done. I think.

As if reading my mind, my phone pings, and I smile at the message.

NICO

Are you nearly ready?

ME

Finished just now.

NICO

We're downstairs. Dallas is pacing like a goddamn cat.

ME

On my way :)

I throw my phone, wallet, and keys into a clutch, snaking the chain over my shoulder before triple checking the locks are set on my door and heading down to where Nico and Dallas are waiting for me.

Dallas is singing tonight. It's kind of adorable that he's so nervous, especially when he's been singing his entire life, but after deciding he wanted to make a name for himself music wise, outside of his family, he's essentially starting from scratch.

Starting tonight.

"Don't you look all cowboy," I tease him when I reach them, wrapping him up in a hug. He smells like smoke and forest. Like a bonfire in the woods.

"Hilarious. Y'all made the name for me, so I figured I'd lean into it." He winks at me as he pulls back from the hug.

"Look, I didn't nickname you, Dallas." I laugh when he rolls his eyes. "I just made the comment about you being named Austin when you're from Dallas. The guys did the rest."

"Yes, we did," Nico chimes in once he's put his phone away and hugs me. "Now, let's get going. I'm starving."

We ride in mostly silence, the music on the radio filling the space as Nico drives us into town in his SUV. I stare out the window from the passenger seat, just like the princess I am, because God forbid I be allowed to drive anywhere, and wonder what life would have been like if I wasn't born Noah Carrington.

It's a nice fantasy to get lost in, one I've been having more and more since what happened with Scottie. Part of me knows what happened wasn't my fault, but another part of me can't help but wonder if it's because of who I am that it happened.

Nico pulls the car into a space in the lot and shuts off the engine, taking the music with it.

"You good?" he asks Dallas, glancing into the rearview mirror.

I turn in my seat so I'm facing them both as Dallas runs a hand through his dark blond locks, which just fall back down into his crystal-blue eyes. "I think so."

"Then let's do this," Nico announces, grinning as he opens his door. Dallas bounces out of the car on my side, opening my door before I get a chance. He offers me a hand and helps me step out of the giant car as Nico joins us. "I would do disgusting things for a good steak right now."

"I don't need to know about you and your disgusting things, thank you," I say, gagging out loud and making them both laugh. They place me between them, almost subconsciously, I'm sure, and lead me into Alchemy.

It's cute, in that dimly lit, upscale, music scene kinda way. It's a mesh of tables and booths, a bar running along the right wall, and a stage across the back. It's not too busy yet, but we're early. Who knows what this place will be like once the crowd finally fills in? Nico speaks to the hostess, who leads us to a table near the stage to the left of the bar and hands us each a menu. "You guys want drinks?"

"I'll take a whiskey on the rocks," Nico says, that stupid brooding smolder he perfected at like, eight, on his face, and she is eating it up.

"Sure thing," she says, blushing as she glances down at her feet, twisting her hands together. "And for the rest of you?"

"Vodka tonic," I say curtly, before looking back at the menu. She didn't ID Nico, so I swear to God, if she asks for my ID, I'll lose it. Even if I definitely don't look twenty-one, and it's definitely illegal if she gets caught— not that that's ever stopped any of us before. While I might not always like the downsides of my life, money does fix a lot of problems so I'm still going to try it. After the day I've had, I feel like it'll help me relax.

"Just a water for me, thanks," Dallas says to her before she rushes away to the bar. I glance over at him and find his signature casual smile on his face. If I didn't know him so well, I'd think he was super relaxed, but there's a tightness to the corners of his eyes and his shoulders are tense, even beneath that plaid button down he's got on over his black t-shirt.

Our server appears with our drinks, looking far more skeptical than the hostess when she gives them to us, but she doesn't comment. We place our orders and I go with the chicken caesar salad because it's a safe option, but I also order a side of fries, knowing even if I don't eat them all, the guys will demolish them. Nico gets his steak and Dallas orders a chicken club.

"I don't wanna eat too much," he explains when the server leaves. "Vomiting on stage isn't the reason I want tonight to be memorable."

"What are you singing?" I ask before taking a sip of

my drink.

He scratches the back of his neck as red creeps up it and onto his cheeks. "An original."

"Oh, well, color me intrigued," I say with a playful wink, squeezing his arm in an attempt to reassure him. "I'm sure you'll be amazing."

Movement at the door draws my attention and I notice Kate entering with her friend, Vann, and the new girl. *Probably should just start calling her Talia.*

They're seated in the farthest corner from the stage in a booth, and I start to bring my focus back to the table when someone else walks in.

A guy wearing a leather jacket with ripped black jeans and Converse, a guitar slung over his back, who doesn't bother to wait for the hostess and walks straight to the bar, embracing a guy working behind it. He runs a hand through his ginger curls which are cut pretty short, and I notice a hint of ink on his hand.

Sweet baby Jesus.

The rocker bad boy type has always been my kryptonite, and this guy has those vibes rolling from him in tsunami-like waves.

He laughs at something the bartender says, and I swear the sound of it makes my toes curl.

"Earth to Noah," Dallas says, chuckling. I shake my head, bringing my attention to him, realizing Nico isn't even sitting with us anymore. "You eye fucking Myles Alden for any particular reason?"

"I was not—" I start, feeling heat blossom across my chest. "Fine, I was, but only because he is…"

"Everything you know you can't have?" he asks, finishing my thought.

I nod, knowing his comment is the truth I don't want to fully acknowledge, while glancing back at Myles. "Exactly that. How do you know him?"

"He organized tonight. His dad owns this place. They're new to Spring Creek. He's in college, but he commutes into the city when he has classes. Just in case you're interested." He smiles at me knowingly and it's like my brain starts up a whole new storyline in the book of my life, one where I get to have the guy I'd like, who is obviously just perfection wrapped in a pretty package. "He's a nice guy."

Letting out a sigh, I pick up my drink and take another sip. "Of course he is."

"Myles!" Dallas calls out, lifting a hand in the air before he stands. "Thanks again for slotting me in tonight, man."

"Sure thing, a voice like yours deserves a stage."

Oh my God, even his voice is orgasm worthy. Smooth but sweet, like a molten lava cake.

Yeah, this guy needs to be on a no-no list.

Though that'd probably make me want him more.

Myles walks away toward the stage, giving me another chance to eye fuck him, and his peachy, biteable ass, some more.

"Oh, you're fucked," Dallas says, laughing as he takes his seat again. "Don't let Nico see, you know what he's like."

"Don't I ever," I grumble. "Where is he?"

He tilts his head back and I see Nico sitting next to Talia in her booth.

"And here I was thinking she was chasing him."

Dallas shrugs as our server reappears with our food. "I wouldn't read too much into it."

But his statement just makes me more suspicious, Nico doesn't do anything without reason. He might be a big soft cuddly bear for me, but he's calculating and cold to the rest of the world. Just how his daddy taught him to be.

I watch him as he stands from their table. He leans down to Talia and says something before sauntering back over to us. Her eyes follow his back, half death glare, half desire.

Typical female reaction to him.

Instead of saying anything as he takes his seat, I take a bite of my salad and glance over his shoulder to where Myles is setting up on stage.

Oh yeah, tonight is going to be interesting.

FOURTEEN

Talia

After a week, that if I had to describe it, 'week from Hell' would be an understatement, I just want to chill out. So when Kate suggested checking out Alchemy, the new place in town that had an open mic tonight, I was fully on board. Tomorrow is a Sunday so I can sleep in. Win..

Vann drove us here and Allie is supposed to be meeting us later on, but what I didn't expect was for us to be seated and for Nico to come and sit down beside me.

He struts over like he owns the place—which, knowing my luck, he fucking does—looking way hotter than he should in jeans, boots, and a t-shirt, with his dark hair pushed back and his whiskey eyes focused solely on me.

"What do you want?" I ask quietly, while Kate and Vann just stare at him.

He leans back, draping his arm across the top of the booth behind me. I sit up a little straighter so I'm not brushing against his arm. Turning slightly to face me, he smiles at me, enough that it touches his eyes, and I feel like I'm a rabbit caught in a trap. "Is that any way to treat a guest?"

I glance over at Kate, who shrugs, wide-eyed. Vann whispers a question to her and part of me wants to glare at him for distracting her so I have to handle Nico alone. Little traitor.

"You're not my guest. You weren't invited to sit with us, you just popped up. Like a bad zit."

He laughs. It's low, and somehow smokey.

Get a grip, Talia. A laugh can't be fucking smokey, you imbecile.

"Touché. I just thought I'd come and say hello, let you know I was here so we didn't have to run into each other in the kitchenette in the middle of the night for you to talk to me."

I quirk a brow and lean into him. "So you *want* to talk to me now?"

His eyes crinkle in the corners as his smile deepens. He lifts my drink and takes a sip of my Coke. The audacity of this asshole. My thoughts must be projected on my face because I swear his smile widens a little more before he says, "Maybe I did."

Pursing my lips, I wait for him to continue while trying to keep a lid on the word vomit that wants to fall from my lips, but he doesn't say anything else. Instead, he locks eyes with me, my drink still in his hand, and lifts it to his lips again.

This freaking guy.

He finishes the glass, his throat bobbing as he does, his eyes never leaving mine, as if taunting me to say something.

I keep my mouth firmly closed, hoping it'll make him leave faster.

After a few beats, he glances over toward the stage, where I notice Noah and Dallas sitting at a table before he slides out of the booth and leans down to speak to me again.

"I'll be watching," he murmurs into my ear before standing and turning his back to me as he leaves. I blink after him as he walks away, confused as fuck about why he even bothered coming over here, mostly wishing he hadn't.

"What, and I say this with the utmost confusion," Kate half shrieks. "The fuck. Was that?"

Shrugging, I sigh as I glance at my glass. "Fucked if I know," I answer, probably more bewildered than she is.

"Guess I'll be ordering a new drink when our food arrives."

"How do you know Nico?" Vann asks and I shrug again.

"I don't," I tell him, and it's his turn to look confused, though he looks more curious than anything.

"Really?"

"Really," I confirm, wishing I had the ability to order something stronger than a Coke.

Our server appears with our food and puts another Coke down in front of me, taking my empty glass away. I glance over to Nico, who is watching just like he promised, and he raises a glass to me, tipping his head in a weird nod thing.

Am I supposed to say thank you?

Kate notices where I'm looking, tuts loudly, then turns back to face me. "The non-relationship you guys have is weird."

"Don't have to tell me," I agree, taking a sip of my drink, wincing when I taste the whiskey in the glass along with the Coke.

Part of me is wary of drinking it, but it's not like he made it or had a chance to do anything to it. Hell, I didn't even see him order it.

Plus, he has no reason to try to do anything to me.

Right?

Putting the drink down, I take a bite of my burger, the

cajun spices dancing over my tongue. Yup, this place just became another favorite. Silence descends over our table as we eat, and when the music funneling through the speakers stops, I look over to the stage, seeing the guy who came in before us. "Evening everyone, welcome to Alchemy's first open mic night. My name is Myles Alden, and this is, *Dare You to Move*."

He waves to someone on the floor, motioning for them to join him, but I can't pull my gaze from him. My throat thickens at the opening chords of Brody's favorite song from the guitar in his hands as the world starts to fade away.

He opens his mouth and starts to sing and tears prick my eyes. I'm held captive by the gravel in his voice as he starts the chorus.

A second guitar joins him, along with a second voice to finish the chorus, and I almost choke when I see Dallas sitting on a stool beside him. The second verse starts and Dallas starts to sing alone, his voice so smooth, each word like a cut on my soul.

"Are you okay?" Kate asks quietly, pulling my attention to her. "You're crying."

Swiping at my face, I nod. "I'm fine," I murmur as my focus is drawn back to the stage as the chorus starts again, and it's like Brody is sitting beside me. I can't even think of how many times he played this song to me.

The song draws to a close and I wipe at my face again

as the crowd cheers and claps for the two of them before Dallas steps off stage, leaving Myles alone, messing with his guitar.

"Hey, guys!" Allie says as she reaches the booth. "What did I miss?"

Her gaze bounces from my tear-stained face to Kate and Vann opposite me, but nobody says anything.

"Okay," she says, drawing out the *A*. "I'm going to go order food, and hopefully you guys will be less weird by the time I get back."

She turns on her heel and heads to the bar while Kate and Vann turn their attention back to me.

"I'm fine, just a song that brings up some stuff for me. It's nothing." Clearing my throat, I take a gulp of the spiked Coke from my glass and spot Nico and Dallas watching me from their table, sans Noah.

Blinking at them for a second, ignoring the concern on their faces and telling myself it's not about me, I pick up my burger and shove it in my mouth, hoping someone else will start talking so I don't have to.

But then the guitar starts again and Myles starts his second song as Allie rejoins us, and I'm thankful for the music so I don't have to speak.

Maybe I should leave so I don't bring down the night, but part of me wants to stay, be normal. Try to forget about Brody—which, in itself, feels sacrilegious— and just enjoy my life.

Because at least I still have one to live.

After having my heart ripped out by Myles and Dallas, several times over because oh man can those boys sing, I laughed at one of the girls who had turned a ton of online hate into a quirky song, then finally started to relax again.

"Ice cream?" I ask Allie quietly, since Kate and Vann seem to be having a moment across the table.

"Sure, let's give those two some breathing space."

We announce our departure, asking if they want anything, and head toward the bar, but the line is nuts. "Want to get some fresh air first?"

I nod at her suggestion, so she takes my hand and leads me through the crowd and out onto the sidewalk. The air is fresh and stings my cheeks as we step out in front of the restaurant, my ears ringing from the change in volume.

"Holy crap it's cold," Allie complains. "What is going on with the weather this year? I swear it's like someone opened Pandora's Box and pulled out the weird weather card."

"I'd agree, but my ears are ringing so bad I'm not sure I heard you right," I tell her, laughing.

She giggles in response, nodding as I try to make my ears pop.

"Fancy seeing you here, Little Spice."

"Dallas!" Allie exclaims, jumping into the arms of the

musical dreamboat. "You did so good!"

His smile as he puts her back on her feet is almost bashful. "Thanks, Allie. I was nervous as hell. Thought I was going to fall off the stage, my knees were shaking so bad."

"You couldn't tell! You were incredible. Wasn't he, Talia?"

He glances over at me, his smile as warm as it was that day he helped me up off the ground when I ran into Nico. My interaction with him since then has been minimal outside of the occasional hello in class.

He does at least seem nicer than his friends.

"You were great," I tell him, trying to swallow past the lump in my throat at the memory of him singing Brody's song.

"Well thanks, darlin'. Somehow, I didn't peg you for a melodic, guitar, ballad type."

I wink at him, trying to push off the emotions and go for playful. "I guess you don't know me that well."

"And whose fault is that?" he teases me right back, and it's like a zip straight to my vagina.

Down girl, we've had enough random fun lately.

"Where's Trey?" Allie asks him when she looks up from her phone.

I don't miss the momentary frown on Dallas's face at the question. "He and Issac had something going on already."

"Well, that dickhead needs to answer his phone before Mom blows an artery. She is all over my phone. Excuse me a second."

She walks away, furiously typing on her phone, leaving me with Dallas.

"So maybe you should tell me some more about yourself, pretty lady."

I burst out laughing as he wags his brows at me. "Okay, one, so much cheese in everything you just said *and* how you said it. I guess those pretty eyes and cheesy lines normally work for you, huh?"

His smile grows and he leans against the wall, chest puffing out. "You think I'm pretty?"

Laughing again, I shake my head. "Fairly certain I said you had pretty eyes. What's up, Mr. Superstar? That ego of yours need boosting some more after all that applause?"

"Nawh," he drawls, winking at me. "But you are real pretty, and I'm sure you could boost more than my ego."

"Gross, Dallas. Leave my friend alone," Allie chides him as she returns. "And keep your ego in your pants. What is it with you guys getting that junk out all the time? I just cleaned up Trey's mess. Please don't give me more work."

He puts his hands up in mock surrender, wide smile still on his face. "No more work coming from me, I keep my ego exactly where it's meant to be." He winks at me as he pauses, and I try to stifle the laugh that threatens. "I'll leave you two ladies to your night, but you know where to find me."

He tips his phantom hat before turning and heading back inside.

"Boys are so freaking weird," Allie sighs. "Thankfully, I got a hold of my brother, and saved you from his friend."

"You clear up their messes a lot?" I ask, more to make conversation than anything, but I can't say I'm not intrigued.

She shakes her head. "Nah, I just like to give them shit. Trey might be my brother, but they all act like I'm their adopted sister. I feel for Noah, cause she gets it way worse than me, but oh boy can they be smothering. Anyway, ice cream?"

"Yeah, I think Kate and Vann will be missing us by now."

We head inside and straight for the bar, which is still just as busy as before. Glancing over to our table while we wait, Kate and Vann are so close, I swear watching them is like edging porn.

So goddamn frustrating.

It takes another ten minutes before we're able to place our order and pay, and as I turn from the bar, a Coke in each hand for me and Kate, I pause to take in the scene before me.

"Why is Noah at our table?" Allie asks, looking confused.

I shrug my shoulders before tipping my head toward the table and weaving us through the crowd. "I have no idea, but we're about to find out."

FIFTEEN

Kate

“We’re going to get ice cream, do you guys want anything?” Talia shouts over the table at us. I don’t miss the coy smile on her face, or the matching one Allie has on.

I’m not stupid, I know what they’re up to.

But also, ice cream.

“You know it! Rocky Road please!”

“Share?” Vann asks and I nod. “For two,” he adds to Talia who nods before her and Allie head toward the bar.

Allie winks at me as they leave and I roll my eyes before turning my focus back to Vann.

“Sorry, what were you saying?”

He laughs, and I swear it lights up his whole face.

This night has been... surprising. Like, obviously, we're just friends, and we're hanging out in a group, but it's like we've existed in our own bubble. I don't want to get ahead of myself or get my hopes up, but maybe I'm not imagining it.

Maybe I'm not the only one with a bit of a crush.

But what if that ruins everything?

Then I hear Josie's voice in my head, quoting Nana, *Regret the things you did, not the things you didn't do.*

Shaking it off, I bring myself back to the present and try to relax. It's so loud in here, but I kind of like it.

Vann leans forward and talks into my ear so I can hear, but the smell of warmth and boy and outdoors comes from him and it's delicious. His lips brush against my ear and I fight off a shiver.

Quit it, Kate.

"I was asking if you wanted to hang out some more tomorrow."

Oh, right. Conversation. That's what was happening. Maybe I should read less romance novels, because the whole friends-to-lovers thing isn't what's happening here. It's just loud, so he has to be this close.

Totally that.

Leaning forward so he can hear me, placing my hands on his chest so I don't actually fall into his lap, because that's definitely something disaster Kate would do, I try to be super nonchalant when I respond. "Sure, I've got a paper I need to start for history, and another for government, but I can make time. Did you have anything in mind?"

The song finishes and my ears ring at the change in volume. I move to pull back from him, but his arm over my shoulder keeps me in place.

He nods, flashing me that traffic-stopping smile again. He tucks some of my hair behind my ear, his hand lingering as he holds my gaze, and for a second, I think he might kiss me as he leans in a little closer again. His heart is racing, I can feel it from where my hands are still on him, and I move a little closer.

He strokes his thumb over my cheek, and I swear I hold my breath as a hoard of butterflies take flight in my stomach.

I have to be imagining this right?

"Kate." My name on his lips is little more than a whisper and his eyes flutter closed.

Holy shit. Is this happening?

"Well, this looks cozy." I startle and look up to see who is interrupting us, and find Noah standing at the end of the booth.

What the hell?

Vann's cheeks heat as he lets out a sigh, and I move away a little, creating some space between us.

Freaking Noah Carrington.

"Noah. How can we help you?" Vann says as he pulls back from me, twisting his body to face her, blocking my sight of her. That hopeless romantic voice in my brain says he's trying to protect me from her, but I push that little shit into her box in my head, slam the lid closed, and lock it before paying attention to reality again.

"Oh, Evander, help little old me?" She flutters her lashes, but it's overplayed, like she's making fun of him.

I don't think so.

"Yes, Noah. Help little old you. What do you want?"

Shock flits through me at the harshness of my tone, and I immediately want to apologize for being rude, but she turns that smile to me, and it's cold as ice. "Oh goodie, you do speak. Because it's you I wanted to talk to. Well, you and your new friend."

"Talia? What do you want to talk to us both about?"

She sighs, lifting her hand as if examining her nails. Like I'm wasting *her* time. She came over here, and this feels a little put on.

Which makes no sense at all.

Glancing over to the bar, I spot Talia and Allie, they're not paying us any attention though. Dallas is with Myles, the guy he sang with earlier who looks weirdly familiar and I can't put my finger on why, and Nico... well, I can't see him anywhere.

"It'd be much easier to speak to you both," she sighs before glancing at Vann and frowning. "And I'd rather speak to you privately."

Vann stiffens beside me, and that pisses me off too.

"Noah, you took time out of what I'm sure is your very busy evening to seek us out. Anything you want to say to me, you can say in front of Vann."

She quirks a brow at me, smiling at me in a way that chills my blood. Like I've played right into her hands. "Oh, really?"

"Noah! You okay?" Allie's question as her and Talia rejoin us draws Noah's attention and I let out a small sigh of relief. I can play tough for a minute, especially when I'm mad, but dealing with Noah one-on-one? Not something I relish the thought of.

"Allie! I didn't know you were here tonight, you should've come and said hi," Noah exclaims, turning instantly into a somewhat normal human as she hugs my small friend.

"I was just hanging with my *friends.*" The emphasis on the end of her sentence isn't lost on me, neither is the momentary frown of Noah's. "Everything okay?"

Talia looks ready to go to war, but Allie's diplomacy seems to be winning out.

You okay? She mouths to me, and I nod, shrugging subtly.

"Yes, just being friendly," Noah says, glancing over at me before looking at Talia. "Hope everyone is having a good night. Wasn't Dallas great?"

Huh. So whatever she was going to say to me, she doesn't want Allie to hear?

Double weird.

Allie manages to steer the queen bee away from us, leading her over to where Dallas and Myles are, leaving Vann and I with Talia.

"What was that really about?" Talia asks.

"No idea," I tell her earnestly. "She said she had something she wanted to talk to us about, that she wanted to discuss privately, but then you guys swooped in and saved the day."

"I'm sure you guys would've handled it just fine," she responds, but her smile is forced. "I know I just ordered ice cream, but I think I'm going to head out. That cool with you guys?"

I frown, worried about my friend. Her tears earlier were... well, maybe the most emotion I've seen from her since I got here. "Yeah sure, are you okay? Do you want us to come back too? Give you a ride?"

"No, it's fine, enjoy your night. I'll see you tomorrow."

"Okay, see you tomorrow."

She leaves the table, heading back to where Allie stands with Noah and Dallas for a minute, before leaving entirely, Allie in tow.

I guess that's how she's getting back.

"You want to go check on her?" Vann asks, and I shake my head.

"No, she'd say if she wanted company." I think. "Plus, we have their ice cream to eat now too."

Moments later, the ice cream is brought to our table, and while I'm glad we're still here, the moment from before is gone and there's a new space between us. Like an awkwardness hanging in the air.

I push out a breath, hoping my disappointment expels with it, but no luck.

I guess Nana wasn't always right, because right now, I'm definitely regretting the thing I didn't do.

SIXTEEN

Talia

After a somewhat quiet weekend since Kate was with Vann for most of it after Friday evening, and an uneventful swim practice Saturday morning, I'm almost surprised at how quiet my week has been so far—Lexi has left me alone, barely acknowledging my existence during practice over the weekend, and while I'm glad, I'm also suspicious as hell about it—quiet, that is, if you ignore today's early morning delivery of purple flowers for Kate again.

Who sends flowers at five in the morning on a freaking Tuesday?

She swears she has no idea who is still sending her

flowers. At first, we assumed it was a bouquet from the staff after what happened with Charlie, but now? I half suspect Vann, but why wouldn't he say something?

I teased her about a secret admirer, but then she pointed out there's never been any note so they could just as soon be for me and I shut up.

Random flowers for her is cute. For me, it's creepy as hell because I hardly know anyone here. Let alone well enough for someone to send flowers. I'm excluding Evan because he knows my favorites are sunflowers, and he'd send those like he used to.

I think.

Leaving the library after getting ahead on homework at lunch, putting that little thought to the back of my brain, I slowly make my way to my afternoon class: music.

Not one I particularly enjoy. While I love music, I'm not exactly gifted, and after Dallas ripped my heart out with his performance at Alchemy on Friday night, I don't really want to see him again.

Obviously, he has no idea what effect his song with Myles had on me, or the fact that the original he played later that night tore my heart out and stomped on what was left of its shredded pieces, but I know.

And I'm discovering that my mask of indifference kind of sucks.

Before Arbour, I had Callie, before that I had Brody,

and well, I never really needed to hide anything because no one really paid attention to me.

But here? It's like an alternate universe. Not quite parallel, but it's definitely not what I'm used to. I miss my wallflower days.

Not that I'm not a wallflower here, I definitely am, but somehow, not to everyone, and I'm not sure that I like it. Attention hasn't ever really been my thing.

Thankfully, it hasn't impacted my whole, get good grades and get the hell out of here goal I set over the summer, and so far, I'm ahead and excelling, even with swim team taking so much of my time. Practice three times a week with daily gym sessions is a lot already, and I can't believe I considered trying out for cheer. I think my plate is quite full enough, thank you.

My inner musings, though bouncing around like my neurospicy brain likes to do, keep me company until I reach the music halls. Heading to the biggest room at the end of the hall, I enter and take my seat in the empty room, trying not to wince at how loud the zipper is on my bag when I undo it to get my music book.

Grabbing my phone and AirPods, I start scrolling through my socials, laughing silently at the dog with a dancing tail as I attempt to not be bothered by the weird alone time in here.

Thankfully, it's not long before the bell sounds and the

teacher, Ms. Ravan, enters along with a steady stream of students. Including Dallas.

Who just happens to take a seat in the open chair next to me.

Funsies.

I keep scrolling until the second bell sounds, then tuck my AirPods and phone away as Ms. Ravan takes a seat on the bench at the piano at the front of the room.

She smiles warmly at us as she softly runs her fingers over the ivory. "Today, we're going to do some vocal warm ups, then I'm going to group you off based on the skills I've seen so far and give you a fun little project, which absolutely will count toward your grade."

Oh, God. What torture.

Upside, I'm terrible, so the chances of me being partnered with Dallas are slim to none. There is no chance he would want his grade dragged by my inadequacies in this lesson, and I'm pretty sure Ms. Ravan wouldn't do that to the top student in her class. Glancing around the room, I see Emma and Vanessa, two of Lexi's besties, motion to each other like their pairing is set in stone, and gulp.

Please don't pair me with them either.

Sending up the silent plea, I turn my attention to the page Ms. Ravan called out and try to run the vocal scales with the rest of the class as quietly as I possibly can.

Screeching cat isn't a pleasant sound and I'm reminded

of why I fought Ms. Feldman so hard about making me take this class. I am so not meant to be here.

We run the scales until Ms. Ravan is satisfied, then she moves toward her desk, grabbing the folder she placed there as she walked in earlier and clears her throat.

"You'll be put in groups of two or three and head to your allocated practice room. There will be no adjustments made to the groups, my word is final." She looks pointedly over to Emma and Vanessa who pout back at her, and I press my lips together to stifle a laugh.

Though, if they're not together, I might be with one of them or, God help me, I could be grouped with both of them. God knows their musical talent isn't exactly stage worthy.

Someone please take pity on me.

"Your projects are in an envelope in your practice room. They are to be kept a secret until you present them to the class at the end of the semester. Do I make myself clear?"

A murmur of agreement sounds around the room, which I add to, wincing at the thought of performing.

Ms. Ravan calls out names and practice room numbers, and students filter out of the room until there are only four of us left.

"Emma and Vanessa, you'll be in room twelve," Ms. Ravan announces.

The two of them jump to their feet in excitement with a hissed, "yes!" Grabbing their things, they scoot from the room as fast as their heels will carry them, leaving me with Dallas and Ms. Ravan.

"I wasn't sure about this pairing," Ms. Ravan says softly. "But, Dallas, your talent is undeniable, and Talia, I have this sneaking suspicion that you're holding back. I've seen Dallas work his musical magic on many people, so this could either be a total disaster or a giant success. Regardless, in this case, your grades will be given with this experiment of mine in mind."

"Fine by me," Dallas drawls beside me, that southern accent of his thick as he smiles at Ms. Ravan. "Where are we heading?"

"You'll have this room," she advises, and my head drops, my chin touching my chest. "Your assignment is on my desk. I'll head down to my office now, so if you need anything, just ask."

"Sure thing," I grumble. She gives us a finger wave and almost floats from the room with one last curious glance back at us.

"I am so sorry," I say to Dallas. "This is going to be a disaster."

He laughs, the smoothness of it like brushing silk across my brain. "I doubt that." Without another word, he stands and saunters over to the desk, picking up the brown envelope with our names scrawled across the front. He opens it, pulls a sheet of paper from it, and laughs.

Curiosity gets the best of me and I get to my feet, moving over to him to read the paper from beside him.

'Original work. Use of at least two instruments. Both vocals are required.'

"Oh, come on!" I exclaim, running a hand down my face in exasperation. "This is going to go so terribly."

"You should have more faith in yourself, or at least in me. Ms. Ravan was right, I can work miracles. You'll see."

Here was me, thinking this day couldn't get worse. Having started with the earlier-than-normal wake up thanks to the flower delivery, followed by my six o'clock swim practice, then a delightful day including chemistry with my newest frenemy, Noah, and being paired with Dallas in music, I was hoping that I could have today's gym session to work out some frustration.

But no.

Apparently, the universe hates me.

Because not only are the swim team in here working

out, but so are some of the other teams, and of course not only Trey is in here, glaring at me as I pause in the doorway with my water bottle in hand, but so are both Evan and Dillon.

Lexi is fawning over Dillon and it's enough to make me want to vomit. That much PDA is... well, I mean, we're here to work out, not work *it* out. So gross.

I smile over at Evan when he waves at me, then move my ass to the last open treadmill while trying to ignore the heated glare I can still feel coming from Trey.

I really wish I knew what his problem with me is. Maybe I should ask?

And maybe he'd be honest... and maybe pigs will take flight too.

I gigglesnort to myself, then realize it might've been a little loud. Glancing around, I'm thankful no one seems to have noticed as I slip my AirPods in and hit shuffle on my *Fuck This (WorkOut)* playlist. *Dirty Little Secret* by All American Rejects starts playing and I grin as the song fills my ears.

There is something about classic rock that makes workouts more fun. Ruby helped me make the playlist at the start of summer, commenting about the fact the songs of her teenage years are my classic and vintage rock making her want to "shrivel up in ancient". The memory still makes me smile.

One of the very few good parts of my summer.

I start my warm up, shutting out the fact that I'm in a room full of people, cranking the speed and incline up.

Once I'm successfully warm and sweaty, I hit the stop button and make my way over to the free weights.

"No," Trey barks at me, stepping in front of the bench I was about to drop my towel on. "Why are you here?"

Rolling my eyes, I sigh at him. "I'm always here at this time. Swim team practice. You're the encroacher, now get out of my way."

"No."

He has got to be kidding. "Seriously? What is your problem with me?"

He folds his arms over his chest, looking down at me like he's trying to be menacing or intimidating, and maybe if I wasn't so annoyed I would be both menaced *and* intimidated, but I'm sick of his bullshit when I've done nothing to him.

Lexi might be a bigger bitch, but at least she has a delusional reason for her crazy bitchiness. Trey has no reason, unless he knows something I don't.

"You exist," he snarks.

"Is there a problem here?" I turn and find the football coach behind me. "Trey?"

"No, sir," he snaps, before turning and moving back over to the weight rack he was at before.

"Miss?"

"Hayes. But no, everything's fine. Thank you."

He doesn't look convinced, but nods anyway and heads back into the little office on the side of the gym. I guess that's where he was hiding before.

I grab a couple of dumbbells and start working on my lat raises once I hit play on my music again, and work through my upper body set until my arms, back, and shoulders are shaking and feel like Jell-O.

"Hey, T."

Oh, someone kill me dead.

"Hey, Dillon," I say, trying not to grimace. "Everything good?"

He lifts his towel and wipes at his face before taking a swig of his water. *Nothing like drawing out this awkwardness, Dillon.* "Yeah, I just wanted to say sorry. About the whole Lexi thing. She shouldn't have done what she did."

"No shit," I mutter. "But you're not the one who should be apologizing."

He shrugs. "I know, but you won't get one from her and I feel like it's my fault. So here I am, I guess. I just wanted to make sure there was nothing weird between us about it all."

"You're off the hook, Dillon. I didn't blame you, I still don't, but if it makes you feel better, which is what I'm assuming this little visit is for, then you're forgiven."

Nodding, he takes another drink, and I really wish he'd disappear. Between him and Trey, this workout session might be the worst one to date.

"Awesome. Great. I guess I'll see you around."

"Sure thing. Bye, Dillon."

He nods again before walking back over to where Evan is waiting for him by the main door. It's only then I realize that the rest of the swim team has already left. My stomach gurgles and I check my phone, noticing the time, and a message from Kate.

KATE

THERE'S TACOS. Let me know when you're done in the gym and I'll meet you in the cafeteria.

ME

Just wrapping up now. Will grab a shower then meet you there in 30?

KATE

Okay. See you soon.

Slipping my phone away, I finish my water and rerack my weights. Hopefully, the rest of this day goes better, because there's no way it could get worse.

"Are you okay?" Kate asks as she slides onto the chair opposite me as I take a bite of my taco.

I glance over at her, noticing the worry on her face. Frowning, I ask her, "Any reason I shouldn't be?"

Pushing off the exhaustion and frustration from today's gym session, I glance around the cafeteria and notice how many people are looking over here, whispering between themselves. Though this *is* Arbour, I could just be projecting and being super paranoid that they're looking at me. People look and whisper all the time here.

"You haven't checked your email in the last half hour, have you?" she asks quietly.

Grabbing my phone, I tap the email app while shaking my head. "No, I had gym after class and then came straight here. What happened?"

The words fall from my lips as my email pings, announcing that she doesn't need to answer.

From: Anon
To: All staff and students
Subject: Student accused of murdering brother in alcohol fueled car accident!

My heart stops and my mouth goes dry as I re-read the subject.

No,

I guess Dillon's apology was a little too early because this has to have been Lexi.

"That's not true," I whisper, my voice breaking as I speak. I fight the tears as they well in my eyes and open the email in full.

Inside, I find a news article, the headline to match the subject line, with pictures from Brody's accident. I haven't seen this article before, but there were so many. Maybe I didn't find this one to flog myself with when it happened. Maybe it's a fake. But as I read it, there are too many half truths for someone to have not researched me if they did create a fake.

"I need to go," I say, pushing my tray of food away before grabbing my bag and hightailing it from the room as fast as I can without anyone realizing that I'm running away.

Reading the details of the crash again, even the lies and half truths in that article, is like I'm back there again. Sitting in the ambulance as a paramedic tries to clean the scrapes on my head while I'm screaming at someone to save him.

The article said I was driving, that I was drinking beforehand... that isn't true.

But it is my fault he's dead.

That much they got right.

I don't even pay attention to where I'm going, but I

find myself in the music hall and take refuge in one of the empty rooms. I close the door and lean my head against it, thankful for the soundproofing as the sobs I fought win and wrack my body.

My arms clutch my stomach as I cling to myself, moving to lean against the wall. My knees fail as the devastation rips through me and I slide down it until I'm curled in a ball on the floor, crying, just like I did the day they told me he wasn't coming back.

I'll never forget the day the doctors walked into his hospital room and told us that he had no brain function. They asked about organ donation, but everything from there is a blur. All I remember is clinging to his warm hand, telling them he couldn't be dead. I'd know if he was really gone, but I could still feel him.

He wouldn't leave me.

He wouldn't let that be the last thing we said to each other.

It wasn't possible.

I begged them to check again, cried hysterically as my parents agreed to let him go, to donate his organs.

I don't think I've forgiven them for giving up on him so easily.

Twelve days, three hours, and twenty seven minutes.

That's how long it took them from the end of surgery to declare that he wasn't coming back.

I'd have given him a lifetime to find his way back to us.

For the first time in my life, I prayed daily, begging forgiveness for a lack of faith, begging for someone to give me my brother back.

So that I could fix what we said.

So that I wouldn't be alone.

But they gave up on him, and then he was gone.

I didn't think it was possible to break again, and yet, right now, I don't know how I'll ever put myself back together. Surviving it once was bad enough, but twice, here, with the whispers I know will come?

I'm not that strong.

"Talia?" I hear the voice but I don't look to see who it is. I couldn't see through my tears right now, even if my eyes weren't so puffy they'd barely open anyway.

The swish of the door closing sounds between my sobs and I'm suddenly being lifted.

"I got you," the male voice murmurs, tucking me against a warm chest, and I cling to him rather than myself. Maybe his lifeline is stronger than mine.

Nico murmurs to me, stroking my hair as I cry until the tears run dry. "What happened?"

I try to clear my throat to speak, horrified I let him see me like this, let alone that I snot cried all over him. Humiliation laces with my devastation and forces me from his embrace to my feet. He scrambles up after me as I use my sleeves to wipe at my face before putting my hair up in a ponytail in an attempt to put myself back together.

"Nothing happened," I say, my voice cold and dead. "This never happened either. We're not friends. You weren't here."

He frowns, his brow furrowing as his dark eyes flicker with bewilderment before they turn stony with anger. "Talia—"

"No, Nico. This was probably you anyway," I retort, my words laced with venom, reason not exactly factoring into my thoughts right now. "This didn't happen. Stay the hell away from me."

Shame fuels my words as I grab my bag and storm from the room, leaving him shouting my name as I head down the hall toward my dorm.

"We're not done here, Talia."

I flip him the finger behind me, not bothering to look back.

The fuck we're not.

I am so done.

With him. With Arbour. With all of this.

SEVENTEEN

Talia

After a way too dramatic start to the week and a meeting with Ms. Feldman about my 'state of mind' and me wanting to transfer out yesterday morning, I was told in no uncertain terms by my dad last night that it would be a cold day in Hell before I changed schools. Which was thoroughly backed by Ms. Feldman again this morning, even with the stupid email that went out to everyone. Along with the pictures that have popped up online, plus the ones plastered through the halls and pushed under our dorm room door and through the grates in my locker…

I'm over this week already.

The people in control of my life are the only reason I'm

still here, backpack slung over my shoulder, more books clutched in my arms as I begrudgingly head to the library for a study session with Kate, Vann, and the rest of their crew, before swim practice in an hour.

I find them in the back of the study area, having pushed tables together so they're all sitting together. Except, when I approach the table, four of the girls, whose names I don't remember, pack up their stuff and leave, glaring at me.

Trying not to think it's about me, I slide into the empty seat beside Kate. "Hey," I say quietly, because well, this is still the library and it's busy as hell tonight.

"Hey," Kate whispers back. "How was your day?"

I shrug as I slide my bag off my arm and pull my books onto the table. There's so much I could say, but rather than explaining it all, I go with, "I'm still here."

Three more people get up and leave the table and Kate frowns.

"What's going on?" she asks Rosie, who looks at me, then to Vann, then back to Kate and shrugs.

Letting out a sigh, I start putting my books back in my bag. "It's fine."

"What? Stop." Kate insists, turning back to Rosie. "What is going on, Rosie?"

"They don't want to associate with her," Rosie replies, pointing at me. "We've all been victims of Lexi's torture throughout the years, we did our time. It's her time to shine right now, and no one wants to get caught in her limelight."

Ouch.

Like, I get it, but ouch.

Clearing my throat, I finish packing up my bag. "It's fine," I tell Kate. "I'm going to study in our room."

"Talia—"

"Don't stress it, I've got to get ready for practice anyway," I mutter as I get back to my feet and leave the library, books back in my arms, head held high.

This is exactly why I wanted to transfer. People don't care about the real story, they believe what's easiest. Outside of Kate and Vann, no one has even mentioned the article to me, but plenty of people have avoided me, even in the halls, like I'm a carrier of the bubonic plague.

Which is exactly what happens as I make my way back to my room. People move out of the way, whispering as I pass by them. Thankfully, I haven't run into Nico since the incident on Monday, because I get the feeling he wouldn't avoid me.

I haven't even told Kate about that yet. Oops.

Once I'm back in my room, I drop onto my bed face first and scream into my pillow, a niggle of rage pushing through the numbness I've been encased in since I woke up yesterday morning. Closing my eyes, I play through that night again, hearing Brody's voice, hearing him shouting. Us arguing.

Then I see him next to me. In the car.

Then there's bright lights and I'm screaming his name.

"Talia!" I suck in a breath as I jolt upright, regaining my bearings, and realize I'm not in the car.

I'm in my room, with Kate shouting at me.

"Shit, I fell asleep." I scramble for my phone, which has messages from Coach.

Fuck, I missed practice.

"I know, you were shouting, but you need to wake up. Something's happening."

Rubbing my eyes in an attempt to wake up, I take the bottle of water she holds out to me. "What's going on?"

"I don't know. The police are here with K9 units. Flashlights all over the back field. It's chaos."

Jumping from the bed, I move to stand beside her at the window, pulling the curtain farther back so I can see what she is talking about.

"Shit!" Kate squeals when there's a bang on the door. I rush to it, unlock it, and find Ms. Feldman standing on the other side, dressed in sweats, hair in a messy ponytail.

Apparently, I'm not the only one who was woken up.

"Good, Talia. You're here. Is Kate here?" she asks, glancing into the room.

"I'm here," Kate confirms, coming to stand beside me. "What's going on?"

Ms. Feldman pauses before letting out a sigh, as if

she doesn't want to say, but this can't be her first time explaining, considering where our room is situated.

"There were reports of screaming and sounds of a fight. Upon checking the student rooms, we found evidence of a struggle. There was also blood."

I glance at Kate who is watching Ms. Feldman with her mouth agape.

"The police have been brought in to investigate further."

"Investigate a fight?" I ask, because that seems a little extreme given what's going on.

"No," she responds, shaking her head. "The police are here because one student was found in the front courtyard, bound and bleeding. He is on his way to the hospital, and the other... well, that student is missing."

With the student—now identified as Laurence Bailor, a senior I don't *think* I've ever met, at least I don't remember if I have—still missing, Arbour has been in major lockdown for a week. No leaving school grounds over the weekend, no practice, no gym sessions, no sports of any kind for anyone, which is honestly kind of a welcome reprieve, even under the circumstances, but it makes the email on my screen seem so... out of place.

From: Ms. N. Feldman
To: All Staff and Students
Subject: Lockdown

Good afternoon all,
With the investigation underway, the authorities have advised we are able to lift the lockdown placed on students from this week, and free movement is reinstated. We do ask you all to stay vigilant and report anything that seems out of the ordinary. Laurence has not yet been located, so please remain cautious when traveling.

If you have any questions, or need to talk, please come and see me.

Yep. Weird.

"Did you get this?" I ask Kate, who's been pouting all morning about missing the concert tonight that she asked me to go with her to last week.

Her eyes brighten as she scans the laptop screen then grabs her phone and checks her email. "I did!"

"You don't think we're being pranked?" I ask, cautiously. It all seems a little too... neat.

She shrugs and taps on her phone before putting it to her ear. "It's a little suspicious, sure, but I'm over being cooped up and there is one way to find o—Oh hi, Ms. Feldman. I just saw the email and I wanted to confirm it wasn't a scam email or something equally ridiculous." She pauses, giving verbal cues as required, nodding despite the fact that it's a call, then gives me a thumbs up with a wide smile. "No, I totally understand, we will be careful. Thank you so much for confirming."

She squeals as she ends the call. "We are freeeeeee! Like, I hope they find Laurence, and that Stuart is okay, but being caged up made me realize I might not be quite as introverted as I thought. Plus, now I can do my own investigation and find out what the hell is really going on. But like, starting tomorrow, because tonight we have plans!"

Jumping to her feet, she does a little shimmy dance thing, making me laugh.

Personally, I'm a little more hesitant to run out into the wild, but considering we've been confined to our rooms outside of classes, with meals being brought to us by staff, it has been a little suffocating.

I wince at the choice of words, considering the student who was found in the courtyard had physical signs of asphyxiation from being hung. He still hasn't woken up, and while nobody has released his name officially, everyone has worked out it's Laurence's roommate, Stuart Hinkley.

Personally, I'm selfishly glad for some drama that isn't mine, that's taking the focus away from me, but I feel guilty as hell for that thought, and for the fact that people had to get hurt for the gossip cycle to change.

Oh, the joys of boarding school.

"So what is the plan, oh fearless leader?" I ask as she bounces around the room, continuing her dance.

She pauses as she turns to face me, all seriousness back. "Now I call Vann and Allie and we start getting ready. After what happened last week with the others, well, they can suck it. We have"—she checks the time on her phone—"T-minus three hours before we need to leave! Let's get hustling!"

After spending the entire time that Kate allocated to getting ready, mostly just laughing at her meltdown over what to wear, using all of half an hour to straighten my hair, I slide on a pair of jeans, a crop tank with a mesh long sleeve over the top, put on a choker and a few random rings Kate practically launched at me.

"You ready?" she asks, practically vibrating with excitement.

I grab my leather jacket, slide on a pair of Cons, make sure I have my phone, keys, and wallet, then nod. "Yep, I'm ready."

"Awesome, Vann said he'll drive."

"Fine by me, as long as we still get to have control of the playlist."

"Of course," she says, grinning. "Let's do this!"

I follow her out of the dorms down to the parking lot where Vann is waiting for us by his car. "Hey!" I call out, waving as I shuffle to the back door, watching on as they hug hello.

Well, that was awkward as hell, what is going on with them? I thought my matchmaker work was done after seeing them at Alchemy, but I guess I need to speak to Kate. Because whatever that is, it is not chill, happy, more-than-friends vibes.

Vann unlocks the car and I climb in, shooting Kate a look as I do. She shakes her head, so I put my questions away, but we are so not done here.

"Remind me who is playing tonight?" I say once I'm buckled in.

Kate grins at me. "You'll have never heard of them, they're a small indie band, but I've followed them since they were just posting covers on their social channels. But you'll love them, I swear!"

"Sounds good!"

Kate hooks her phone up to the car and starts playing *Ready For It* by Taylor Swift. Vann groans, which makes me laugh, because how did he not know that Kate is a straight up swiftie girl?

We sing and dance the entire ride to the gig, and once Vann has the car parked, we head inside. "Please, no more Swift on the way home?"

"I'm making no promises," Kate teases as we walk toward the guy at the door. She flashes her phone at him so he can scan the tickets and let us in. It's a super small venue, like almost a hole in the wall, but the energy inside is great.

"Drink?" Vann shouts, trying to be heard over the volume in here.

"Water, please!"

Kate asks for the same, then tells him we're going to find a spot near the stage. The band is already up there, setting up their gear as we elbow through the crowd.

We reach the front, so we're practically leaning on the stage, and Kate looks back at me and grins. "Thank you for coming tonight!"

"As if I'd miss live music!" I grin at her as she bounces on the spot. "Want to tell me what's happening with you and Vann yet?"

She shrugs and her smile drops a bit.

Don't like that at all.

"I think he was going to kiss me at Alchemy, but then Noah appeared, and it's been a little weird since. Tonight is the first time I've seen him properly since the lockdown, so

I'm hoping it'll ease off and go back to normal."

Fucking Noah Carrington.

"Okay, so no wingwoman moments?"

"Please, God, no. I think it's easier if we're just friends, ya know?"

Nodding, I give her a one arm hug. "I get it. I will keep my nose out of it!"

The band starts moving and the background music cuts out.

"Wait, is that?" I shout to Kate, pointing at the guy front and center of the stage.

"I KNEW I RECOGNIZED HIM!" she squeals.

"Ladies and gents, it's great to see you all out tonight! We're so grateful for the support. I am Myles Alden, we are Alive For Tonight, and this is *Living for You.*"

He starts playing his guitar, the band joining him, and Vann finds us just as Myles starts to sing. "I found someone," Vann shouts, and I turn to find Dallas standing beside him.

Of course he is.

"Evening," he hollers, though I barely hear it over the song. So I join Kate in waving at him quickly before turning my attention back to Myles and the band.

So much for a fun night with Kate, now I have Dallas here too…

Though, I guess he's here for Myles, so really, what's

the worst that could happen?

Trudging downstairs at three in the morning wasn't how I saw this night ending, but once again, my nightmares haunt me and I can't sleep. Which is why me, my fluffy socks, and my robe are stumbling through the dark. After Kate researched how to help me sleep following the leaked article, I've kept the sleepy girl mix she found with her hidden stash for times of dire need. I've never been one to self medicate, and I don't intend on starting now. I'd hoped I would pass out after such a busy night, but no. Sleep is an elusive bitch, apparently. Though, that could be overthinking all the singing and dancing with Dallas.

He was actually really fun tonight, but I have a feeling that when I see him in class, we'll be back to normal. Tonight was a glitch in the matrix, a blip of time in a different timeline.

At least, that's what I'm telling myself, because there's no way his hands felt that good on my hips as he stood behind me while we danced.

A shiver runs down my spine as I enter the kitchenette, cold despite my socks and robe. Maybe I should start sleeping in more than boxers and a tank, but I get so hot when I sleep that I can't bring myself to do it.

Shaking it off, I grab the tart cherry juice, a can of raspberry lemonade, and the magnesium powder. Mixing them in a glass with ice from the freezer, I jump up onto the counter and scroll through social media while I sip the sour concoction, hoping to whatever god that might be listening that it works.

The sound of footsteps makes me pause. Who the hell else is down here?

Then I hear the voice.

Why am I cursed?

I haven't seen Nico outside of class—where I managed to get in just at the second bell then hauled ass to be first out the door—since the whole crying thing, and a part of me was really hoping to keep my streak up.

"Talia, I'm beginning to think you're stalking me down here. Waiting for me?" Nico stands in the doorway, leaning on the frame, dark eyes watching me closely. His jab riles me, even though I know I shouldn't react. I've dealt with enough of the Arbour bullshit by now to know reacting isn't going to work... but then, neither has not reacting so it's kind of a lose, lose thing.

Though I wonder if he knows I spent the evening with his friend. The jab is on the tip of my tongue but I decide against it.

"I was here first. Maybe you're stalking me," I retort

instead as I slide off the counter, finishing the dregs of my drink. "This isn't the first time you've found me. Did you ever consider that I *don't* want you?"

Part of me wants to kick myself for hinting at Monday, but I try not to let it show. A smile tugs at the corner of his mouth as his eyes raze over me. The predatory stare makes me want to pull my robe closed where it's fallen open, but that feels like letting him win. Instead, I fold my arms over my chest and jut out my chin.

"It looks like you want me. Kind of hard to hide," he purrs as he stares at my chest. So what if my nipples are hard? It's freaking cold, dammit.

"You really are full of yourself, aren't you?" I question as I step toward him. Maybe playing his game will make him back off. Then I can run away. Again.

Placing a hand on his bare chest, I smile as goosebumps appear on his skin before dragging my nails down his smooth flesh to the waistband of his shorts. "I guess having everyone throw themselves at you has helped your ego grow just a little too large. Not used to someone like me walking away from you."

I finish the taunting whisper, my eyes darting down to where his dick is very obviously hardening before leaning in closer. "But maybe that ego is just a little too out of control for me."

Quick as a snake, his hand is on my throat as he pushes

me back into the room and up against a wall, pressing into me. "Oh, I get the feeling you'd enjoy getting a little out of control, new girl. Can't run so easy now, can you?"

"That's not my name," I hiss at him, pushing against his hold, despite the fact it restricts my air. "And maybe I would enjoy it, but with you? Unlikely."

For a minute, I think he's going to let me go. That he's going to let me run again.

His lips twitch, almost like he's toying with a smile, but then his lips are on mine, his chest pressed against me. My hands are in his hair, pulling him toward me like I've lost my mind. Like I'd rather his kiss than oxygen. His touch is hypnotic, enthralling, like a poison that I didn't know I wanted. His hand presses on my throat, the other gripping my hip as his cock presses against me, pulling a sound from me that I'm not sure I've ever made before.

"Tell me to stop," he says when he pulls back, resting his forehead on mine. "Say it."

"No," I respond, watching the torture of want mixed with something I don't recognize play out on his face.

He pulls back just enough so his body isn't on mine, though his hands are still pressing on me. "This is your last chance, Talia. Tell me to stop. I won't let you run after this, not without a chase."

Part of me feels like he's begging me to give him the out, but no part of me wants this to stop. A shudder runs down my spine, like my body is betraying me, but maybe it's my mind betraying my body. Because this? It's exhilarating. It's forbidden. And, well…

"No. Just this once, then never again."

The words fall from my lips, a promise of yet another thing between us to never be spoken of again, and his hold on my hip tightens for a moment, like the last test of his resolve. "Don't say I didn't warn you. Once won't ever be enough, but you had your chance to run."

His words finish with his lips back on mine and fire shoots through my veins as fingers tighten around my neck. This definitely shouldn't be happening. I can't stand him, and he very obviously hates me, yet I can't make myself stop. It feels too good.

Forbidden fruit always does.

Only once he releases me does his tongue plunge inside my mouth and take complete and utter control. It's as if dominating this kiss will dominate me.

Well, fuck that. No one controls me except me.

My hands let go of his hair and with my palms against his hard, naked chest, I push him back once, twice, the third time he's forced to catch himself on the kitchen counter.

In the dark, his black eyes narrow like he wants to bend me over and slap my ass for daring to challenge him.

Jutting out my chin, I match his stare. "We're doing this my way."

"Oh no, Talia, that's not how this works. You had your chance to talk on Monday. I gave you a chance to run from me again a moment ago. You didn't take it. We're doing this my way." In a flash, I'm slung over his shoulder with my head so close to his ass that I don't even hesitate. Pulling his boxers down, I bite his ass cheek hard enough to make him curse. His response is instant as he exposes my ass and smacks it like I'm an unruly kid who needs putting in line.

I'm not proud to say I squeaked but also, my pussy got real wet, real fast.

"I hate you!" My words are laced with venom, but he laughs like he knows they're a lie. My frustrated cry at him completely loses its impact when I rub my thighs together looking for more friction.

"It doesn't matter what you say out loud, I already know that you and your cunt want this, want me, and that's good enough for now. You can hate me all you like, you'll still be screaming my name soon enough."

Part of me wants to argue with him, but before I get the chance to open my mouth again, he reaches the kitchen table and lays me out like a fucking buffet. Before I can throw out more insults to his face, rather than his ass, he's got my robe open and my underwear around one ankle.

"See? Your pussy is so fucking wet for me, it exposes your words for the lies we both know they are." I growl at him in frustration, but it quickly turns into a moan as he hooks my knees around his forearms as he sinks to his own, and starts attacking my pussy with his talented tongue. If I thought he was a great kisser before, boy did I know fucking *nothing*.

I've been eaten before, but that's like comparing a pee-wee game to the Super Bowl, and this... this is my own personal Super Bowl. This is fucking out of this world. Not that I'd ever tell *him* that. He doesn't need his ego boosted any more than it already is.

Reaching up and over my head, I curl my fingers around the edge of the table to stop myself from reaching out for him. Touching him would only make me want him more and this can *not* mean anything. It won't. I refuse to allow it.

This is nothing more than want.

Frustration.

Pent up anger.

And working it all out in the best fucking way.

But when his tongue thrusts inside my pussy, my body reacts viscerally, despite how I feel about him. My treacherous body only wants pleasure and this motherfucker is giving it to me in spades.

It's like punishment through positive reinforcement.

Fuck, I really wish I could say he's lousy at this but clearly, he's got my body writhing and shaking, searching for anything and everything he's willing to give me.

"Oh, God," I groan, biting on my lower lip to try and stop from crying out as I grind my hips on his face, feeling his smile against my sensitive skin. I feel my orgasm cresting, building up, like a tightening of my spine as I rise up from the table, and just as I'm about to come all over his face, he stops.

That bastard fucking stops.

And I lose my ever-loving shit.

"What the fuck, Nico?" I sound possessed, like a tiny demon is trying to crawl out of my chest and throat punch him.

"Only good girls who beg get to come. Are you a good girl, Talia?"

My mouth drops open and my eyes go wide. His wicked, dirty words are enough to steal my breath, and somehow add to my frustration.

"Are you fucking serious?" I hiss.

What an asshole.

But also, I want his mouth back on my pussy.

"I'm always serious when it comes to orgasms." The bastard licks his lips like he's a fucking porn star as I glare at him while he holds me firmly so I'm still laid out wide before him.

I want to slap him then push his head to my pussy so he can finish what he started.

"Fuck it, I'll just finish myself off. I don't need you for this."

Without another thought, I bring my fingers to my clit and start rubbing, another hand on my breast, teasing my nipple, the perfect mix to help finish me off.

Except it's all wrong.

I'm so fucking pissed off, or frustrated, that I'm rubbing too fast, too hard, and without concentrating on what feels good.

That has to be it.

I refuse to believe that it's because it's not him.

When I look back up at him, that fucking smirk on his face only makes me want to try harder. But, somehow, that almost makes it less fun.

"You're such a fucking asshole." The exasperation is so obvious in my breathy tone, but I don't drop his gaze while I try to picture him licking me again. Except, it's like when you've got a word on the tip of your tongue but it just won't pop back into your head. That's what's happening with this fucking orgasm. It. Just. Won't. Come.

Banging my head back against the table, I groan out a few choice words that only make his smug face grow more satisfied.

"So, Talia... are you a good girl?"

Motherfucker.

Fine. It's all in the name of getting myself off.

"I hate you but yes, please, Nico. I'm a good girl. Now, please make me fucking come." *Or else I will cut off your dick while you're asleep.* I don't actually say the words but the way he's shaking his head at me, pressing his lips together like he's trying not to laugh, it's like he heard my silent threat.

"It'll do, but next time, I want you to be more convincing."

"There won't be a next time." I retort, but he doesn't say a thing as his hand slaps mine away right before he plunges two fingers inside my pussy and toys with my clit like I'm his favorite game.

I cry out silently as I arch off the table again, and this time he doesn't stop.

He takes me all the way to the crest, curls his fingers just so, and sends me crashing onto the other side of Nirvana.

With every silent cry from my mouth and twitch of my body, he drinks what he pulls from me like a man desperate for water after a drought.

I fuck myself with his fingers without an ounce of shame as I ride the wave, and when I come down, I open my eyes to find him staring at me with pupils so dilated it's almost as if his eyes are entirely black.

We both freeze for half a second before he grabs me by the throat again and kisses me like I'm the ice to his burning skin. I'm so consumed by the ferocity of his mouth, by the taste of me on him as his lips slide against and nip at my skin, that I don't realize he's pushed his boxers down. His hand has his dick poised at my entrance until he pulls away and grins once more.

"Are you going to be a good girl for me again, Talia?" As if I weigh nothing, he grabs me by my hips and flips me around on the table, my knees wide and my robe discarded long ago along with my tank. He pushes my very round ass up until I'm completely exposed to him, waiting for his cock.

The wait feels like it lasts forever.

To the point that I'm close to begging.

One second I'm about to ask him what the fuck he thinks he's doing, and the next I'm gasping at the sheer fullness of his cock slamming into my pussy.

I lose my fucking breath when he bottoms out, my pussy stretching as far as it's ever had to.

He stops, grinding against my ass as he presses his bare chest to my back, his mouth at my ear and one hand finding its way back to my throat.

"Beg me, Talia. Be a good girl. Beg me to ruin you with my cock." I'm about to shake my head, my brain wanting to refuse him once again, not wanting to give into him despite my current position, but my traitorous body reacts to his filthy words by pushing against him, silently begging him to fuck me senseless.

Fuck it.

If given the choice between my dignity and a really good orgasm, apparently I'm *that* girl. The one who chases pleasure, all consequences be damned. At least right now. These last few weeks have me wound up so tight that I don't think I'll even care later that I caved to him so easily.

"Please, Nico," I beg, my words strained by his grip on me. "Ruin me with your big, fat cock."

Okay, so he never said I had to be sincere about it.

"One day, you're gonna pay for that smart ass mouth of yours... maybe even with your ass."

I don't have the chance to retort and tell him that my smart mouth pays for itself when he pulls out quickly and slams the breath right out of me once again with his cock.

I don't have time to breathe in some much needed oxygen before he does it again, his fingers squeezing my throat to the bite of delicious pain.

Our bodies are flush against each other as he holds me to him by the throat, his mouth whispering delicious threats in my ear as he destroys me.

Threats of things he's going to do to me.

Of all the ways he's going to ruin me.

Of how many times he's going to make me come before he's done with me. I soak up every fucking word, my pussy getting wetter and greedier and aching for more.

Always fucking more.

"God, yes, please! Fuck me harder, Nico. Fuck. Me. Harder." The words fall from my mouth like a betrayal of myself, but he rewards me with a bite to my earlobe, and who the fuck knew that could feel so fucking good?

My body acts without thought, the pure, carnal need so fucking primal and instinctual that my mind completely shuts off as I let go, handing myself over to Nico to fuck me with his oh-so-beautiful yet cruel intentions.

"Fuck, Talia. Scream for me, like a good girl. Say my fucking name."

"Don't stop! Yes! Yes! Yes! God yes, Nico!"

My words are like the answer to his prayer and with one more thrust, I'm gone.

My orgasm washes over me like a tidal wave taking everything in its path and soaking me with pure, unleashed bliss.

I'm panting, my chest heaving and my throat sore from his hold, when Nico stills behind me, his fingers impossibly tighter around my neck and his dick so goddamn deep I can feel him in my chest.

"Fuuuuuuuck." It's just one word, drawn out and low, but it's the sexiest sound I've ever fucking heard because I know when he starts going harder, like I've unleashed some beast inside of him. I know for a fact that I just made this asshole come too.

He slows to a stop, sending ripples of pleasure through

me before he releases my throat and toys with my earlobe as he kisses down my spine.

"It'll never be just once. Don't say I didn't warn you." With that, he pulls out of me, grabs his things, and walks away, leaving me naked, spent, and dripping.

Typical asshole.

I clean myself up, grab my clothes, and wrap my robe around me, a smirk on my face. Yes, he fucked me, and it was amazing, but regardless of what he says, it was a one-time thing.

And who knows?

Maybe I'm the one who's ruined him, after all.

EIGHTEEN

Talia

"You did what?" Kate looks at me, a mix of horror and fascination staring at me. "I thought you couldn't stand Nico?"

"I can't, and he doesn't like me either," I tell her, shrugging into my uniform blazer. "I only told you because you're my friend, but after this, it will never be spoken of again."

"But—"

"No," I state, interrupting her as I turn to face her head on, pointing to emphasize my point. "Never. Again."

"Spoil sport," she pouts and drops back onto her bed. "But fine. Way to end the night with a bang." She winks at me and I can't help but laugh. "Yeah, that's right, I'm awesome *and* punny."

"You're definitely something," I tell her. "Did you and Vann have fun yesterday?"

"Swift change up. Don't think I didn't notice it," she teases. "But yeah, he's helping me with my philosophy project. Got to love extra credit."

"Extra credit?" I balk. "It's so early in the semester!"

"Yeah, but I like to get ahead. I want to go to a top school for journalism, get on the right track for what I'm hoping is a Pulitzer-worthy career."

I smile at her as I check and make sure I have everything I need for this dreary Monday. I think my history book is still in my locker, and I have that first thing with Mr. Lancaster. Need to grab that after I get coffee. "Dream big. Got to chase that good life."

"That we do," she says, before shifting awkwardly. "So, erm, I know we've still not really discussed the whole article thing outside of you not leaving Arbour, but Allie and I looked into it. It was a fake article pieced together from a dozen sources, but your reaction... I won't push, but when you're ready to talk about it, I'm here."

Nodding, I try to swallow despite the lump in my throat. "Thanks," I croak.

Part of me wants to tell her the truth about it, but talking about Brody? Not something I'm so great at anymore. Not outside of my journal, but I'm not sure that counts.

"That's what friends are for," she says softly. "Now let's go grab some breakfast. They say it's the most important meal of the day, you know?"

"Uh-huh. As long as I grab coffee, I'll be powered up plenty."

Kate gigglesnorts as she grabs her bag. "Yeah, whoever put history first thing on a Monday for you is an evil mastermind."

"Tell me about it," I say, sighing. "Could be worse, I suppose."

"It could," she says, frowning. "I have a free period, then history, and then calculus. Way worse except for the free period. Maybe that was their goal for seniors? Make Mondays *really* suck so we appreciate the rest of the week. I have gym on Mondays too, though you go to gym at the end of every day except Thursdays, so I might not have that quite as bad as you. However, I am still thoroughly convinced of my new theory. Evil runs this school."

"Why are you even up if you have a free period?"

"Library, duh," she teases as she grabs the last of her things.

Laughing at her, I make sure I have my phone, wallet, and keys. "Ready?"

"Let's do this," she says before practically bouncing from the room. Oh, to have that much energy and pep naturally. I used to, I think. At least, compared to Brody I did, but I'm beginning to think I've either absorbed his personality and become less peppy, or Kate really is just *that* optimistic and happy.

Kate chatters away about her day with Vann yesterday and I think that my matchmaking thing might not be needed anymore. She hasn't said anything happened, but they're hanging out a *lot*. She disappears to grab food and I detour to get coffee from the cart like usual, only to find Nico and Isaac at the back of the line as I get there.

Keeping my head down, focusing on absolutely nothing on my phone like it's the most important thing in my life, I step behind them to wait for my coffee.

"Talia," Isaac says, emphasizing the 'a' at the end. "Fancy seeing you here this morning."

Glancing up, I give him a smile. "Yup, imagine that. Me, a student, getting coffee on a Monday morning."

"Oh, your sass really does something to me," he says, a wicked glint in his eyes as he leans into me. "Maybe I could show you."

"Unlikely," I retort, trying to keep my answers short and hoping something else steals his attention.

"Maybe Talia is too good for the likes of us," Nico says, a knowing smile on his face.

Isaac clasps his chest. "Say it ain't so!"

Rolling my eyes, I sigh, pocketing my phone in

surrender to them having my attention. "That must be it."

"Well, I've always been one to rise to a challenge," Isaac says, grinning, grabbing his dick. "We do like to rise."

"I'm sure you do."

He rubs his hands together while Nico chuckles as the line moves forward. "That's it, make it harder."

The double entendre isn't lost on me, but it's way too early for this. Part of me wonders if Isaac knows about Saturday night and this is some weird test from Nico to see if I'm going to talk about it. Little does he know that when I said only once, I meant it. That includes keeping it to myself—well, excluding Kate, but that's just girl code.

"I'm not sure it's all that difficult to entice you, Isaac. Like a dog with a bone. Easily pleased."

Nico laughs, just once, but Isaac grins wider. "Oh yeah, definitely a dog with a bone. Breaking you is going to be oh so sweet."

"Good luck with that," I retort as they reach the front of the line.

"Double espresso and a red eye," Nico says to the guy at the cart. "Plus a vanilla latte with an extra shot of espresso."

I blink at him in surprise.

He knows my coffee order? Yeah, that's not giving stalker vibes at all.

"You don't have to—"

"Just accept the coffee, Talia." Nico interrupts, so I clamp my jaw shut and nod.

So, so weird.

Is this like a truce? Not that they were awful to me before, but well, kinda.

The guy makes the order, handing me my coffee once Nico pays.

"Thanks," I say, though it comes out as more of a question. A flash of red draws my attention and I realize Kate is standing by the wall, watching the exchange with rapt fascination. "See you around."

I head over to my friend, who looks at me pointedly, lips pressed together and brows raised, so I just shake my head. "That looked cozy."

"It was weird, like I stepped into the twilight zone or something," I reply. "But I have coffee, so I'm happy."

"Uh-huh. One time, my hiney. He's still watching you, by the way. They both are." She pauses and I fight the urge to look back. "Oh, I grabbed you a bagel," she says, handing me the paper bag. "To class?"

"Thanks, and sure," I agree, feeling their eyes on my back as we walk away. Part of me wonders if Isaac's fascination with me is because I stood up to him for Kate in the library, or if it's because I'm a shiny new toy, or if it's because of Nico.

Whatever it is, I don't want it.

Any of it.

"Any updates on the missing kid?" I ask Kate, knowing that she's been looking into it all herself, claiming journalistic curiosity.

"Some," she says quietly. "I found out Stuart is still in a coma, medically induced. They're not sure if he'll survive. Evidence is minimal, so if he dies and no one finds Laurence, the police basically have nothing."

Shock flits through me. How is that even possible? "Seriously?"

"Yup," she says, smacking her lips together. "Weird, right?"

"Definitely."

"I'm going to keep nosing around because there's no way that no one saw anything, right? And the weird Medusa mask they found just seems off."

"Wait, what?" I ask, pausing as we reach my locker.

"Right, I didn't tell you that bit yet. Yeah, they found some weird red cloak under Laurence's bed, along with a snake, Medusa mask thing, same blood-red color. The snakes resemble the school sigil thing, which is also weird. No one seems to know why a jock would have that, or if they do, no one's talking. I tried to speak to the baseball water guy, but he's about as in with that group as I am. It could be something, but it could also be nothing at all other than some fetish thing."

I chew on my bottom lip, mulling over the option in my head that seems like a really bad idea. "I could speak to Evan. Or Dillon…"

Her eyes go wide and she shakes her head. "Dillon? Do you *want* Lexi to keep gunning for you? She seems distracted since the whole police thing. Her and Dillon made up."

"Oh," I respond as I grab my history book. Something like hurt sparks inside me but it's faint enough that I dismiss it. "I didn't know that. Social pariah, remember?"

"Oh, hardly," she says with a snort. "And even if it was true, if Lexi has a new place for her attention, then that wouldn't last much longer anyway. Don't get me wrong, she's still a bitch when she's with him, but if she was coming after you because of him, well, she'll likely think having him back is a big enough win to snub you."

"I so don't understand mean girl politics."

"That's not a bad thing," she says with a shrug.

Finishing the last of my coffee, I drop the cup in the trash. "Well, I could still ask Evan. He stepped in after the whole Trey thing, and it's not like he's a bad guy. He just... well, he didn't care about me all that much in the end. You don't have to be a terrible person to treat someone terribly."

"If you say so," she says, disapproval rich in her

tone. She hasn't really been team Evan since I told her about our entire thing. Apparently, dropping me for the ex he swore he was over, then telling me he didn't want to give me up but didn't want to be with me fully either, is enough for her to put him in the "fuck boys can fuck off" category. I don't entirely disagree, but when he was good, he was…

"Earth to Talia." Kate clucks, snapping her fingers in my face. "Where did you go?"

"Just thinking about the Evan thing."

"Pfft, he was a dick. And even if he did help you with Trey and you guys had a moment, I don't trust him. Unreliable source if you ask me."

"You don't think it's worth asking him?"

Shaking her head, she loops her arm with mine as I close the door to my locker. "Nope. I think steering clear of him is for the best, especially with Nico."

"There is nothing with Nico," I hiss. "Nothing."

"If you say so." Her words are practically sung and I roll my eyes as we reach the library. "Time for me to depart, but seriously, don't worry about it. I'll find another way. It probably isn't anything anyway."

She waves before walking into the library and I move down the hall, still thinking about the mask. Something about it is niggling at the back of my mind, but I don't know why. Maybe I will ask Evan, and if it's nothing,

Kate doesn't need to know.

Why does the mask sound so... familiar? I ponder on it as I glide into history and take my seat.

Maybe I'm losing my mind, but whatever it is, I can't remember for the life of me.

Mr. Lancaster breezes into the room like a whirlwind of sweater vest and papers, followed by the stragglers just making it as the second bell rings.

"Time to get your critical minds ready for the day. I have an assignment for you all, and this one is a doozy!"

After classes and my workout session, where Coach pushed us *way* harder since we missed time due to the lockdown, I decide to go for a walk to stretch out and unwind. I find the lake Kate mentioned weeks ago on the school map, and since I haven't ventured out this way, I figure why the hell not? Something about today has me wanting to be by the water. Grabbing my phone, I pull up my thread with Kate, remembering to check in with her. Our new agreement since the lockdown happened.

ME

Heading down to the lake, want to clear my head.

Smiling, I grab my AirPods, slide them into my ears, and play *(Don't) Love You Like That* by Someone Else's Rain as I start the slow walk away from the masses gathered out on the green. The sun is shining despite the weather starting to turn. Fall is coming quickly. I swear it was just July, and I blinked and all of a sudden it's almost October.

I'm not a typical fall girl, give me winter any day, but I'm a little sad that summer is coming to an end.

What has gotten into you today?

Shaking off the weird feeling, like I'm not entirely myself, I follow the signs to the boathouse, assuming I'll find the lake that way. Of course, this place has a lake. Sailing is probably part of the gym curriculum. I bet Kate just loves that, she who fears the water with a passion.

It occurs to me that's why she didn't just automatically suggest meeting me at the lake.

My bad, but also, I really do just need some decompression time after today. I hid in the library at lunch again under the guise of getting started on my history assignment, but really, I scrolled through videos on my phone the entire time while eating chips.

These last few weeks I've been so wrapped up in everything happening to me that I haven't really had a chance to reflect on who I'm becoming here. I haven't even journaled since I got here. Part of me feels like I should be happy about that, like I'm finally moving through my grief, making friends, having a life, and getting on with school so I don't fall behind, but there's a niggling part of my mind that keeps saying I'm still running from everything.

Hence my little excursion to the lake.

Eventually, I find the boathouse, which is basically just a giant wooden shed that has two jetties that lead to the lake. I keep following the path and find a deserted spot. Grabbing my sweater from my bag, I lay it on the ground and sit on it, staring out over the still water as *Gone or Staying* by Sleep Theory starts to play.

A smile creeps onto my lips as a memory of Callie dragging me to their show last year plays out in my head. When the song finishes, I shut off the music and enjoy the quiet.

Brody would've liked it here.

An urge I haven't had in forever strikes me, so I pull my notebook from my bag, pop my AirPods back in, hit shuffle on my playlist, and start to sketch as *Atom Bomb* by Boy in Space starts playing. I'm terrible at drawing, but it's always just been something fun and grounding for me.

Brody had music, singing, playing, and I had this.

I try to capture the sun as it starts to set, the boathouse to my left, and add a little boat out in the distance just because I can.

The lights flicker on around me as the sun sets, casting an almost eerie glow in the darkness. I take out my earbuds, realizing sitting out here alone with headphones when students were attacked recently really isn't the smartest idea I've had.

After dropping a message to Kate letting her know I'm still alive, I pack up my stuff and start making my way back toward the school. My stomach gurgles and I divert, heading toward the cafeteria rather than the dorms, cutting through the woods in hopes of avoiding the masses who are also likely heading that way.

Voices in the distance catch my attention, mostly because it sounds like people arguing. I ignore it and keep walking until movement and a flash of red to my left, further in the copse, catches my eye.

Weird.

Pausing because I know it's stupid to go and see who's over there—typical stupid girl in a horror film move—but also, curiosity has always been a downfall of mine.

Fuck it.

Detouring from my path, I head toward the voices, my pants getting caught in the underbrush as I trudge through the overgrown wilderness. After a few minutes, I start to think I imagined the whole thing because there's no one else out here.

I keep trudging through until there's a sort of clearing, then a giant freaking hedge, when I hear voices again.

"You shouldn't be here."

I turn at the voice and find Isaac in the tree line, leaning against the trunk of a tree.

"Oh, really?"

He smirks at me and a shiver runs down my spine, like a primal alert to danger. "Really. How'd you get this lost?"

"Who said I was lost?" I ask. I don't know if it's the predatory aura he has, but something about him brings out my defiant side, even if I am wary on the inside.

"I did," he starts as he walks toward me. "Wouldn't want to get lost in the maze, would you? Especially when this is a dead zone for cell signal. Could be lost for days and no one would know where to find you."

My breath hitches as he stops a step away from me, his threat not missed.

"You should go back to campus. Much safer for you there."

"After everything lately, campus doesn't seem that safe either. And hell, if someone could get lost out here, maybe that missing kid is out here."

"Go back to campus, Princess." He practically snarls

his last word.

I laugh at the attempted insult. "Oh, I'm a princess alright, dainty and delicate. Perfect words to describe me. Try again, Prince Charming."

He opens his mouth to speak but an alarm blares in the distance.

"I guess we should both head back," I say and he nods, grabbing my elbow and dragging me back into the woods.

He grunts as I stumble, holding me tight enough to ensure I don't fall. "I think I'll escort you and make sure you don't get lost again."

"I'm pretty sure I can find my own way," I say, wrenching my arm from his grasp and stumbling again with the force of the movement.

He catches me again, grumbling as he does, so at odds with how he acted toward me earlier in the cafeteria. "Then maybe I'll just make sure you make it back in one piece."

We get back to the main campus, Isaac not having said a word since he stopped me from falling, and my phone starts to ring. Pausing, I look at the screen and answer warily since I don't know the number. Isaac shrugs when I glance up at him as if expecting him to have some magical insight. I swipe on the screen and hit the speakerphone symbol.

"Miss Hayes?"

"That's me," I reply hesitantly.

"This is Ms. Bassett Posey. I need you to come to my office, immediately."

Worry flickers through me and I notice Isaac's brow furrow as he listens. "What's the issue?"

"I'd rather not discuss it over the phone. I'll be waiting for you. Please, come quickly."

The line cuts off and I pocket my phone as I chew on my lower lip. "I'm going to go," I say to Isaac, taking off for the main building without waiting for him to answer. Not that I wanted him with me in the first place.

He falls into step beside me, his stride longer than mine since he's so much taller than me. "You don't need to come with me, I made it back safe and sound."

"You nearly broke your ankle a dozen times," he retorts sharply. "Plus, I want to know what's so urgent."

He taps away on his screen, opening the door for me when we reach the school before falling into step with me again as I hurry toward Ms. Bassett's office.

We turn the corner to the hall where her office is located and find her pacing outside her open door. "Talia, there you are. Thank goodness. I tried to call a few times." She eyes Isaac beside me hesitantly before looking back at me, obvious concern on her face.

"What's wrong?" I ask, and she smiles tightly.

"It's Miss Galloway. Kate. There was an incident."

"What sort of incident?" Isaac asks before I get a chance.

"She's on her way to the hospital," she starts. My heart pounds in my chest and it's like there's an air bubble around me, her words becoming muffled. "She was found unconscious in the pool."

NINETEEN

"She was what?!" I screech. "Kate hates the water, there's no way she'd have gone in the pool."

"We don't know any of the details yet. Nobody else was there when she was found. We've called her parents, but I know from my meetings with her that the two of you are friends. I thought you'd like to be with her."

"I'll drive," Isaac says as I nod at Ms. Bassett. "Come on, Talia."

He tugs at my arm and I follow him in a stupor.

What the fuck is going on in this place?

Could this be linked to Laurence and Stuart?

Or is this something else?

A million thoughts whirr through my mind, to the point I hardly realize we've walked across the school grounds and parking lot as Isaac opens a car door for me and ushers me into the passenger seat.

"—no idea." Isaac says, and I realize he's on the phone as he buckles me into the car. "Yeah, I'm taking her now."

I close my eyes for what feels like a second, but when I open them, we're coming to a stop at the hospital. It doesn't even occur to me that it's weird for Isaac to have brought me here, because once we go inside, the smells hit me and it's like I'm thrown back in time.

Brody.

Except no.

This is Kate. She's not dead.

Please don't let her be dead.

"We're here for Kate Galloway." Isaac says at the nurse's station. "Ms. Bassett called ahead to notify you that we'd be coming."

I wrap my arms around myself, trying not to freak out, and Isaac is standing before me again. "She's okay."

"She's okay?" I ask, looking up at him, feeling lost.

He nods once and repeats the words again. "She's okay. I've got her room number, come on."

Relief filters through me, but I still feel like I'm walking around in a daze as he leads me to the elevators. The sounds of the ER are like an attack on my senses and

I close my eyes again until the ding signals the arrival of the elevator. Isaac waves me in before following me, and when the doors close, shutting out the noise, it's like I can breathe again.

I crouch down into a ball as he hits the button to the floor we need.

"Are you okay?" he asks, and I nod, unable to form words as the night of the accident plays on loop in my head.

Fuck, I hate hospitals.

At least Kate is okay. That's what I need to focus on.

We ride up the rest of the way in silence, and when the ding sounds as we reach our floor, I stand back up and follow Isaac through the chaos up here.

"Jake?" Issac says, and I notice Mr. Hall standing just ahead. "What are you doing here?"

"I brought in Ms. Galloway. Why are you here?"

Isaac nods toward me and the shock on his brother's face is palpable.

"Your friend is just inside with the doctor," Mr. Hall says to me. "If you knock, you can probably go in."

I nod at him, trying to work up the courage to go into the hospital room when I hear Kate through the door.

"I am fine, will you please stop prodding me? Your hands are *cold!*"

At the sound of her voice, it's like someone flipped a

switch. She really is okay. This isn't like last time. She's okay.

I let out a deep breath of relief, hearing her screech some more, smirking as she tells off the doctor again. I knock on the door and push it open a little.

"Kate," I start as I put my head in the gap.

"Oh, thank God," Kate says, trying to climb out of the bed.

"Miss. You need to stay put," the doctor says, attempting to stop her from moving, so I enter the room and move to the bedside. The doctor lets out an exasperated sigh and Kate settles down. "Thank you."

"Are you okay?" I ask her as the doctor finishes whatever it is he's doing.

"I have no idea," she replies. "I think so." She looks at the doctor and asks, "Am I?"

He frowns, glancing at me before looking back at her. "You were without oxygen for an unknown amount of time, so I want to keep you in at least overnight to monitor you. You don't appear to have any physical injuries from it, but this could be an adrenaline surge, so I don't feel comfortable letting you return to your school yet. Especially since you don't remember what happened to you, before or during your accident. I've ordered tests just to be sure there's nothing going on that's potentially been overlooked, but your vitals look good for now."

"You don't remember?" I say to Kate, who shakes her head.

"Not a thing." That's a little concerning, but I try to focus on the fact that she's okay. She glances over at the door and her eyes go wide. "Wait, is that *Isaac*?"

"Yeah, he was with me when Ms. Bassett told me what happened. He gave me a ride here."

The doctor clears his throat, drawing our attention. "I'm going to go and update your teacher and your parents. If you need anything, press the call button. A nurse will stop by regularly to check in on you."

"Okay, thank you," Kate says, way more politely than she did before, then yawns. "I think I might actually be kind of tired after all."

"That's to be expected," the doctor says with a smile. "I'll check in on you before I leave for the night."

When he leaves, I spot Isaac and Mr. Hall outside, talking quietly to each other, glancing in the room in turn.

"So why were you with Isaac?" Kate asks when the door shuts fully.

I remember the weird hedge maze and Isaac finding me in the woods, but push it to the back of my mind for now. "That's not what's important. Do you really not remember what happened to you?"

She shakes her head. "I really don't. I remember finishing class, heading to our room, texting you, and then nothing until I was in the ambulance. Apparently, I wasn't breathing for at least three minutes. Mr. Hall did CPR and resuscitated me after he hauled me from the pool, but he didn't know how long I was in the water."

"That's fucked up."

She nods in agreement. "That it is, but there was no bright light that I remember either, so you're stuck with me for a little longer."

She laughs and I join her in her morbid humor. "I can deal with that."

"Now," she starts, glancing over my shoulder again. "Tell me why you were with Isaac."

After spending some time with Kate, I left when her parents video called, but not before mentioning that she thought she remembered seeing Lexi before everything went dark for her. It could mean anything, but considering Lexi's vendetta against me so far this year, and Kate's friends saying they didn't want to become a victim again, I can't help but wonder if this is my fault.

When we pull into the school parking lot, I feel awkward as hell. Isaac drove me back to Arbour in silence. Mr. Hall was still there talking to the doctors when we left, otherwise I'd have tried to ride back with him.

"Thank you," I say as I climb from the car.

"Don't mention it," he says, that sharp tone back in his voice as he glares at me like I'm his enemy.

I swear today is giving me freaking whiplash.

"Right, whatever."

He slams his door shut and moves around the car to stand in front of me, towering over me as he glares. "I mean it, don't fucking mention it. Ever. And forget earlier too. Do not test me, Princess. You won't like what happens."

"What exactly am I supposed to forget?" I ask, rolling my eyes, refusing to back down from his menace.

"Do not be a smart ass, it won't end well."

"If you say so," I utter, stepping to the side and walking away. "It's been a long day. See you around I guess."

I wave over my shoulder without looking back, wondering just how much chaos can happen this semester. Hell, I've only been here four weeks and I feel like I'm an extra in *The Hunger Games* or something, running a chaos gauntlet that I definitely didn't sign up for.

Like, if someone is testing me, I'm failing, cause I'm over this shit. Can I tap out yet?

Just looking back over everything that's happened since I came to Spring Creek, I half wonder if I'm being punked. Between summer with Dillon, Evan showing up, Lexi being a bitch, and my weird back and forth with Nico and his friends... it's just fucking weird. I feel like my life doesn't make sense.

Not that life has felt like it made much sense since Brody died, but this is like someone turned the weird dial up to three thousand and forgot to mention it to me.

By the time I reach the dorms, my stomach is rumbling, so I detour to the kitchenette, make myself some ramen, and flick through my socials. There's nothing about what happened to Kate, which I'm taking as a positive, but like, how does no one know? Or is it just that no one is talking about it?

"Talia."

I turn at my name being called and find Vann in the kitchenette doorway. "Hey, Vann, you okay?"

"I heard about Kate, as in like, ten minutes ago because she called me."

Shit.

"Sorry, I didn't even think to message you. I was kinda in shock. I'm surprised Ms. Bassett didn't call. That's how I found out."

He shrugs before stepping into the room and sitting on one of the chairs at the table.

The table I got thoroughly fucked on.

Not the time to think about that, Talia.

"It's okay," he says quietly. "Do you know what happened?"

"No idea," I tell him. "Kate says she doesn't remember."

"And you believe her?"

Eyeing him suspiciously, I fold my arms over my chest. "Why wouldn't I?"

"I don't know," he says, letting out a sigh as he runs his hand through his hair. "It's just weird. And weird that she sounds so okay on the phone after something so... big. It doesn't make sense to me. It's not that I don't believe her, but my brain is screaming at me that it doesn't all add up."

"Nothing in this place adds up," I mutter, and he nods. "But I believe her. Mr. Hall is the one that found her, he has no reason to lie about it."

"No, but him finding her is weird too. Like, why was he there? Where was Coach Summers? She's the one that's responsible for the pool and that entire area, so where was she? Why didn't she notice anything? Why is nobody asking more questions, especially after everything with Stuart and Laurence? Like, why is no one making a bigger deal out of that either?"

I grab my noodles and take the seat next to him. "It doesn't make sense to me either, but I'm not a detective, I'm not a teacher, hell, I might almost legally be an adult, but I don't *feel* anything close to like an adult. Maybe that's why none of this makes sense. We just don't understand the scope of it."

"But aren't you at least curious?"

"Oh, I'm curious as hell," I tell him. "It gets me into way too much trouble though. And after everything that I've already handled since I got here, maybe I'm being indoctrinated by Arbour to not ask questions. That's the way of life here, right?"

He shrugs again, but I can tell he doesn't like my answer. Hell, *I* don't like my answer, but I am not Nancy Drew. Even if I like to look into stuff a little more than others. Kate is the investigative journalist, she's the one that would usually look into this.

"Wait, has Kate still been digging into the missing student thing?" I ask Vann.

He nods, fiddling with the strings on his hoodie. "Yeah, I think so. Do you think that's linked to this?"

"I have no idea," I tell him honestly. "This could be my fault, it could be a mean girl thing, and they didn't know Kate can't swim."

"It's not like Lexi hasn't done worse."

We sit quietly for a while and I finish my noodles, thinking over everything. The chaos at this place is nuts.

"This isn't weird at all." Noah walks into the room, staring at us. "Who died? Actually, I don't care."

She heads over to one of the cupboards, grabs a bottle from it, then turns to leave. "No wait, I want to know."

"No one died," I tell her, rolling my eyes. I am way too tired to deal with the bitchiness of the girls at this school.

"You can go back to obsessing about yourself now."

Wincing, I pinch the bridge of my nose. "Sorry, that was uncalled for. Long day."

"Don't stress it, new girl," she says, shrugging before leaving the room.

"I need to sleep," I mutter, and Vann stands.

"Yeah I should go. See you later, Talia."

Deciding that hanging around down here much longer isn't a great idea, I head up to my room, where I lie back on my bed, rubbing my temples and trying to process through this day.

I need to shower, go through my notes from classes today, and prep for tomorrow. I want to check in with Kate tomorrow too, but my mind is a whirr with so much stuff.

Why is nothing going to plan, dammit?

My moment of peace is interrupted by my phone ringing, and I smile when I see Callie's name on the screen.

"Are you psychic?" I say as I answer. "Because I really needed to talk."

"I mean, no, I am magical though. What's up, T? More queen bee drama?"

Taking a deep breath, I start telling her the entire bullshit parade I've been through since I arrived at Arbour, and miraculously, she stays mostly quiet until I finish telling her about today with Kate.

"Wow. Someone painted a target on your back, huh?

You sure this is all from this Lexi chick?"

"She's known to be a grade-A hag, so probably."

"That doesn't explain the missing dude, or the one from the past, the weirdo mask and cloak thing—though, masks and fetish play is fun, you might be right with that—or the guy being gnarly about the hedge maze thing. You sure that place isn't some front for a fucked up cult?"

"Honestly, it wouldn't surprise me. People with this much money are *weird*. But it mostly just seems like a school, bullying bullshit included. I just... I wanted a quiet year."

She laughs loudly, and I smile because only she would laugh at that. "Yeah, I didn't think for one second you'd get a quiet year when you told me that Evan was there and besties with your summer fuck buddy. And now Evan is out here saving you from the big bad football player; knight in shining armor shit. Maybe he really does regret what happened with you guys."

"Maybe," I say, sighing again. "But really, what does a girl have to do to get some peace? I know I'm not behind on my school work, which is the only thing I'm ahead on, and swim practice has been going okay, we have our first meet in two weeks. But socially, it just seems like a *lot*."

"That's what happens when you make friends, T. Life gets messy. You've got to learn to let go a little. I know after Brody, you spun out, you wanted to control *everything*, but maybe, just maybe, you need to loosen your grip on life a little. Try to embrace the chaos rather than fight it."

"Dude, you really have been going to therapy, huh?"

She laughs again. "No, but I did meet someone and it's like a whole new world I didn't see before."

"God, I'm so selfish, I didn't even ask why you called!"

"Don't sweat it, but yeah, I met someone."

The smile on my face is wide and I'm genuinely excited for her. "Well, come on then, tell me!"

Drying off after my shower, I pad through the locker room to grab my clothes and get ready for food. Coach called for an extra practice tonight and it was *brutal.* I'm not convinced that my arms and legs aren't just Jell-O now, but I need food then sleep.

Someone slams into my back and I stumble, falling into a locker and stubbing my little toe in the process.

Goddamit that hurts.

"Oops, I guess I didn't see you there. Surprising, considering you're so hard to miss," Lexi snarls at me. "Your times are getting sloppy. You're going to be dropped from the team if you don't, maybe, I don't know, work out more, eat less, actually lean up so you're not dragging so much dead weight through the water. You'll drag us all down at the meet at this rate."

Of course she called me fat. I guess she's had enough of calling me a slut.

The room is dead quiet except for the sounds of running water from the girls still in the showers and it's hard to miss the fact that everyone is staring at us.

At me.

Waiting for me to respond. Do they expect me to curl up and cry because Lexi said something about how I look? I might not exactly love my body, but I'm way more secure than that.

Swallowing the petty comment on the tip of my tongue about Dillon enjoying my "extra dead weight" just fine, I decide to try and not feed her fire.

"Sure thing," I retort instead, rolling my eyes and moving past her to get to my locker.

Whispers start around us and I can feel the death glare from Lexi on my back, but I try to ignore it and just get dressed. Maybe Callie was right, calm and chill is the way forward. I can't control what Lexi says or does, the same goes for Noah, Nico, all of them, but I can control how I respond.

No more taunts. No more random fuckery with guys who dismiss me as less than. No more looking into random shit that doesn't involve me—including the weird hedge maze thing and the disappearing students.

None of it helps me. It's just adding to the chaos.

I spent a long time journaling last night and it helped me see the forest through the trees.

It's like I've been trying to distract myself from Brody, from my anger at my dad, by filling my brain with so much noise that I don't have time to pay attention to the things actually going on with me.

Avoidance at its finest.

Obviously, not all of it I can control, like the stuff with Lexi for example, but I can try to minimize the outside stuff and get my life back on the track I wanted it on when I arrived at Arbour.

Summer was meant to be my time to blow off steam and get lost in any distractions I could find. Which I did. A Lot.

Now is not the time for that.

Now I need to focus on myself, what I actually want from life, how to get there, and work out a plan.

Sure, there's still a gaping hole in my chest from Brody being gone, but that's always going to be there. I need to adjust to the new version of me and work out how to move forward as I am now, rather than floating along behind him, which I've come to accept is what I did before. He led, I followed.

I don't have that anymore.

Once I finish getting dressed, I pull my wet hair into a messy bun on top of my head and gather everything up into my bag.

Looking around, I realize most people have already left. I guess not reacting to Lexi worked. Now just to keep riding this zen train I've managed to get a ticket on.

Way better than the hot mess express so far.

Long may it continue.

Heading out of the locker room, I spot Coach talking to Lexi, and they're obviously disagreeing about something, but I repeat my new mantra in my head.

Not my circus, not my monkeys.

Leaving them to whatever that is, I make my way to the cafeteria, dropping Kate a message on the way.

ME

You break out yet?

KATE

No :(but apparently everything is still fine, so as long as tests come back clear in the morning I'm free.

ME

Your folks stop threatening to take you home?

KATE

Yeah. Part of me would love to go home, but
the thought of a new school for senior year in
an entirely different country with a totally
different school curriculum? No thanks. I
think that's the only thing that got my mum
on board. Dad talked her round too
according to Josie.

ME

Well, selfishly I'm glad you're sticking around.

KATE

Can't get rid of me that easy. Anything new at
school?

ME

Nope, it's been weirdly quiet today. You
remember anything else yet?

KATE

Still a mystery, buttercup. Doctor says I might
never remember. School says there's no
footage on the security system, the pool isn't
covered for privacy reasons or something. So
no clues. Mum and Dad are pissed at the
school, so not sure what Mr. Teller will do
about that considering the donations, but I
guess we'll see.

ME

Well, I'm glad you're feeling better, and that
I'll be seeing you soon. Do you need a ride?

KATE

No, Vann is here. He came by last night, offered to stay the night, and then bring me back to school in the morning if everything is good.

ME

Staying the night? How scandalous.

KATE

Stop it. We're just friends.

ME

Yeah, if you say so.

KATE

We are, and he didn't stay so stop it. If you want to talk about boys, we could discuss Nico... or Isaac.

ME

Nothing to discuss. Two random one off events, my friend.

KATE

Yeah, if you say so.

I laugh at her parroting and join the line in the cafeteria. The smell of melted cheese wind fries is enough to make a girl weak at the knees. I'm sure Lexi would love me to eat dust and lettuce, but she can shove her opinions up her ass.

KATE

Dinner is here, talk soon. Yay hospital food.

ME

Gag. No thanks. Enjoy your not scandalous night ;)

KATE

You too. No more kitchenette hookups :p

Laughing again as I shake my head, I pocket my phone and practically drool over the food available. Ordering way too much, I grab my tray and head over to an empty table. After the shit with Kate's friends, I've avoided sitting with them. Tory has been quiet company at the table sometimes, but she's absent tonight.

Not complaining.

I pull up my e-reader app on my phone and dive into a book Callie mentioned on our call last night while I eat. Before I know it, I'm eleven chapters in, my food is demolished, and an hour has passed.

The cafeteria is much busier than it was. Stifling a yawn, I clear my tray, glad I had a quiet hour to myself. Though, after practice and eating, I'm beyond ready for bed. I step back to put my tray by the trash and groan as something wet spills over my head and down my back.

"Oops, my bad. Guess I didn't see you again."

Wiping what seems like water from my eyes, I take

a deep breath. Then I see the red puddle surrounding my feet. Glancing at my hands, I notice they're also stained red from wiping at my face.

Which means my face and back are likely stained too.

Just awesome.

The zen I was embracing is holding on by a fraying thread as anger floods me. I am so over this shit. I clench my fists and try to take another deep breath. Calm and collected is the goal.

I stumble forward as I'm shoved from behind, and I only just catch myself from falling into the trash can full of discarded food.

Nope. Zen is gone.

Turning, I face off with Lexi, who is smirking at me, her friends at her back. Of course she isn't alone. Fucking coward. "What the fuck is your problem?"

"I don't have a problem. I told you, I didn't see you." Her face is a mask of innocence as she flutters her lashes. "Not *my* problem you're where you're not wanted."

"Yeah, well," I start, telling myself this is such a bad idea, but I'm over it. "Want this."

My clenched fist collides with her face and sweet satisfaction flicks through me as her nose crunches, blood splattering from it. Pain rips down my wrist, but I refuse to acknowledge it. "Oh look, now we match. Red accessories for us both."

"You bitch!" she screams and attacks me. We end up on the ground, her on top of me, pulling at my hair as her blood drips onto me while I try to fight her off.

"That's enough of that," I hear before she's lifted from me. Scrambling to my feet, someone grabs me from behind.

I push my hair out of my face and spot Dillon holding Lexi. "Keep your bitch on a fucking leash," I snark, before pulling free of the hold on me. Spinning, I find Evan, hands up in surrender. "You leave me alone too."

Grabbing my bag from where it fell to the ground, I storm from the cafeteria, not feeling proud of what just happened, but too pissed off to chastise myself fully.

I think I might be proud of you.

The words in Brody's voice make me smile as I head to the dorms. He *would* be proud of me. Hell, *I'm* kind of proud of me for standing up for myself. I just kinda wish the zen way of life had lasted longer.

And that I'd reacted better... or not at all.

Tears prick at my eyes from the sheer level of anger coursing through me. Ugh. I hate when I angry cry.

I stomp into the seating area that joins the girls' dorm to the boys' and find Noah, Nico, and Dallas talking by the door to their dorms.

They stare at me when they spot me and I realize I must look an absolute mess.

I need another fucking shower.

"Should we ask?" Nico asks, trying not to laugh.

Noah nudges him, shaking her head. "Lexi?"

"Got it in one," I respond before heading up to the showers.

Once I'm there, I groan as I take in my reflection. Thank God for dark hair, because if I was blonde... yeah, I don't want to think about it. I'm just hoping whatever she dumped on me washes off easily enough.

Grateful I still have my shower stuff from the pool, I jump back in the shower, scrubbing myself down. It's not until I'm done and wrapping my damp towel around myself that I realize I don't have another change of clothes with me.

Awesome.

Sticking my head out of the stall, I make sure no one is around, wanting to kick myself for not heading to my room first.

"Truce," Noah says when I spot her standing by the sinks. "I thought you might need this."

She holds up a black robe and offers it to me.

"Thank you?" I say, hesitantly. "Why are you being nice to me?"

"Being a bitch is exhausting," she admits. "Plus, I realized the other night that you really aren't interested in Nico, or the others, so I figured I should apologize for earlier. I'm a little protective."

I take the robe, wrapping it around myself before letting the towel drop to my feet. I tie the sash then grab my towel, still unsure if I should trust this olive branch.

"I also kind of feel responsible for Lexi. I created that monster, so her mess is ultimately my mess."

"I don't think anyone can create that level of insecurity, it's like, from birth," I reply and she shrugs.

"Maybe, but still, I'm sorry. I heard you got a good shot in though. Good for you for standing up for yourself."

"Thanks, I think." I pause before moving to leave, then stop again. "Why did you think I was going after Nico by the way? And why did you really change your mind? You don't even know me."

Though, I'm guessing from her truce and statement that she doesn't know Nico fucked me into oblivion a few days ago.

"The enemy of my enemy is my friend…" she trails off and my eyes widen in shock.

"I'm kidding. Call it experience." She shrugs like that explains everything. "I'm good at reading people, and you're not like other people here. I was just on guard that first night."

"I don't know what that means."

She smiles sadly, moving past me to the door. "Be glad for that. Some things are better left unknown."

She leaves the room, heading down the hall in the opposite direction from me, leaving me with even more questions.

So much for no more curiosity.

They say it killed the cat, let's just hope mine doesn't kill me at Arbour.

TWENTY

"**F**reedommmmmm!" I shout in my best *Braveheart* impression as I bounce into our room. Talia stares at me like I've lost my mind, and maybe I have, but hospitals are gross. The beds are uncomfortable, the food is disgusting, and well, I'm lowkey hoping that being back at school might help me remember what the hell happened Monday night.

It's driving me nuts not remembering, but I'm trying to play it off like I don't care.

There's too much weird shit happening at Arbour this year, and maybe looking into that is *why* Monday happened. Maybe that should be enough for me to stop looking, but it goes against my entire nature.

"Welcome back to the real world, roomie," Talia says with a grin as she gets up from her bed and hugs me. "Where's Vann?"

"He had to go to class," I tell her. "Speaking of, why aren't you in class?"

It's only then I notice the red tinge to her skin. "Erm, why are you a different color, Smurf?"

"Smurf? Aren't they blue?"

"Hence the different color. Why are you red?"

She huffs as she steps back. Closing the door, I bounce over to my bed, groaning as I lie back on the mattress. This might not be top luxury, but the hospital was like sleeping on a cement slab. I turn to my side, ignoring the soreness of my body like I have since I came around from CPR, and look back at Talia, who is now sitting on her bed watching me.

"Well?" I ask again.

She shrugs, flexing out her right hand. "Lexi. Which is also why I'm not in class. I am, er, suspended from lessons for the rest of the week."

"Erm, why?"

"I punched her in the face."

I push myself to sit up, bewildered and full of joy. "I'm sorry, you did what now?"

"Not proud of it," she replies, though the smirk on her

face says differently. "She dumped something over me in the cafeteria after dinner, hence the red, and then she pushed me, so I punched her. We ended up fighting, Dillon pulled her off me and I had an email from Ms. Feldman by the time I got back to the room."

"How do you say all of this so nonchalantly?" I ask, puzzled. "That isn't like, oh yeah, I had a quiet night, read a book, got an early night. That is... well, it's kinda awesome and I'm sad I missed it."

"Eh, I was trying for calm and peaceful."

I burst out laughing, holding my aching ribs as I do. "Oh, goal achieved. So well."

She joins me in the laughter.

"At least I won't be lonely this week. I'm excused from classes too. Teachers are emailing me the work."

"Oh no, two days of dorm, TV, and snacks. How awful for us both," she says with a grin. "Want me to make a fort? We can move the TV down and binge something!"

"Yes!" I exclaim, happier than ever to be back, and that my parents shipped me a TV for this room. "That sounds perfect. Do you not have practice?"

"Nope," she replies, wincing. "Went to practice yesterday morning and Mr. Teller pulled me aside after that and told me I'm out for the week. Fun stuff included."

She gets to work while I rest. My offers to help are waved off, which I'm quietly thankful for, because damn

I hurt. Playing down the pain probably wasn't my greatest idea, but I really didn't want to stay in the hospital. Turning down the painkillers probably wasn't a stellar move either, but can't pretend I don't hurt then accept the pills.

I might be foolish, but I'm no fool.

"I'm going to go grab snacks. Any requests? Other than cheese puffs and Coke?"

I love that she knows me so well already.

She might be the first real best friend I've ever had. It's new, but I like it, not feeling so alone. Grinning at her, I nod. "M&M's too? Chocolate ones though, not the other types. Oh, and maybe something with cheese."

"Most random requests ever, but sure. I will do what I can." She grabs her phone, wallet, and keys then heads out of the room.

I wonder if she cares that she's still in her pjs?

She's gone before I can ask, so I leave it and close my eyes.

Racking my brain for more information about what happened Monday is futile, but I try anyway, hoping to find something more than dead space, but I come up empty. Frustrated, I grab my phone, remembering to text Mum and Dad to let them know I'm back at school, dropping the same to Charlie and Josie. The family group video call last night wasn't the most fun I've ever had, but I had to concede and promise to try and stay out of trouble.

Not a conversation I've had to have before, but this year is all about new things it seems.

New roomie.

New bestie.

New mysteries at Arbour.

So much new. I miss the comfort of boring a little, but I also like that Talia being here has spiced up my world a little. Not that I think it's all because of her, that would be nuts, but being around her makes me want to open up my world a bit. Be more adventurous. There's just something about her that makes me want to be more. To live my life to the fullest.

It doesn't make complete sense to me, but I figure that's okay. Senior year is meant to be about figuring yourself out and getting ready for big life decisions, I guess the universe sent her to me to help me find myself a little easier.

Who knows?

I'm not about to question it.

A knock at the door pulls me from my thoughts, so I stumble across the room to open it. "Did you get too much to—"

My words trail off, jaw slacking when I look at the person standing in my doorway. A person who definitely isn't my roomie.

"Kate. We should talk."

I watch the giant football god as he glances around the room, that eagle eye of his taking in every detail. "So erm... why did you want to talk, Trey?"

He runs a hand over his head, shifting from one foot to the other like he's feeling awkward. He doesn't get to be awkward right now. Him being at my door wasn't expected, and after his manhandling of Talia, I'm not exactly thrilled he's in our room.

Allie might be awesome, but her big brother? He seems like a jerk. I've not had a ton of interaction with him before, but I never thought he was a terrible guy. Sure, him and the fantastic five have had their moments of ruling Arbour like giant bags of dicks, but this is high school. There's a hierarchy. It is what it is. But manhandling Talia? Yeah, that was totally out of line.

Am I a hypocrite for thinking that, but being so thrilled she punched Lexi? Maybe, but fuck it.

I hate being so cynical, but Monday has me shook, and him being here unexpectedly isn't exactly filling me with the warm fuzzies.

"Allie told me what happened. Vann told her. She's worried about you, and I'm worried about her. I don't want anything happening to her."

"Right…?"

He lets out a huff. "Do you know what happened? Allie said you didn't, but that just doesn't sit right with me."

I shift awkwardly where I'm sitting and shrug, wringing out my hands. "I don't know what to tell you."

"Tell me the truth," he demands, taking a step closer to me.

"Why the hell are you in my room?" Talia demands as the door swings open. Her arms are laden with snacks, which she deposits on her desk, before turning her attention back to the behemoth of a man in our room. "Did you go mute?"

Her sass kills me sometimes, but right now, I'm beyond grateful for her. Trey is kind of scary. It's not even his size, it's just the aura he puts out. Like he's not afraid to get down and dirty to do what needs doing. Isaac and Nico have a similar thing, but theirs are more focused. Less unpredictable. Trey seems like an unstable chemical compound that could go off at any time without warning.

"Don't be such a twat," he growls at her. "I was just asking her what happened."

"Why?" she asks, cocking her hip as she folds her arms over her chest. "Why do you even care?"

"Because of Allie," he retorts sharply.

"Well, you can leave," Talia says, motioning to the door. "We can speak to Allie."

He clenches his fists as he stretches out his neck and butterflies start in my stomach. This isn't going well. "I just want to know what happened."

"Don't we all, buddy. She doesn't remember, now you should really leave. Don't you have class?"

He turns back to face me with a frown. "You don't remember?"

"No," I reply, shaking my head. He just stares at me so I shrug. "No memory at all."

His shoulders drop and I can't tell if it's defeat or relief. *Did he do this?*

That would be weird though, right?

"See?" Talia snarks. "Now leave."

"I'm going," he snaps at her before turning back to me. "I hope you feel better, Kate. Can't have us London kids dropping off."

He leaves without waiting for me to say anything, slamming the door behind him loud enough that I flinch.

"What a jackass," Talia mutters as she picks up the snacks and puts them on top of the blanket pile she made before. "Here was me thinking the Brits were meant to be gentlemen. Anyway, back to our relaxing day."

She moves the TV down to the floor and I grab my pillows, shimmying down to the blanket fort and grabbing a bag of cheese puffs as I get comfy.

"That was weird," I comment as she locks the door

before joining me.

"Everything in this place is weird," she says, shrugging it off, so I try to do the same.

Except that nagging thought haunts me the entire day.

Was that relief? And if it was, did he…

Did he try to kill me?

TWENTY ONE

A call to the principal's office wasn't exactly how I expected to start a new week, especially after my suspension. I was hoping for a better, quieter few days, but here I am, sitting down, legs swinging, rather than being in History.

No one has told me *why* I'm here, but I'm assuming it's about the Lexi thing again. Because why wouldn't something in my life be about her? I am so over it, but I guess while I'm here, I have to accept that she's going to be a thorn in my side.

Though I should probably try to find a better way to deal with it than throwing hands.

Satisfying yes, but long term, probably not great for future prospects.

But that was nearly a week ago and life has been obscurely quiet since. No bullying, no bullshit, nothing.

I mean, that Stuart guy is still in a coma, and there's been no word on the missing student either, but that still leans into the quiet thing.

Our first swim meet is this week, so I've taken advantage of the peace and spent a ton of extra hours training in the pool. It's been so nice starting and ending my days with a swim. Even the days when I have practice, I make sure to be in the pool more than once.

I passed my chemistry lab with Noah, and that class has been almost pleasant since her truce.

I've had minimal run-ins with the other Elites.

Hell, even Evan has stayed away like I asked.

Kate is suspicious as hell about it all, but I've just tried to accept my what-will-be-will-be attitude and roll with it. Personally, I think it's balance.

With so much chaos must come some peace.

At least that's Callie's theory, and I'm clinging to it for dear life.

The phone on the receptionist's desk rings, jolting me from my thoughts. She answers and hums into the handset before looking over to me and hanging up. "They'll see you now."

They?

They who?

"Okay, thanks," I say with a smile, figuring it's pointless asking when I'll find out in a few seconds. Picking up my bag, I move to the door, knocking once before opening it and walking into the office.

I find Mr. Teller sitting behind his desk and Coach leaning against the wall behind them.

My stomach sinks because this can't be good.

"Good morning, Talia. Please, take a seat," Mr. Teller says.

I do as I'm asked, trying to smile as I attempt to get comfortable in the hard wooden seat.

"Thank you for coming down. I'm sure you're wondering why you're here."

I nod at Mr. Teller. "I am. I have no idea why I'd be here, with both of you."

They glance at each other and Coach pushes off the wall, looping her fingers together in front of her as she lets out a sigh. "Talia, your drug test came back positive."

"I'm sorry, what?" I ask, because I had to have misheard that.

"The test results were positive," Mr. Teller says sternly. "This means you are disqualified from the meet this week. It also means that your spot on the team is suspended."

I sit back in the chair, absolutely stumped. "But I don't

take drugs. How was it positive? Could it have been a false positive? Can we retest? I've never touched drugs outside of prescriptions."

"Unfortunately, the school's policies on this are very clear. The test was run three times to confirm the result, all showing as positive. So you'll need to do weekly tests, and when you have eight clear in a row, your suspension will be lifted," Coach explains, smiling sadly. It's like she knows this is bullshit. She knows I don't take drugs for fuck sake.

Eight weeks? The season is basically over by then.

"This is insane," I say, letting out a deep breath. Wait. "Is this going to go on my record?"

Mr. Teller nods. "It will, as will the follow up results."

"Can I appeal this? Or see the results? I'm happy to retest right now," I argue. Less about the swim team, and more about the drug test being on my transcripts. Not exactly going to look great for college applications.

Fuck my life.

"You can, and we'll do another test today, but that doesn't change the policy or the results being on your file in the meantime." Mr. Teller leans forward, folding his arms on his desk before him. "I understand your frustration, but between this and your recent behavior, this isn't something that we can overlook."

Lexi.

This has to be her.

I don't know how, but my entire being is screaming that she's behind this.

"If you want to retest now, I can escort you to collect your sample," Coach offers.

"Is that all?" I ask, glancing between them both, feeling helpless. I don't know how to fight this sort of thing, but it's something that could steal my future. Might have already.

"That's all," Mr. Teller says, excusing me from the office.

"Let's go," Coach says softly, leading me from the room. I follow her to the bathrooms where she supervises me peeing to collect a new sample to be tested. I hand her the cup and head to the sink to wash my hands.

"You know I didn't do this right?" I ask her, and she nods.

"I don't believe you take drugs, Talia. I've seen your performance, but my hands are tied. The results are what they are. I pushed for the third retest, because usually they only do two, but every result was positive. Are you sure no one has been slipping anything into your food or drink?"

Shaking my head, I finish cleaning my hands, feeling my future slipping away. "I don't think so. I have no idea how this is possible. What should I do? This could ruin me."

"I'll do what I can to help," she says, trying to reassure

me. "Now head to class and try not to let this interfere with your lessons. I'll get in touch once we have the results, but if you have someone you know in the legal system, it might be worth putting in a call."

A dry laugh escapes me as she leaves the bathroom. I know one of the top lawyers in the country. She's my mother.

But there's no way she's taking my call.

She'd just as soon see me rot as Lexi would.

I went through what was left of history and US Government in a daze, avoided everyone at lunch then wandered to the music room where Dallas was waiting for me for our afternoon class.

"You're distracted." He frowns at me and I shrug.

"No shit, Sherlock."

He leans back in his seat, watching me closely. "Anything I can help with?"

"I doubt it," I reply, trying not to sound as hopeless as I feel. I haven't felt this dejected since... well, I don't remember when. Probably after Brody died.

"Want to talk about it? A problem shared and all that."

His smile is warm and his blonde hair falls into his

pretty eyes. Everything about him is inviting. Like he's the guy to keep you safe and protect you from the world while staying soft and gooey.

Except he isn't that guy.

Not for me.

Even if we did have that moment at the Alive For Tonight concert, we've hardly interacted since then.

And yet, somehow, I find myself telling him what happened this morning. He listens so well, chiming in only when I need a minute to gather myself. I hadn't realized he was this... nice, I guess.

He stands and wraps me in his arms, hugging me tight. Usually, I'm not a huge hugger, but he's big, broad, warm and his hug is like everything I need right now. I feel small and safe, like I could stay here forever. Protected from the big bad Arbour. "I'm sorry, darlin'. That sounds awful. Is there anything you can do?"

He murmurs the question into my hair and I shake my head. "This is great, thank you. I'm sorry for unloading on you like that. We hardly know each other."

"I don't know about that," he says softly. "We've spent plenty of time together, more than I spend with most people. But I like that you feel like you can talk to me. We all need that."

Why is he so nice when I am feeling so low?

So weak.

He can't be this nice to me.

"You can always talk to me if you need to."

I push back out of his arms, because I can't feel like this about him.

I slept with Nico for God's sake... not to mention that Noah *just* started being nice to me, and Trey *despises* me.

"What are you, my white knight?" I tease, trying to lift the mood and put some space between us.

He winks at me and I can't help but laugh. "I can be whatever you need me to be, darlin'."

"So you're cheesy too, good to know."

"As long as you're not lactose intolerant."

I laugh again, hard enough that I have to wipe away a tear from my eye. "Yeah, that was awful.

"It was, but you laughed, so mission accomplished." His cheesy grin still somehow looks good on him, when it should look dorky.

Yeah, I need to change the direction of my thoughts, because if I keep thinking about that smile, and how hard his chest felt when his arms locked around me... about how he hides what is obviously a ripped as hell physique below his uniform...

Yeah, no. Bad Talia.

"Shall we get on with this assignment?" he asks, still watching me, that teasing smile of his making me feel gooey, especially when it's so obviously real because it reaches his eyes.

"Sure," I mutter, thankful for the change of direction. "This is going to be so bad though. Singing is not my thing."

"Then let's start with composing. I have something I've been messing around with, let me play it to you." He moves to the piano, taking a seat on the bench, and starts fingering the ivory.

Nope, can't watch those strong hands work.

I move to stand at the far end of the piano, but he shakes his head and taps the bench beside him. "Come sit with me, darlin'. I want to teach you some chords so Ms. Ravan can't accuse you of riding on my wagon."

Devious move, Dallas. I see you.

Really, he's probably just being nice after I broke down on him, but the delulu is real right now.

Begrudgingly, I move to sit next to him on the bench, perching on the edge rather than brushing against him, and he starts to play.

The melody is haunting and beautiful, and I lose track of time as I close my eyes, listening to him play. When he finishes, I let out a sigh, almost sad it's finished. "That was... incredible. How is that something you're just messing around with? You really are talented."

His cheeks flush red as he ducks his head. "Thanks, darlin'. It's rough at the moment, but hopefully we can turn it into something."

I scoff at him. "Yeah, no, that is already something. I am going to ruin your grade."

"Nawh, we got this. Come on, let's focus, try to get some lyrics down, and then we can tidy up the melody."

Groaning, I cradle my face in my hands. "I am going to be so bad at this."

"Believe in yourself," he says, winking at me.

We spend the next twenty minutes trying to piece together lyrics that make some sense, but I really do suck at this. I have no idea how he hasn't given up on me yet. I pace back and forth by the window, trying to come up with something to add, then throw my hands up in frustration.

"You should ask for a new partner," I whine as I walk from the window to the side of the piano and hop on top of it. The black top is cold on my legs and a shiver runs down my spine.

"Or we could focus," he counters, and I glare at him where he's sitting across the room with his notebook.

"I don't think focusing is going to help me."

"We could focus," he says, moving to stand in front of me. "Or I could help to... inspire you…"

Tilting my head, I look up at him, a playful smile on his face. "Inspire me how, exactly?"

He takes a step forward, between my legs, placing his hands on the cold top to either side of my thighs. "I'm sure we can think of something."

"You want to fuck around?" I ask, brows raised. "Here was me thinking you were the good guy."

"Oh, I am, darlin'. I can be *real* good." That drawl of his does something to me. It could be that or the smell of bonfires that is wrapped around him as he leans into me that has me tilting my head back.

"Why?" I challenge, because this seems very out of the blue. Sure, we flirted a bit, and he has me feeling all kinds of weak, but this doesn't seem like a him thing.

"Why not?" he retorts and I smile. "You need some inspiration and I need to run my tongue up that creamy thigh of yours and see if you taste as good as you look."

My eyes go wide at his words and I jolt when he strokes a thumb over my thigh.

Wearing a skirt today was apparently a good move.

"Who am I to deny you?"

"Good answer, darlin'. I'm sure I can inspire you in all the best ways." He grins at me, adjusting me so I'm closer to the edge. The top of the piano bites at the bare skin of my legs again, but with Dallas standing between them, his lips on mine, I can't find it in me to care. I didn't see my day going this way, but I am definitely not mad about the beautiful, crooning, cowboy type wanting to worship my body.

Absolutely not.

I'm delusional occasionally but I'm not crazy. And this doesn't mean anything.

Sex is just sex.

His fingers trace up my bare thighs and I've never been happier that I chose to wear the skirt that came with my uniform than I am right now.

I tip my head back as his lips work down my neck, pants falling from my lips as I clutch the edge of the piano. My fingers almost hurt with how tight I'm holding it, but I know if I let go of it, I'm going to fully lose control.

"You good, sweetheart?" he asks as he looks up at me when he sits on the piano bench, a smile on his face that reaches his pretty blue eyes as his fingers make fast work of the buttons of my blouse.

"Oh, I'm fantastic," I respond, my words little more than a whisper as his lips press on my skin softly, kissing just above the material of my bra as his fingers toy with my panties.

"Good," he murmurs as he brushes a finger through my wetness, groaning as he does. "So responsive."

I whimper as he gently toys with me with one hand, the other pushing off my blazer before undoing the buttons on my shirt. Reaching back, I undo my bra, and he takes full advantage, licking, biting, and kissing my nipple. "You like that?"

Another whimper escapes me as I nod. "Yes."

The single word is little more than a breath, but I feel him smile against my skin. "Oh, I'm going to have a lot of fun with you, darlin'."

I glance over at the door, safe in the knowledge that he locked it and that these rooms are soundproofed, then decide to let go.

What's the worst that could happen?

Pushing me back a few inches, he presses his palms against my open thighs and spreads them farther apart. This is the part where I should feel self-conscious, but for some reason, I don't.

Something about him puts me at ease, despite the circumstances. The only thing I feel here with him is wanted, so instead of getting lost in my head, I bask in the attention from this gorgeous guy who is obviously turned on by what he sees. At least, that is if that huge tent in his pants is anything to go by.

For a second, he holds my gaze, heat burning like gas flames in his bright blue eyes, before he drops his stare to where my thighs part for him.

"There's something so sexy..." he starts, one of his knuckles sliding along the seam of my panties on one side, then the other. "About a wet spot slowly getting bigger and bigger... and I've barely even touched you yet." His voice is soft, so much so that it's like he's talking to himself. He presses his knuckle against my panties and I whimper again.

I need more, otherwise, I might just combust and I have no qualms with begging right now, not even a little bit. "Please, Dallas."

"Please, what, darlin'?"

My breath hitches at the dominant tone of his voice. Suddenly, he's not the gentle giant who hugged me so tight I felt safe. No, right now, he is so much more.

"Touch me." A smile toys at his lips as I beg.

"Oh, I definitely like that." His voice is so low it's almost gravelly, and I swear it turns me on even more, if that's even possible.

He sneaks one of his fingers between my pussy and the panties, sliding inside of me oh so slowly, before pulling it back out and making a slow circle around my swollen lips. I'm sure I should be embarrassed at just how turned on I am, at how wet I am for him, but it's like his touch washed away any shame or inhibitions I had before this.

"I'll do more than just touch you, darlin'."

Before I can register his delicious promise, I'm pushed onto my back with my legs over the broad expanse of his shoulders, feet hanging on the other side and my skirt hiked up to my waist. Panting, I lift my head just in time to see the devilish grin on his face before he ducks under my skirt and rips my panties off in one quick motion. My gasp at the brutish move doesn't faze him and when the heat of his mouth takes my clit hostage, any protest that might have existed disappears from my mind.

My chest juts up from the piano like something from *The Exorcist* as I slam my palms on the shiny, wooden surface, as he toys with my clit. "Oh my God!"

"Oh, I love hearing you scream, Talia."

I open my mouth to respond when he thrusts two fingers inside my pussy and curls them just enough to make my hips follow the movement as my heels dig into his shoulder blades, making all thoughts but the feel of him disappear.

He sucks on my clit with the perfect amount of pressure to push me toward oblivion.

Clutching at his shoulders, my nails digging into him as my body arches as he pushes me closer to the edge, as I desperately try to catch my breath, until I'm almost begging him to stop. "Too much, oh God, it's too much."

Dallas doesn't relent, he just keeps on sucking my poor, aching clit.

"Dallas!" His name is like a prayer on my lips but he doesn't respond, just hikes me up farther so his entire mouth is on me and his fingers are no longer fucking my pussy, but nudging the tight hole of my ass.

"Dallas!" I've never... fuck it. "Yes!"

Using one hand to pull me up by the fabric of my bra resting between my tits, he releases my pussy and kisses my mouth like he can't stand going one more second without my kiss.

Our tongues battle it out as he breaches the entrance of my ass, using my cum as lube. It stings, the burn almost unbearable, but I'm so fucking distracted by his mouth devouring me that I can't find it in me to ask him to stop.

Slowly, he begins to fuck my ass with his middle finger in time with his tongue fucking my mouth. His movements hypnotize me until I'm nothing but a writhing mess, and when his thumb pushes into my pussy, I lose my fucking mind.

The familiar tingle at the base of my spine turns into an electric spear that runs straight up my back, breaking into a scream that makes my throat burn from the ferocity of it. Except there's no sound because Dallas has his mouth on mine in less than a second, swallowing my screams as I come all over his hand.

"That was a sight to behold, darlin', but I think we can do better than that." My body is jelly after that breathtaking orgasm, so I can't find the motivation to argue with him.

He steps back, watching me like I'm an art display just for him as I'm laid out on the piano.

"Dallas?" I push up onto my elbows, starting to feel a little conscious of being so bare, his eyes burning into my skin.

"Shhh, baby girl, it's time to show me how far you can go."

"What does that mean?" I ask as a slow grin tilts up the corners of my mouth.

Dallas takes each of my legs off of his shoulders and props my feet on the piano, exposing my pussy to him before pressing on my chest so I'm lying back down. Being spread wide for him like this gives him an unhindered view of me from my exposed nipples to my swollen pussy and newly breached asshole.

"You're about to find out."

Fighting the urge to squirm as he darts his eyes from one intimate place to another, I take this time to admire him as he slowly, teasingly, unbuttons his shirt, leaving it open but not taking it off completely. His talented tongue sneaks out, licking his lips as if still tasting me on his skin before he pops open the button of his pants and pulls his zipper down as slowly as humanly possible.

This is the best kind of fucking torture, but there's only so long I can stay here under his gaze.

Propping myself up on my elbows and looking down the length of my exposed body, I watch, enraptured, as his dick springs out from his boxers all thick and veiny with a drop of precum teasing the tiny slit at the head. I'm vaguely aware that I'm licking my lips, realizing it only when his eyes flash at the sight.

"You like what you see, darlin'?"

I nod in response, not trusting my voice.

"Good." The word almost sounds like a promise, a threat, but either way, I am here for whatever is about to happen.

Reaching into the pocket of his slacks, he pulls out a square foil, rips it open with his teeth, and slides it onto his dick with ease and precision. For some reason, that move is so fucking hot I almost come a third time just watching him.

The head of his cock slides up and down my wet lips, only teasing my entrance and circling my asshole before returning to my pussy.

"Brace yourself." I frown as he grips my hips, not sure what he means for a second until his cock doesn't just slide into me but slams inside of me.

My breath catches in my throat as the sheer size of him fills me completely. Pausing once he is nestled inside my pussy, he leans in and sucks one of my nipples into his mouth. Somehow, him not moving is making me as crazy as his tongue on me.

I want... no, I fucking *need* him to move.

To fuck me in all the ways my body is begging for.

He looks up at me with a devilish grin and moves right over to my other tit, biting down on my sensitive flesh.

"Fuck!"

"You make the prettiest sounds, darlin'." His voice is strained, and I'm glad that he's not as composed right now as he seems.

Being the only one of us coming entirely undone isn't as much fun.

Pulling away, he rises back to his full, over-six-foot height, and circles my thighs tighter with his arms.

Dallas slowly pulls out until all I can feel is the tip of his cock at my entrance before he thrusts right back inside, using my legs as leverage, making my world tilt on its axis. The entire room is filled with sounds of skin slapping against skin and grunts echoing along with my moans. My hands reach out to grab onto something, anything, but only one finds purchase on the edge while the other grasps onto the shiny surface.

My tits bounce with the force of his thrusts as he destroys me so forcefully I know for a fact I'll have bruises somewhere. It's so at odds with his usual demeanor that it's somehow even hotter than it should be.

"Fuck, Talia, your pussy is so fucking tight. You're squeezing my cock like a fucking vice." His words are strained, the veins in his neck bulging with the effort of fucking me. I love that I can bring this beautiful man to his knees. It's a power rush I wasn't expecting.

"Dallas, I'm..." Oh fuck, I'm so close again.

"I know, darlin'. I fucking know." Keeping one arm around my thigh as leverage, he reaches up with the other, his fingers finding my nipple and pinching the tight nub between his thumb and forefinger.

Every time he bottoms out, he pinches, over and over again until my body begins to shake, the nerve endings from my nipple traveling straight to my clit and causing me to vibrate uncontrollably as I milk him, tighter and tighter.

"Goddamn, this cunt was made for me." And those words, that single possessive claim, is what throws me overboard.

My back arches off the piano as every one of my muscles contracts, my pussy throbbing and squeezing everything Dallas has to give me.

"That's it, take me, baby girl. Fucking, take it."

My orgasm rips through me, but he doesn't slow. I open my eyes and see the exact moment Dallas loses all semblance of control. His big shoulders squared, his head thrown back, and his Adam's apple bobbing up and down as his hips piston in and out.

Then he stills, frozen in time like a Greek god, a roar ripping from his throat as he comes.

It's a sight to behold.

We're both panting, our chests heaving at the same rhythm, and our breaths the only music in the room. When Dallas blinks, the haze of a powerful orgasm dissipating, he turns those powerful blues on me and grins.

"Feeling inspired yet, darlin?" Licking his lips, he

slowly pulls out, and I can't help but laugh.

"Inspired? Yeah, sure, that's totally what I'm feeling right now."

He removes his condom and zips himself up before handing me my clothes from the floor. "Then mission accomplished again."

I push off of the piano and grab my panties, cringing a little at the wetness before getting dressed again.

"We should probably get out of here," Dallas says, nodding toward the clock on the wall.

Shit.

Yes, yes we should.

"I'm looking forward to our next class, darlin'. I'll see you real soon." He tilts his imaginary hat and leaves me staring after him as he leaves.

Well fuck. I guess that really just happened.

TWENTY TWO

"Remind me why we're going to some random party?" I whine at Kate as she browses through the rails of BoHo, her favorite boutique in Spring Creek. "These people don't like me, you just nearly freaking died, and well... a party just doesn't seem, I dunno, on brand?"

"One," she starts, pulling out a cute dark green crop top that she slings over her arm before continuing her hunt for something to wear. "Some of them seem to like you a whole lot of late. Maybe they *don't* like you, but fuck them and I nearly died. How better to show the haters that you're a real person, and that I'm not afraid. Two, you just got suspended from the swim team, you need a way to unwind, and three, it's Dallas's party, he invited us after you guys hooked up—which we are not done discussing yet, just B-T-dubs—and four, well, I don't have a four, but it will be fun. Plus, I never get invited to parties."

I groan as I drop into the chair in the corner. "It being Dallas's party is exactly the reason I shouldn't be going."

I haven't seen him since our hook up, and I *might* be feeling a little awkward about the fact that I've now screwed him and Nico. Sure, there's nothing wrong with sex, and I'm not ashamed of any of it, but screwing two guys from one friend group can't end well, surely?

Yeah, I might have a little regret now that I'm out of the post-orgasm haze. Especially because I don't know if Dallas knew I'd screwed his friend before we hooked up.

Or if he even knows at all.

"Nope, we're going. You don't have to stay long, but you *do* need to show your face. Even if it's just so people don't think you're hiding after everything that's gone down. Show them weakness and they'll eat you alive."

Groaning, I tilt my head back and stare at the ceiling. "I so hate that you're right."

"Oh, I know." Her response is just a little too cheerful as she bounces over to me. "I found outfits for us both. Come on, let's ring it up and go grab coffee and food before we get ready."

"You found me an outfit? Shouldn't I see it before we

buy it?"

"Nope," she practically sings as she skips to the checkout. "You're being a party pooper, so I'm picking for you. That's my new rule. Call it your early birthday present to me."

"Your birthday isn't until next year."

She grins wide at me when I join her at the counter. "I know, that's why I said early. Can be a Christmas present if you'd prefer."

Rolling my eyes at her, I let out an exaggerated sigh. "Fine, fineeeeee."

We argue over her paying for my outfit, but I cave, because as nice and sweet as Kate is, she fights dirty. Once we're paid up, she snakes the bags from the cashier, then skips from the boutique, while I follow behind, trying not to dread tonight too much.

Hell, if she can be cheery Miss Daisy when she nearly died, I can suck up my unease about seeing a guy.

Soooo easy.

Not.

Shaking off my funk, I loop my arm with hers, trying to draw in some of her cheer as she chatters away about her face-off with Erica this morning about the school paper— something about a flopped edition and being asked to come in to save the day.

By the time we reach the Brew Barn, I am beyond

ready to eat.

"It's so busy in here," she says as we scan the room for a table. "Ooh, in the back!"

I follow as she darts through the crowded tables, laughing when she does a happy dance as she takes a seat at the last open table. "Yes, this is going to be my day, I can just feel it."

"I'm glad the universe is giving you the good juju. Lord knows you deserve some."

She grabs the menu and nods. "You're damn straight I do."

A big group at the table next to us leaves, and for some reason, it makes me feel better. This place is really small and it's almost claustrophobic with this many people in here.

I scan my own menu, deciding on the Cuban sub and fries to go with my latte, when someone knocks my chair from behind. Turning to cuss someone out about being more careful, I find Nico, Dallas, Isaac, and Trey taking a seat at what *was* the empty table.

Two guesses on which one of them it was that hit my chair.

I really wish Trey would get over himself. Especially when Allie and I are becoming friends. His issue with me makes zero sense.

Turning back to face Kate, I can see her grin even as

she tries to hide her face behind her menu.

"Don't."

She lowers her menu and sticks out her tongue. "I have no idea what you could possibly mean."

Glancing over my shoulder, she waves to the guys behind me. "Happy Birthday, Dallas!"

"Thanks, Kate," he replies, but I keep my back to them.

This is so not fun.

Thankfully, our server appears and takes our order, returning quickly with our drinks.

The guys all stand behind us as the server moves to them. "Sorry, we need to go," I hear Nico say to her.

"See you two later?" Dallas asks, but I lift my drink as an excuse to stay quiet.

Kate grins up at him. "Wouldn't miss it."

Traitor.

"Great," he replies before catching up to the others who are already by the door waiting for him. I can feel Trey glaring at me as I turn back to face Kate.

"I really don't understand why Trey hates you so much."

I shrug before putting down my drink. "No idea, wish I did. I also wish he'd get over it."

"Maybe Allie or Noah might have some insight. Noah was nice to you, right? Called a truce?"

"Yeah," I say, wincing. "But that was before I slept

with Dallas. She might not be so nice if she finds that out."

"I don't think she'd care. It's not like she's into any of them, and sex isn't dating. It's not like you're playing them off of each other. One roll around with Nico and Dallas does not a relationship make."

"Let's hope you're right. Anyway, can we change the subject? Maybe back to you and Vann. What's happening with you guys? I feel like y'all have been on a rollercoaster and I can't keep up."

"You're not the only one. We're friends. Nothing has happened since the almost kiss. Even after my brush with death. I can't decide if that's for the best or not, but honestly, it's taking up too much brain space trying to work it out. If he wants us to be more, he'd make another move, right?"

"Right... or he could think the same about you."

"I am a girl. We do not make the first move."

Grinning at her, I roll my eyes. "What a statement for the girls can do anything movement."

"Oh hush," she jokes, waving me off. "I am not the girl that makes a first move."

Our server reappears with our food and all conversation ceases as we eat.

"Okay," Kate announces as she finishes her food, leaning back and rubbing her stomach. "I'm officially bloated, so let's walk this off then go get ready. I am ready to dance the night away."

Laughing, I agree as I scan the code on our check and pay for the order. "Alright, Cinderella, let's get this party going, shall we?

"I still can't believe you convinced me to wear this," I grumble as I follow Kate down the dark path, lit with lanterns on each side, as we head toward the boathouse, which is apparently where Dallas's impromptu birthday party is being held.

The thump of the bass is already audible and I can't help but wonder how they got approval for it because there's no way the staff can't hear it, but not my circus, not my monkeys.

"You look hot!" Kate exclaims as I tug on the skirt again. "Your legs are incredible, especially with those shoes making them look longer."

"Uh-huh." The mini skirt and heels admittedly do look good, especially with the bandage crop top with ribbons that wrap around my bare waist, but this is not my usual go to. "Says the girl in jeans and flats."

"I just can't pull off what you can," she says, laughing softly. "Plus, I'm fairly certain Dallas will thank me."

I knock into her with my shoulder playfully. "I'm fairly

certain I'll be avoiding all of the Elites until I leave."

"Spoil sport," she teases, sticking her tongue out.

"That's me, Captain Downer reporting for duty."

We head inside the boathouse and I'm amazed at how they've dressed the place up. It looks like an actual club in here, not some wooden shed that's usually full of crap. There's a DJ booth set up in the back corner, a makeshift bar opposite it, a VIP runner closing off the stairs, with what looks like security by it—not over the top or anything— then the rest of the place is just a makeshift dance floor.

"Bathroom?" Kate yells as we enter, and I nod in agreement. She takes my hand and weaves us through the crowd to the bathrooms on the other side.

I didn't even realize there were bathrooms out here. Though, this is only my second time here, so not that shocking.

Once we're done, we head to the makeshift bar, where I grab a bottle of water for each of us. There's a dozen or so kegs behind it, along with a line of bottles of spirits and mixers.

Booze on school premises? Who the hell did they pay off?

Then again, Kate said Noah was behind the party and I get the feeling people don't really say no to her.

"Let's dance!" Kate shouts, grabbing my hand again and pulling us into the crowd of writhing bodies.

We spend the night dancing, ignoring the rest of the crowd, and just living our best lives. The music is incredible, bouncing between vintage and new stuff, and I sing at the top of my lungs so much that I might lose my voice.

I'm not that concerned about it, and despite my bitching and moaning, I really needed tonight. After everything that's happened so far this year between Lexi, the swim team, the fake article, and the other bullshit, this feels good.

Kate was right, this has been fun.

Vann appears behind her, so I point and she turns, hugging him tight.

"I'm going to pee and grab more water!" I yell at her, leaving her with Vann. It's not meddling, I really do need to pee and hydrate. I check my phone and realize it's almost one in the morning.

Holy crap, I'm going to be wiped tomorrow. Kinda glad I don't have swim practice.

I push through the still-insane crowd and let out a whoop when I see there's no line for the bathroom.

"Ouch," I yell when I walk into the door and it doesn't open more than an inch.

What the hell?

I slam against the door with my shoulder when I hear voices from inside.

"No, stop,"

"Don't be such a cock tease. You know you want this."

Panic fills me and I hit the door harder. After two more shoves, I fall into the bathroom and find Noah trying to push off some guy I don't recognize, cornering her, his hand up her skirt.

"Hey!" I shout, and he glares over his shoulder at me. "Get off her."

"Fuck off," he grunts before turning back to Noah.

"Stop," she slurs, and I notice her glassy eyes and the fact that he's mostly holding her up.

Shit.

She is wasted.

A second passes and I consider getting someone to help, but that might take too long. Instead, I storm over to him, grab his hair, and yank with every ounce of strength I have.

"You bitch!" he roars as he stumbles backward. Noah falls to the ground and I step between them.

"Get the fuck out of here, you asshole."

He steps forward and swings for me. I see stars for a minute after his fist connects with my jaw, but I grab onto him and shove my knee into his dick. He crumples to the ground, holding his crotch while he groans.

"Come on," I say quietly to Noah, trying to lift her from the ground. I manage to drag her from the room, just hoping to get her out of here before the guy in the bathroom manages to stop being a little bitch.

"Noah?" I glance in the direction of the voice and find Nico striding toward us. He looks at her before looking at me. "What happened?"

My jaw is throbbing, but I manage to answer him. "Guy had her in the bathroom, I stepped in, but I don't think she's in a good way."

He takes her from me, lifting her into his arms just as she passes out. "Come on."

I follow behind him, dropping Kate a message to let her know what happened and that I'm leaving with them. Nico pauses at the bottom of the stairs by the exit, speaking to the giant guy standing there, who nods, before he steps outside.

"Where are we going?" I ask as I kick off the heels to keep up with him.

"To her room." His response is clipped, anger dripping from every word. "Then I need you to stay with her until I come back."

I try to respond, but my jaw hurts too bad, so instead, I just follow behind him until we reach her dorm room. He lays her on the bed then grabs a bottle of water and hands it to me.

"Do not leave her alone," he orders before storming out of the room.

I salute his back as the door slams. "Aye aye, Captain

Grumpy Pants."

Noah groans on the bed and I look around for a bucket, settling on a trash can that I empty and take over to her just in time for her to lose the contents of her stomach.

Awesome.

She glances at me, eyes still glassy. "Talia?"

"Nurse Talia, reporting for duty," I joke, but it's lost on her. "You're okay, Noah."

I open the bottle of water, trying to get her to drink some, but she falls asleep as I'm trying. Letting out a sigh, I move to sit on the end of the bed, wondering how I keep ending up in the middle of their group when her eyes flutter open again.

"I think he drugged me," she mutters before passing out again. "I wasn't drinking."

Well fuck.

TWENTY THREE

Noah

Oh, God. What the fuck happened and why does my throat feel like I swallowed the fucking Sahara Desert?

I groan as I flutter my eyes open, the light stinging them as I do.

"Noah?"

Who the fuck is that?

My stomach twists and I shoot up in bed fast enough that the room starts spinning like I didn't already need to vomit.

"Shit." I hear the hiss before my trash can is thrust into my hands, just in time for me to lose the contents of my stomach.

Why do I feel so fucking awful?

"You should drink some water." The trash can is taken from my hands and replaced with a bottle of water. As much as I want to drink it, because oh, holy hell that taste in my mouth is vile, the thought of swallowing the water makes me feel sick again.

Finally, I muster the courage to open my eyes a little wider to see who the hell is in my room. My eyes water as the light hits them, the sting making my blurred vision seem worse somehow. Blinking rapidly, I try to clear my sight, but it makes the room start spinning again.

Jesus fucking fuck, why do I feel like this?

"Are you going to spew again?"

I try to gain my bearings, gripping the water bottle like it's a lifeline, and finally look over at whoever is talking.

Wait, what?

"Talia? Why are you in my room?"

Her eyes go wide as she stares back at me. "You don't remember last night?"

I try to think back, and groan as a stabbing sensation rips through my head. "Nope."

"Shit. I should go get Nico."

I attempt to lie back down, but the motion makes me queasy again, so instead I stay sitting upright and close my eyes. "What happened, Talia?"

"It was Dallas's party."

Annoyance flickers in my chest as anxiety makes my heart race. Not knowing what happened, but knowing that something obviously happened is fucking me up.

It's almost as bad as when Scottie…

Yeah, no. Not going there.

"Yeah, I remember that much. I've been planning it for weeks."

She sucks in a breath and I swear, even with my eyes closed, I can feel the unease rippling from her, like it's filling the room and suffocating me.

"Well, I don't know how your night started, but it ended with me finding you in a locked bathroom. Some guy had his hands all over you, you were telling him to stop, but he wouldn't leave you alone."

Oh fuck. No.

Please God, no.

"I stopped him, got you to Nico, who brought us back here and told me to watch you."

My heart races so fast I think I might pass out. Finally, I open my eyes again when I'm more sure I won't pass out, but the pity on her face makes me wish I hadn't. "Where is Nico?"

"I don't know," she stutters. "He said he'd be back, but that was hours ago."

A tear slips down my cheek and I bat it away, betrayal

slicing through me at my own bodily functions. "Call him."

My demand is short, but she nods, taking my phone and calling him. I'd do it, but the thought of looking at my phone screen. Yeah, let's not.

I lie back again, staring at the ceiling, wondering how I'm here again.

I wasn't even drinking last night, so my drink must have been spiked, but I don't understand how, it was never left unattended; I made sure of it after what happened over summer.

Attempting to remember anything feels futile, but I try nonetheless as I hear Talia speaking on the phone. My memory is blank, and I want to shout, scream and cry in frustration, but I know that won't get me anywhere.

I need a shower.

I feel dirty.

Whose hands were on me?

Fuck, I hate that I don't remember. Somehow it's worse than remembering, and I didn't think that was possible.

"Okay, bye." Talia says before handing my phone back. "He's on the way."

"I need you to help me to the bathroom," I say through gritted teeth. I hate having to ask her for help, someone I barely know. Usually, I'd wait for Nico to get here, but I need to scrub my skin until it's raw.

Until I feel clean again.

"Oh, erm, sure."

"You are not this feeble," I snap at her. "Stop acting so meek and help me."

Her eyes go wide as I bark at her, but she nods. "Sorry, this is just—"

"Yeah, it's fucked up. I know." I let out a sigh as she moves to help me from the bed. I try to stand with her help but I feel weak as hell, like my legs won't hold me.

What the fuck was I given to make me feel like this?

I drop back onto the bed with a huff as Nico opens my door. He strides across the room and Talia moves out of the way as he crouches in front of me. "How are you feeling?"

"Like someone wiped my mind and stole all function of my body with it. Like I want to tear off my skin." Tears well in my eyes as I clench my fists. Somehow, him being here makes everything better and worse all at once. "Why does this keep happening to me, Co?"

"Shhhh." He stands and wraps me in his arms, holding me so tight that it feels safe to fall apart.

"I'm going to go," Talia whispers, and I feel him tense as he holds me.

"What happened to your face?"

"It's nothing," she says, dismissing him. "I'm really sorry last night happened, Noah."

Her words are quiet, but I hear them as though she shouted them. Nico bristles against me and I hear my door open before he says, "We're not done talking."

She sighs before responding, "Yes, we really are."

The door clicking shut follows her words, leaving the two of us in silence.

"Sorry, Noah. I am so fucking sorry I wasn't there. That this happened."

"It's not your fault," I say, sniffing as the tears run silently down my face. "I just need a shower. So bad."

"Okay," he murmurs, running a hand up and down my spine. "You need help? I can get one of the others?"

"No," I sigh as I step back. "Just help me in there and I'm good from there."

He nods and helps me into the bathroom, letting me lean on him as he half carries me to the shower. "I'll be just outside."

"Thanks, Co."

He kisses the top of my head before leaving me in the bathroom. I turn the water on full, stripping out of my clothes as fast as my body will allow before stepping beneath the scalding water and breaking entirely.

After my shower, my skin is sore, my tears have run dry, and I feel a little hollow. But hollow is better than before.

Numb is better than what I could be feeling.

I don't want to break again.

Nico is waiting for me in my room as I exit the

bathroom in the pj's he'd handed to me a few minutes ago. Thankfully, it's a Saturday and I have absolutely nowhere to be.

Having plans might be best, a distraction of sorts, but all I want to do is climb into bed and rot.

"How are you feeling?" he asks, concern lacing his tone as I climb onto my bed and pull my blanket up to my chin.

"Better than I did."

He's watching me like I'm made of glass and about to shatter. Which I guess is fair, but I don't have to like it. He's always seen me as delicate, and I go along with it, but you don't live the life I have and be that way.

Resilience is a key to surviving being a Carrington.

"What are you up to with Talia?" I ask him, wanting to change the subject. "And don't play stupid like you don't know what I mean."

He rolls his eyes as he leans back on my sofa, letting out a deep breath. "Honestly, I don't know. I can't be up to anything, she's off limits."

"What does that mean?"

He looks at me in that, please don't ask because I can't tell you way, and I tut at him. "So freaking typical. One day I'll get to the bottom of the cryptics."

"Don't, Noah. Trust me, you're better off not knowing. I wish I didn't."

So freaking cryptic.

"That still didn't answer my question."

"I know," he says, shrugging. "But it's all I've got."

He grabs the remote and turns on the TV before climbing into bed beside me. I cuddle up to him like the big brother he basically is to me. I hate how déjà vu this feels after what happened with Scottie, but I'm not sad he's here.

I feel safe with him, which isn't something I can say about a lot of people.

And considering last night, whether I remember it or not, my cynical non-trusting ways are going to be remaining firmly in place.

Arbour was supposed to be a safe haven, but I'm beginning to realize that nowhere is truly safe, and maybe building my walls higher might be the only way to get through this life in one piece.

TWENTY FOUR

Nico

Once Noah is sleeping, and Dallas is with her, I step out, trying to decide what needs my attention first.

The guy who attacked her that Isaac currently has tied to a chair out in the maze, or speaking to Talia to get a better idea of what happened.

And to find out what the fuck happened to her face.

I hate that my entire focus should be Noah, and Talia is there on the outskirts, a distraction. How she scaled my walls escapes me, but she's there, peeking over the top and I don't know if it pisses me off or if I like it.

She might be off limits, but that just makes her more intriguing.

Fuck it. Talia first. It'll give Isaac and Trey more time to play with the douchebag that attacked Noah. Maybe I won't have to get my hands dirty this time. I've never had a problem with it, and I will never have a problem getting them dirty for Noah, but I'm barely eighteen and my soul already feels like it's been shredded to ribbons.

I check my phone to make sure I haven't missed anything while Noah has been sleeping. Relieved my screen is empty, I head down the hall toward Talia's room.

This is probably a really bad fucking idea, but like a moth, I'm drawn to her flame.

Except it'll be her who ends up getting hurt.

Even that knowledge isn't enough to keep me from going to her.

I knock on her door, and after waiting a second, it occurs to me that I have no idea if she's even here, but the handle turns and I see her face, that purple mottled bruise on her cheek pissing me off all over again.

"What do you want, Nico?" she says, sighing, almost deflating.

"Can I come in?"

Usually I'd just walk in the room, but she helped Noah, so I'm trying to be less of an asshole.

I watch as her thought process plays out on her face, and for a second I think she's going to tell me to fuck off. She should. But instead, she relents and steps back, opening the door to let me in.

Stepping into the room, I take in the space on instinct. Old habits die hard. "No roommate?"

"She's out with a friend."

Her voice is almost monotone and it occurs to me that she's probably exhausted. She was up with Noah most of the night.

"I won't keep you long," I tell her, trying to soften my voice, but her defeated stare as she takes a seat on her bed bugs me.

"Okay." She's usually far more combative, and I think I prefer her that way. This meek, feeble act isn't her at all.

"What happened to your face?" I ask her again, and the roll of her eyes makes me want to smile.

There she is.

"I already told you it's nothing."

"Talia, your jaw is fucking purple. Don't tell me it's nothing."

She sighs, folding her arms across her chest, some of that fire back in her eyes. "The guy hit me when I stepped between him and Noah. It's no big deal. I iced it when I came back here earlier. I'll be fine."

No big deal.

No. Big. Deal.

I guess I'll be getting an extra hit in on the dick that attacked Noah after all.

"How is Noah?" she asks before I have a chance to speak again.

"She's asleep," I respond, not wanting to talk about Noah, because well, Noah is private. The fact that Talia was witness to something so... violating... will be bad enough. I'm not about to cross any lines. "I'm sure she'll reach out if she wants to talk."

She nods once, her jaw ticking at my dismissal. "Okay. Was that everything? I really need to get some sleep."

"I just need to know what happened last night. Anything you remember."

She relaxes a little, letting out a deep breath. "I don't know much more than I already told you."

"Tell me again, so I take it in."

It's a request, even if it doesn't sound like it, but she just nods, relaying the events of last night, rubbing at her shoulder as she does.

I have a feeling her jaw isn't the only thing that's bruised.

When she's finished talking, and my anger is fully stoked, I move to leave. "Thank you."

She follows me to the door before saying, "I didn't do it for you."

Pausing, I turn back to face her, the urge to kiss the sass out of her rushing to the surface, but I shove it down. Now is so not the time. "I meant for telling me what happened."

"Whatever. Just go, Nico." I hear the words she doesn't say. The ones asking me to leave her alone entirely. I'm not unaware of what she's suffered in the small amount of time since she arrived at Arbour, and while I might not be responsible for some of it, I also could have stopped it.

But that wasn't the plan.

If she's broken, it would make my life easier.

Or so I thought.

That was before I knew her.

Everything is different now. And so fucking messy.

"Bye, Talia."

She closes the door behind me, the click of her lock sounding louder than it should. Shaking it off, I shove down that part of me and call on the darkest parts instead.

Making my way out of the dorms, I head toward the maze, systematically disassembling the most human parts of me and placing them in the boxes they need to be in for this. I have a job to do, and being human won't get it done.

I wash the blood from my hands, leaving a groaning Daniel to Isaac. He'll deal with cleanup and make sure he's afraid enough to never try what he did last night again. Hissing at the sting of my knuckle as the soap enters the broken skin,

I'm almost thankful for the sensation.

Monsters don't feel pain.

So if it hurts, I must still be me.

My phone buzzes in my pants pocket, so I dry off my hands and check it, just in case it's Noah.

s

It's nearly time. Make sure you're ready.

Grunting, I pocket my phone again. Like I'm ever not ready.

Leaving the bunker, I make my way through the maze and back to campus, finding Dallas on the quad. He beelines for me and I prepare myself for whatever else is coming at me today.

Running a hand down my face, I let out a breath while I wait for him to reach me. I'm exhausted, but being up for days in a row is something I've been conditioned to endure.

"What happened?" he asks when he reaches me, and we walk into the treeline to avoid the passing students.

"It was handled. Isaac is cleaning up."

He nods once. "Good. Also, you need to speak to Trey, he's going to fuck shit up. He lost it at Talia about half an hour ago. She was just cutting across the quad, heading for her car, and he flipped."

"For fuck's sake," I groan. "He's going to make himself

prime suspect number one if he's not careful."

"Speak to him, he listens to you." Dallas insists, and I nod, adding it to my never ending mental to-do list. "What is the plan with her?"

Shrugging, I start walking back toward the dorms and he falls into step beside me. "I don't know, but I was notified earlier to be ready. Whatever they have planned, it's coming soon."

Shock flicks over his face as he pauses momentarily. "They haven't told you?"

"Not a thing. Plausible deniability I guess."

"That's fucked up."

"Isn't it always?"

He nods, then shrugs. "I still don't get why her."

"Me either. They're playing this one real close to the vest."

"But it's never a daughter."

"I guess she's the exception to the rule."

His laugh in response is dry. "Isn't she just?"

"You're into her?" I ask, surprised. I know they've hung out, but we haven't really discussed her.

"I can't be. She's been tapped. But that doesn't mean I'm not." I look at him and realize he's fucked her too.

"We could share her?" I offer, half joking.

He looks me over and laughs again. "You too?"

Nodding, I shrug. "Not usually one for sharing, but

like I said, she's the exception."

"I guess we'll have to see how this all plays out. If we all survive, then we can figure it out."

He's not wrong, there's a good chance we won't all survive. It's exactly why Noah is kept fully in the dark. Other than it being our law, her being off limits is something I bartered for. It's the one thing I don't mind paying for. She's worth the stains on my soul if it keeps her free.

Unfortunately, Talia... well, I can't make the same deal for her.

She was tapped before I knew her.

The only thing I can do is help her when the time comes.

If I can.

"I guess we'll have to see what happens," I tell him, a stone settling in my stomach.

Hope isn't something I hold on to anymore, but this entire conversation just reinforces what I already knew deep down: I need to push Talia out of my head and make her a nobody to me.

Except I have a feeling she's already buried under my skin, and this is going to hurt more than it should.

TWENTY FIVE

Talia

ONE MONTH LATER

The last few weeks since Dallas's party have been pretty quiet. Lexi backed off with her shit, I've been doing my drug tests for swim team, classes have been pretty standard, even Nico and Co. have steered clear of me.

Apparently, saving Noah from the dude at the party has made it so everyone is leaving me alone.

Well for the most part.

No one has spoken about what happened to Noah since that night, so other than me telling Kate, I'm not sure anyone else even knows. Which makes people leaving me alone weird, but I'm trying not to question it.

I tried to speak to Noah the following week in chemistry but she just told me to shut up, so I dropped it and haven't mentioned it again. Kind of weird, but I get it. Having everyone know your business is no fun.

The weirdest part is that even in class, Dallas and the guys have barely spoken to me unless they had to, which has made music so much fun.

I don't understand it, but I've stopped trying.

In fact, the only thing of note in the last few weeks is that Stuart woke up from his coma, but he has severe amnesia. Like, he thinks he's seven years old and has lost the last ten years of his life. I really feel for him and his family, but they've taken him out of the hospital and withdrawn him from school. The police have basically quit looking for Laurence, which is freaking awful for his family, but with no input from Stuart and no other leads, they have nothing to work with.

More than a little terrifying, but no one is really talking about that either.

This place is weird sometimes. Like, almost a little cultish. Who doesn't talk about missing students? It's like the lockdown was just for show, but nobody really cares.

"You heading out?" Kate asks when she gets back from studying with Vann and finds me packing a bag.

"Yeah, I want to swim. I might not be on the team, but Coach told me I can still use the pool. I figured it would be empty this time of night."

"Talia, it's nearly ten on a Wednesday. Of course it's going to be empty." She drops her bag onto her bed and groans as she drops down beside it. "Oh, another letter arrived for you. I put it on your desk."

"Another one? You'd think Theodore would get the picture." I grab the letter from my desk, realizing I haven't even read the last one, but decide not to read this one either. My family has had my entire life to reach out to me. Just because I'm now close enough to be convenient for them, doesn't mean I want them in my life. "I see you got more flowers too. Any idea who they're from yet?"

"This set came with a note. Turns out they were for you." She mutters as she lies back. "Just had your name on it, and was signed from S."

"Who the hell is S?"

"I was kinda hoping you'd know."

Shrugging, I drop the envelope in the drawer on my desk and grab my swim bag. "Not a freaking clue. You okay?"

"Just have cheese for brains. Studying for AP chemistry exams is cruddy."

I frown, because yeah. "Sounds it. I'll try not to wake you when I get back."

She gives me a thumbs up, her eyes already closed, and I laugh as I sling my bag over my shoulder before leaving.

I'm fairly certain she'll be asleep before I even leave the building. Late nights are not even a little bit the norm for Kate.

By the time I reach the pool, it's empty and silent.

It could be eerie, but it's just peaceful. I rush to the locker rooms, changing into my suit and shoving everything into my locker, then head out to the pool.

The water is cold as I drop into the pool, but it wakes me up a little and helps clear my head.

Yeah, I need this.

Almost too much.

Taking a deep breath, I force all of my thoughts away and push off the wall, slicing through the water. The rest of the world fades to nothing and for the first time in weeks, I find a little bit of true peace.

Stepping out of the pool, I grab my towel and wrap it around myself, noticing the time.

Wow. I was in there longer than I thought.

I hurry into the locker rooms, take off my swim cap, and head toward the showers, but Nico steps into view and halts me in my tracks.

Unease flits through me. The last time we spoke, he

was *pissed.* Then after Trey bitched me out later that day, they all stopped talking to me. Him being here is weird as hell.

"Talia."

A shiver runs down my spine at my name on his lips "Nico? Why are you here?"

"I wanted to come and make sure you're okay."

"And you had to do that now?" I tighten my hold on my towel, despite the fact that he's seen me in much less. I'm feeling a little vulnerable right now and the minimal coverage is making me feel a little better.

"Yes. This doesn't mean anything," he says and I roll my eyes. "I just wanted to say thank you, again... for helping Noah."

"So you're here to make sure I'm okay, or you're here to thank me again for helping Noah? Nico, you've ignored me for literal *weeks.* You being here now makes no sense. But like I said last time we spoke, I didn't help her for you. I did it because it was the right thing to do," I retort firmly as he takes another step toward me. It's weird, him being here. I thought I was alone, nobody comes to the pool this late, and well, this is the girls' locker room. "You can go now, preferably before someone sees you in here."

"You and I both know there's no one else around right now," he responds, that calculating smile of his gracing his lips. I hate that I know his different smiles, that I've paid enough attention to notice, but he's kind of hard to ignore. Even if he is an asshole.

But something about what he says, and how he says it, is unsettling. A shiver of unease trails down my spine, but I try not to let it show. "Maybe, but you still shouldn't be here."

His eyes flash, like my words are a challenge to him. Sometimes I think that's why we keep ending up in situations like this. Because I'm a challenge to him.

"Plus, your *friend*"—I overemphasize the word friend, just because—"already told me to keep my distance from you and yours. I don't want any drama here."

"Friend?" he questions, taking another step toward me and caging me against the wall with his arm above my head.

"Yes, your friend. The football brute. Trey. He was so nice to scream at me on the quad in front of everyone and tell me that what happened to Noah was my fault and that I should stay away from you all."

His eyes flash again, with anger this time, the lines in the corners tightening as he frowns momentarily. "Trey is my friend, but he isn't my keeper. I'll be wherever I want to be."

"And you want to be here?" I ask, poking him because a twisted part of me wants to see what it would take to watch the unbreakable Nico shatter to pieces.

"Oh, Talia, what is it about you that gets under my skin?" His words are almost a purr as his lips move against my ear. His fingers toy with the bottom of my ponytail, before he wraps the hair around his hand and tugs until I'm looking up at him. "You're supposed to be off limits. I definitely shouldn't be here. What have you done to me?"

Off limits? What does that even mean?

I suck in a breath at the almost venomous tone as his obvious conflict plays out on his features, but then his lips are on mine again, scorching my skin as my fists clench in his hoodie.

"You said just once," I pant as he pulls back, loosening my grip.

He pauses then grins down at me. "No, *you* said just once. I told you that you were wrong. This definitely shouldn't happen again, but there is something about not being able to have you that makes me want you more."

He kisses me again, and a guttural moan pulls from me like he's breathing life into me with every touch. He might have lied, but I've been lying to myself. He releases my hair and strips my swimsuit from my body, then watches me, that predatory stare of his back in full force as I fight the urge to cover myself, despite the chill in the air.

"Oh, yes. I definitely want you," he says before tearing off his hoodie and t-shirt. He watches me as he undoes the belt on his jeans then lowers his zipper. "Kneel."

The word is a command, a compulsion I want to fight, but the way he looks at me makes me want to do as he demands, so I find myself kneeling before him.

I will likely hate myself for this later, but right now I'm willing to risk that for the promise of what he has to offer.

"I knew you could be a good girl," he murmurs and a thrill runs down my spine at the words as he strokes a thumb down my face. It's almost enough to distract me from the pain of the cold bumpy floor on my knees.

I'm torn between keeping my eyes on him and looking down at his cock. I've seen it, had it inside me. I've come all over it. But I've never *tasted* it. Hadn't even really thought about it before now, but damn. Now that he's said it…

Fuck, I really want to taste it.

Nico wraps a hand at the base of his shaft, just able to circle his fingers around it, then pushes it down so the head is lined up with my mouth.

Our gazes lock, mine searching, trying to figure him out, if this is for real, while his is almost calculating with just a hint of sadistic pleasure. As he rubs the tip of his hard cock across my lips, I open just enough for him to push inside and stifle the moan as wetness floods between my legs.

"Such a pretty little mouth made just for sucking. Tell me, Talia, do you like sucking cock? Are you going to be my little cock whore?"

Instead of being outraged at his demeaning words, I keep my stare unwavering, pulling back enough to answer him. "I love sucking dick. Doesn't have to be yours."

Whatever tenderness he was demonstrating is gone in a blink. The hand caressing my cheek is suddenly back to my ponytail, wrapping my strands around his palm and yanking me back so hard that my head stings.

In this position, all I can see is him. The tight line of his lips, the dark pools of his eyes, which are filled with a mixture of rage and lust that only makes my pussy pulse with need.

Why am I like this?

Pissing him off shouldn't turn me on but holy shit, it totally does. Stealing power from him really does something to me.

"Want to change your answer?" He grips my hair a little tighter, his tone laced with venom, and it sends another thrill of excitement down my spine. This position might hurt, but I'm definitely still in control here.

"Nope." I open wide, a silent invitation to see if I've pushed him too far.

Part of me wants to have done so, to watch him shut down and leave me alone, but a bigger part of me wants him.

Bad.

There is definitely something wrong with me. Stupid forbidden fruit.

His brows shoot up to his hairline, but he quickly drops his cold-as-ice mask back in place before he smiles. A smile that promises punishment and maybe just a little pain.

Yes, please.

The way he's holding me is the perfect angle for him to push his cock inside my mouth. Which he does, until the tip hits the back of my throat. I'm taken by surprise, not just by the stretch of my lips, but by the initial gentleness of the movement.

He holds his dick in place, stretching my throat, withholding air. "Such a good girl. I'm going to make you regret having such a smart mouth."

Tears gather in my eyes, one falling down my face, but I don't care. My main focus is not choking as he pushes even further, finally making me gag. No doubt, that was his intention…

Even though I can now only see him through the haze of unshed tears, the determination and unmasked need are written in the heat of his eyes and the tightness of his jaw.

He wants me, but he doesn't want to want me.

Me too, Nico. Me too.

Pulling out his cock until only the head is between my lips, he slams back in, fucking me deep with long, measured strokes. Every time he hits the back of my throat, he stills, testing my gag reflex, pushing the limits of it.

My hands reach out to touch him, to steady myself against his onslaught, but he slaps them away like he wants me to be uncomfortable.

Asshole.

I glare at him, but he tips his head back, moaning as he fucks my face, and I almost hate how wet it makes me.

Hate sex never felt so good.

It takes everything in me not to rub my thighs together or press my fingers against my aching, swollen clit.

God, I need a release, but at the same time, I can't help but love the power he exudes with every thrust he takes inside of me.

"Such a pretty little mouth, Talia. So fucking plump and willing. I want to see how far I can go."

One of his hands latches onto my throat and squeezes and I swear to fuck, it feels like his dick gets thicker. I know it's because he's closing up my airways, but holy fuck, my gag reflex can't handle this level of face fucking. I start to cough, choking on him, but he doesn't relent, he doesn't even blink.

I can't look away from his boring gaze as he calculates everything, every move, every inch of him keeping my mouth open and my windpipe closed off completely.

Why is this so fucking hot?

And why the fuck do I want more?

Just as spots start dancing in my vision, he pulls out and helps me while I cough as I try to suck in air.

My throat is raw, but the burn feels so good.

"Such a good little whore. Fuck, Talia, your mouth makes me want to do very bad things to you." I look back up at him and grin.

"What's stopping you?"

His eyes flash at my sass and excitement ripples through me.

"Absolutely nothing."

The next thing I know, he's lifting me from the ground, the sting in my knees finally registering as he tosses me over his shoulder—fucking again—as he takes me to the nearest shower stall where he puts me down and bends me over. "Brace yourself on the wall and spread your legs."

I don't speak, glancing back at him over my shoulder as I place both of my palms on the wall and watch him as he looks around the stall. This is why I don't miss the slow creeping grin that forms on his lips.

"Oh, this is going to be fun." I tense at his words as he eyes my ass. I've never... Dallas only used his fingers. Holy shit. I open my mouth to protest but he speaks before I get the chance.

"Relax, I'm not fucking your ass." I sigh with relief

until his next word has my heart rate beating double time. "Yet."

My mind reels but I don't have time to question anything else as his dick pushes inside my pussy, his girth stretching me more than I remember it doing last time.

"Fuck!" The word sounds like a mix of moan and prayer, and I almost hate that he makes me feel so good.

Pushing back against his every thrust, I get a thrill when his moans match mine as he fucks my pussy like he owns it.

"Fuck, you're so fucking tight, Talia. It feels so good, too fucking good. How do you do this to me?"

I love that he hates the pull between us as much as I do.

He pulls out of my pussy before he pushes one finger inside my asshole until his knuckles are bumping against my flesh. That's when he plunges his dick right back inside, fucking both of my holes in rhythm.

Pleasure rips through me, overriding any pain, and I moan at the bliss of having him fill me entirely.

"Fuck, Talia. You're so fucking tight, so full of me. Tell me how much you want it. Beg me to keep going." I almost lose my mind at his words, especially when he stops all movement.

"Please, Nico," I beg, wishing I had the power to refuse, but right now, I want the orgasm more than I want my dignity. "Please. More."

Nico responds like I just unleashed the last strand of his restraint by rearing back and slamming inside me, both his cock and his finger. Over and over again, he fucks me like it's his mission to ruin me.

I move my grip to the shower bench, worried I'm going to slip, but even then, I'm afraid it might give way with the power of his thrusts.

"Ready?" he asks, not telling me what he's up to before the fullness in my ass increases as he adds another finger.

The stretch stings, but in the best kind of way. I never realized being so full could feel this good. "Oh, God!"

"That's right, baby, call my name." His other hand snakes around my waist and lands on my clit, flicking and pinching and rubbing circles until I lose it.

I come so fucking hard that I begin to slip, but Nico braces me with his legs until I find my footing again.

His thrusts become frantic, almost unrecognizable as he loses control until he cries out. Stilling behind me, he keeps one hand on my clit while the other is clenching my waist as he spills inside of me before we're both collapsing onto the shower floor, panting.

With chests heaving and our gazes locked, we're both asking the same silent question.

What the fuck just happened?

TWENTY SIX

Halloween is finally here, and it's turned Arbour into more of a madhouse than usual. There's a Halloween party tonight, put on by the school for all years, but I get the feeling that it'll be the afterparties that are more fun.

Somehow they managed to make this place creepier too. The halls are lit by flickering candles that make the shadows dance, decorations line the ceilings, and almost everyone has spent the day in costume.

"Boo!"

I let out a squeal as the bozo dressed up as Frankenstein jumps out at me from a classroom. He and his friends laugh loudly as they pass me, heading down the hall in the opposite direction.

I am so over this day.

Halloween has never been much fun for me. Just like horror movies aren't my favorite. Masks just give me the creeps, as do dolls, and everyone seems to use this day as an excuse to be an uber asshole.

Turns out that Arbour is no different.

Heading up to my dorm room to meet Kate, I'm on high alert for any more assholes trying to scare the crap out of me, but make it to the room with no more drama.

"I LOVE HALLOWEEN!" Kate exclaims when I finally reach our door and take refuge in our room.

"Of course you do," I grumble. "Do we really have to go tonight? I can think of so many better ways to spend a Friday night."

"Yes, we have to go!" Her exasperation at my grumpiness is almost frustrating, but I shove it down. It's not her fault that I hate this supposed holiday. The only good thing about Halloween is the candy that goes on sale the day after. "I got us costumes and everything!"

"I thought you and Vann were matching?"

She grins wide as she bounces over to me as I drop down onto my bed. "Oh, we are, but I knew you wouldn't get a costume. You haven't exactly kept your disdain for Halloween a secret. So I got you one too. Don't worry, you don't match us, and I haven't gone over the top either. But please come? It won't be as much fun without you."

I fake a cough and hit her with the puppy dog eyes. "But I feel sick."

"Do not get into TV or film, because your acting skills are lacking," she deadpans. "Cheer up, buttercup. Everyone will be there."

"That's half the problem," I grumble.

I've successfully managed to avoid Nico since our weird little hook up on Tuesday, and while most people have been giving me a wide berth since what happened at Dallas' party, putting myself in close proximity to them is just tempting fate.

"You are not the person that runs and hides in a corner. You are not meek, or feeble. You do not exclude yourself from life to avoid potential problems. I don't know what's got into you lately—other than Nico," she teases, winking as she says it. "But whatever is going on, snap out of it. You've been in a funk since Dallas's party, and I get that what happened to Noah was absolutely bloody awful, but it is no reason to stop living."

"You're right," I admit, sighing. "I've been checked out, mostly, just floating through the last few weeks, surviving rather than living. I guess the thing with Noah made me realize that this isn't a safe little bubble. Not that bad shit hasn't happened to me since I got here, hell that student is *still* missing, but nothing that happened to me was even close to what happened to Noah. I tried speaking to her about it, just checking in with her, but she shut me down and hasn't spoken to me since."

Not that I blame her, I wouldn't want to relive it either.

But I've just been living in a daze since then.

"I'm sorry."

Kate sits down beside me, taking my hand and squeezing it. "You don't have to be sorry, just bring back the Talia that I know and adore. And come to this party with me. It'll suck without you. Vann is fun but he won't dance like a goon with me."

"Fine," I tease, drawing out the word as I bump my shoulder with hers. "What is this outfit anyway?"

She claps her hands together excitedly as she jumps to her feet. "Yes!" Scurrying to her closet, she rips the door open and pulls out a hanger before turning back to face me.

I facepalm when I see the costume in her hand, but I can't help but laugh. "Seriously?"

"Yes, seriously!" She giggles as she bounces on the spot. "Zombie cheerleader for the win!"

The music in the auditorium is so loud that I can feel the thump of the base under my skin. Between that, the lights, and the heat from so many people in here, it's almost a sensory overload. I've never been to a school dance where almost everyone actually showed up.

In fact, the only people who appear to be missing are the Elites.

Not all that surprising, I can't imagine Nico or Noah dressed up in Halloween costumes.

I laugh as Allie and Kate do the monster mash—nothing like kicking it old school—and motion that I need a drink.

They give me a thumbs up and I head out of the dancing masses to the refreshment table that Ms. Ravan is supervising.

No spiked punch tonight.

"Talia!" She waves as she shouts when she sees me. "Are you having fun?"

Nodding, I return her smile. "Just hot! Could I have a bottle of water?"

"Sure!" She crouches down to the mini fridges that are beneath the table and grabs a bottle before handing it over to me. "Have fun!"

"Thank you," I holler back, before turning around, trying to spot Kate and Allie again.

It really is hot in here. I'm fairly convinced the zombie makeup that Kate basically glued to my face earlier has all but melted away. Grabbing my phone, I pull up my group chat with Allie and Kate.

ME

> Grabbing some air. Be back soon!

Once it shows as delivered, I make my way out of the gymnasium. The cold, fresh air hits me and it's an instant relief. I am hot, sticky, and gross.

It wasn't such an issue when I was dancing and distracted, but now that I'm aware, I just feel nasty.

Maybe the girls won't mind if I cut out early, grab a shower, and go to bed.

I chug back the entire bottle of water before grabbing my phone again, and I send another message to the group chat.

ME

> Too hot. So gross. Cutting out, I'm sorry! Hope you guys have fun!

I know they'll moan at me tomorrow, but that's tomorrow me's problem.

Once I've found a trash can for my bottle, I cut through the lantern-lit walkway from the gymnasium toward the quad. The breeze picks up, goosebumps erupting over my bare skin, but the cold is a welcome sensation.

"You!"

The voice sounds like it's coming from the woods and I pause, turning to see who is out there, but I can't see anyone.

Could've been an owl. Yep, that's what I'm telling myself.

Why did I walk back alone in the dark?

Idiot.

Picking up my pace, glad that my zombie cheerleader costume came with sneakers, I pull out my phone and hit the flashlight button.

Not that it helps even a little, but it makes me feel a tiny bit better.

My senses are heightened and I swear, every rustle of leaves in the breeze sounds like someone following me. I keep my head on a swivel, but I can't see anyone else out here. This is exactly why I hate Halloween. Everything feels more... creepy.

Spotting the dimly lit dorm building in the distance makes me feel better, and I move a little faster, pretending to myself that I'm not scared out of my mind for absolutely no reason other than my overactive imagination.

I make it to the building and let out a sigh as I lean against the door once it's firmly closed behind me. Taking a minute to catch my breath, waiting for my heart to stop racing, I chide myself mentally for being such a drama queen.

Shaking my head, I push off of the door and walk through the common room toward the stairwell.

"Talia."

I let out a squeal, turning to find the source of the voice, when arms lock around me from behind. I struggle and scream as someone else steps in front of me, a red mask covered with snakes obscuring their face. "You should've stayed at the party."

I know that voice. Why do I know that voice?

"Let me go, you asshole!"

The hold on me is unmoving, even as I throw my head back, and they lift me from the ground, despite my kicking.

The masked figure lifts a cloth to my face, smothering my mouth and nose with it. The chemical smell makes me gag as I try and fail to get out of their grasp. My eyelids start to droop despite my panic, and as much as I want to keep fighting, I lose control of my body.

"Welcome to the club, little Serpent. It's your turn."

SIGN UP FOR MY NEWSLETTER TO HEAR ABOUT UPCOMING RELEASES

ABOUT THE AUTHOR

Lily is a writer, dreamer, fur mom and serial killer, crime documentary addict.

She loves to write dark, reverse harem romance and characters who will shatter your heart. Characters who enjoy stomping on the pieces and then laugh before putting you back together again. And she definitely doesn't enjoy readers tears. Nope. Not even a little.

Visit her website at http://www.lilywildhart.com to sign up for the newsletter or find her on social media through the links below.

ALSO BY LILY WILDHART

THE RUIN OF SERPENTS

(Dark, Bully, High School Reverse Harem Romance)

Kneel

Plead

Crave

Reign

THE KNIGHTS OF ECHOES COVE

(Dark, Bully, High School Reverse Harem Romance)

Tormented Royal

Lost Royal

Caged Royal

Forever Royal

THE SAINTS OF SERENTIY FALLS

(Dark, Bully, Step Brother, College, Reverse Harem Romance)

A Burn so Deep

A Revenge So Sweet

A Taste of Forever

THE SECRETS WE KEEP

(Dark, Mafia, Reverse Harem Romance, Duet)

The Secrets We Keep

The Truths We Seek

THE SHADOW WALKERS SAGA

(Dark, Paranormal/Fantasy Why Choose Romance)

The Ruin of Souls

The Birth of Chaos

The Secret of Pain

The Misery of Shadows

The Reaping of Envy

The Rise of Dawn

THE SHADOW LEGACIES I

(MF, Rejected/Fated Mates, Paranormal Romance)

Luna Rising

Alpha Bound

Alpha Born